ONCE A GYPSY

the IRISH TRAVELLER series
BOOK 1

DANICA WINTERS

DIVERSIONBOOKS

Fic
Winters

Diversion Books
A Division of Diversion Publishing Corp.
443 Park Avenue South, Suite 1008
New York, New York 10016
www.DiversionBooks.com

For more information, email info@diversionbooks.com

First Diversion Books edition November 2016.
Print ISBN: 978-1-68230-307-8
eBook ISBN: 978-1-68230-306-1

But I, being poor, have only my dreams;
I have spread my dreams under your feet;
Tread softly because you tread on my dreams.

—William Butler Yeats,
Aedh Wishes for the Cloths of Heaven, 1899

CHAPTER ONE

To most people, the green steel doors of Limerick Prison were just ugly riveted doors, but to Helena O'Driscoll, they represented everything that was wrong with her world. Their chipping paint, the color of sickness, only brought thoughts of a system that imprisoned almost every gypsy man, and often their women.

A few meters from the doors ran a black wrought iron fence, tall and brooding, tipped with dangerous spikes. The fence's gate stood firm as Helena pressed her face against it, the cold metal chilling her skin.

Helena tried to imagine her da coming out of those doors, walking down the steps and through the iron gate that stood guard around the prison. Would he still be the strong, work-hardened man she had known as a child? Or would the time behind bars have changed the man who had been the center of her world?

A lump caught in her throat. Helena missed him with every ounce of her being. It had been over three hours and yet there was no sign of him. This damn place and those doors were a constant in her life. Almost every Traveller she'd ever known had spent more than their fair share of time in a place like this—away from the world and out of sight of the country folk.

Her mobile phone buzzed, and she reached down into her fake-diamond-encrusted purse, jamming her fingers on the Post-Leaving Certificate exam textbook she'd brought along to study. Ignoring the pain in her fingers, she opened the mobile and pressed it to her ear. "Aye, Mam," she said, half breathless from nerves. "How's the party coming along?"

"This ain't Mam. She's... busy," her sister replied.

"What has she gotten herself into now?" Helena tapped the pointed toe of her silver heels against the spiked fence.

"Well..."

"Don't tell me she's knackered already. I told you to keep her out of the whiskey."

"It wasn't the whiskey. It was ale," Rionna snapped back in her shrill, over-the-top teenage voice.

"Whiskey or ale, I told you that ya needed to take care of her." The cold steel chilled her flesh as she wrapped her fingers around the bars. If Da were around, things would change. Mam would be different. "I shoulda known this is what would be happenin' when I left you in charge."

"You knew as well as I did that she was going to be a right mess today," Rionna challenged. "You should've taken her with ya."

Rionna was right, but Helena couldn't bear the thought of Da's first sight as a free man being the staggering mess Mam had become—not after everything he'd been through.

"You need to calm her down before the party tonight. I'm relying on you. Have the guests started to be about?"

"Not yet."

"Good. If Da doesn't get out in the next hour, we'll still have time to call it off."

A jingle of metal drew Helena's attention. An old gypsy woman wheeled a little cart down the sidewalk on the other side of the road. Her leathery skin folded into deep wrinkles that cascaded down her neck and disappeared under the edge of a brown, handcrafted shawl. She looked like the fragile cornhusk doll that Helena had played with as a child, as if one hard jolt would send the woman to pieces. The crone sent a black-toothed smile Helena's way.

Turning back to the sight of the green doors, Helena squeezed her eyes closed and prayed Rionna would cooperate with her in handling the twisted wreckage that was Mam. "Look, just make sure all the food is in place and the booze out of Mam's reach. Can you do that?"

"I'm not stupid, Helena. I'm not just some child you can be orderin' round."

"I know." Helena could almost see her sister rolling her eyes. Rionna was far from the type to take orders—even when she had been a wee babe. "I need to get goin'."

"Well don't let me stop ye. I'm sure Da's chomping at the bit waiting to see his favorite little lass." The phone line cut off.

Helena pinched the bridge of her nose as she tried to stave off the beginning of a headache. Some things never changed. Closing the mobile, she stuffed the phone in her purse. The reverberating sound of metal trinkets clinking together echoed toward her as the wool-haired old woman made her way across the street. Helena didn't have to look closely at the cart to know it jingled with typical Traveller wares—baubles and ornaments and wooden knickknacks—whatever could be made from what others had pitched as trash.

Hoping that the woman was targeting someone else, Helena nonchalantly checked over her shoulder, but she saw no one. The woman would undoubtedly recognize her as kindred and want to have a wee chat, but Helena cringed at the thought. She didn't want to have to talk about why her da had been forced to serve time.

The wheel of the crone's cart caught on the edge of the sidewalk, and the woman crashed against the buggy, sending her tripping facedown. Glass cat-eye marbles spewed from her pockets as she flailed and tried to stop herself from falling. The marbles rolled wildly in every direction as the woman tumbled to the ground.

"Oh," Helena gasped as she rushed to the woman's side. "Are you okay, my friend?"

"Oh that damned old bucket o' mine. Always trippin' me up... Almost like a bad man. Always underfoot and only a pain in me arse." The woman gave a wicked, cackling laugh; her breath smelled of onions and vinegar. "Not that you would know about bad men... not a young lass like you, Helena. Aye?"

Helena dropped the woman's leathery hand. "What are you talkin' about? How do you know my name?"

Her black teeth shone from behind her age-creased lips as she smiled. "I got my ways, lass. 'Tis nothing to be afraid of."

Her simple words did nothing to quell the fear that

rose within Helena. "You need to answer me. How do ya know my name?"

The crone wiped the dust from her brown broom skirt. "Now, lass, don't get upset with me."

"What's yer name?"

"Ogak Beoir… Make sure to tell yer da 'ello for me."

From one of Da's many fireside tales, Helena recalled him saying there were three stages in the female form: the young maiden, the mother, and the old woman. Ogak Beoir was the Cant word for the last. The crone had to be teasing.

"Yer puttin' me on."

"Nah, Helena. I's just like ye, I's got the gift—the forshaw." The woman squinted up at her. "But you gots somethin' more. You gots the touch as well." Her lips curled into an out-of-place smile.

Helena thought back to her early childhood when she had gotten lost in one of their camps and found her way to a wise woman's wagon. Inside the havari were bottles of seeds, drying roses, and, along the top shelf, rows of the most beautiful tea cups she had ever seen—their edges were painted with gold and the sides with dainty pink roses and blue cornflowers. That day was the first time she'd ever met someone who had the forshaw.

Even then she had known the psychic gift was special. Forshaw kept many Travellers with jingling pockets and full bellies, but few were truly gifted. Those who were blessed with the gift received reverence and respect amongst her gypsy clan, the Pavee. Every Traveller believed in the power of sight—it was as natural as the rain. Yet it was an ability that could tell of things as dark as night or bright as the sun, so most tended to avoid the power out of fear. One might not like what they came to know.

"Nah, ma'am, ya got me all wrong. I'm just Pavee," Helena said. "Nothing special."

"There you're wrong. Being Pavee *is* special. There's no one out here who can love ya as much as your family. No matter where ya be, we will always be a part of ya. And no matter the trouble ya find, we'll always have your back. You'll soon find out."

The woman was wrong. All Helena had to do was take one long look at her older sister to know that they didn't always stick around. When things got hard, and her older sister had made choices that their culture didn't believe in, the people who were supposed to have her back were the first ones to get to running. The only thing the crone had been right about is that they would always be Pavee. No matter where they went, they would be outsiders—never to be accepted amongst the country folk.

The crone stared at her, her beady, bloodshot eyes never wavering. Helena looked away, but could still sense the woman's gaze upon her.

"What're ya doin' here? Did you come to meet someone?" Helena asked, in an effort to draw the woman's attention from her crazed prophecies and the pain they caused.

"I only wanted to come meet you for myself. I've been hearin' things about your fam."

Nothing good was ever said about her family—not since Da's bit in the clink. "Look, I don't know what you heard, but my da's an innocent man. He done what any other *grand* Traveller man woulda done. If you're here to say something against him, you need to pick yourself up and get to movin' on. I don't want to hear it."

The crone's laughter echoed down the quiet street. "I knew I was gonna like ya." She collected the rest of the scattered marbles and stuffed them into the pocket of her dirt-smeared skirt. "There are good things comin' in your future... though there'll be plenty of madness." The crone's lips peeled back from her gnarled teeth.

If Helena had to guess, the madness sat before her. She turned back to the bars.

"Those bars are a mockery. Aren't they?" The crone laughed. "Those country folk just can't leave well enough alone."

The woman was right. Her da was a good man, a right man, a man who had gone the extra distance to protect his family.

There was a thump from behind the doors, and Helena held her breath. The sound of grinding metal filled the street as the green doors opened, painfully slowly.

Helena almost forgot about the strange crone at her feet. It had been so long since she'd last seen Da. Would he even recognize her? Her fingers found the edge of her black miniskirt and pulled it down her leg.

The doors opened a fraction farther, and the back of a dark-haired man's head came into view. "Absolutely. Thank you, Warden, for seeing me on such short notice. I appreciate your making things happen." His voice echoed out into the street.

From the other side of the metal came the rumble of a deeper, older voice that Helena assumed was the warden.

"Thanks," the dark-haired man said, and he turned with a quick backward wave.

It wasn't Da. Helena's breath caught in her throat as she stared at the man who had gotten her hopes up. His face was the warm caramel color of someone who spent his days in the sun, and his lips where dry and slightly chapped. They perfectly complimented his aquiline nose and deep-set, chocolate-colored eyes.

A country man, a *gorger*. Helena could practically smell the world on him and see it in the way he moved, the confidence with which he stepped. The man was handsome for a country man, even though he wore a red Manchester United football jersey and a pair of wool trousers that looked far too warm for the tepid spring weather. He smiled down at her, his brown eyes sparkling with far too much delight.

The doors clinked shut behind the man and a bolt slid into place. The sound echoed through Helena. Her da was still in there. Didn't they understand that she and the family were waiting? They had been waiting so long.

A gust of wind blew a few stray strands of hair into the corner of her mouth, sticking to her lip gloss. The jingle of the gorger's keys echoed down the steps as she pulled the wild hair from the sticky trap of her lips. He seemed to mock her with his freedom as he sent one last look back at the closed doors.

The man turned, and their eyes locked. His chapped lips twitched into a smile and the cleft in his chin disappeared; he reminded her a bit of the actor Hugh Grant, with his perfectly disheveled hair. She dropped her gaze to the ground out of fear that he would read something into the brief moment of eye contact they had shared. She could have nothing to do with a country man. No matter how much he looked like a movie star.

The crone's cackle broke into her thoughts. "Be careful now, you two little devils." The woman took a hold of her buggy. "Things aren't as they seem." The trinkets within her buggy jingled as she toddled away.

"Hey, lass." The man's voice was deep and rugged, matching the stubble-ridden cheeks of its owner. "Was that woman bothering you?" His footsteps clicked on the concrete steps as he made his way out of the prison's gates.

The overwhelming desire to escape filled her, but it wasn't out of fear.

"Don't you talk?" He seemed to puff up like an overly prideful schoolboy.

"I do," she said, struggling to find words in the soupy jumble of emotions that boiled away within her. He couldn't think she wanted anything to do with him, but on the other hand, she didn't want to stop talking to the handsome stranger who stood before her. She pointed at his shirt to draw his attention away. "Don't you think you should be wearing the Boys in Green's colors?"

He deflated slightly as he looked down at his shirt and smoothed the fabric. "Manchester United is, and will always be, God's gift to the football fan."

She tutted. "You're a disgrace of a Southerner."

"That's not what the women normally say." He gave her a sexy half grin.

Helena held back a snicker. Did he really think that smile would get the gals running? He must have been scuttered. She leaned toward him just far enough that she could take a sniff, but there wasn't a whisper of drink upon him; instead he smelled of the stale air of the prison. Beneath it was the scent of fresh cedar and sweet grass.

"From the looks of you, you ain't no Southerner neither. What are you, a gypo or something?"

The hair on Helena's neck stood on end. When someone called her a gypo, especially a single man, nothing good would come of it. "Born and bred free like the River Shannon. Now if you'll excuse me, I need to get back to waiting for my da—he's getting out of prison after he beat up some nasty gorger."

She gripped her purse tightly as she let the subtle warning sink into the handsome gorger's over-confident thoughts. No matter how good-looking he was, no man was going to get away with calling her a gypo.

"Hold on, don't get your pretty little skirt all ruffled. I'm just trying to chat with you." He stood up a bit straighter.

"Shag off!"

The crone laughed as she weaved away from them and down the sidewalk.

"I'm sorry, I just thought..." The man paused.

"Thought what? That you could go talking to me like I'm some kind of street woman?" She was getting angrier by the second. "Well, I ain't. And I ain't no *pikey* neither."

"I'm sorry. I shouldn't have said that about you. I thought you were a gypsy."

She pulled her purse higher on her shoulder. "So what if I am?"

The man shifted nervously. "I don't mean anything. Really. Let's start over. My name's Graham Kelly." He stuck out his hand, but Helena only stared at his fingers. If her da walked out and saw her talking to a non-gypsy man, they'd probably have to lock him right back up.

"I'm Helena and I'm a Traveller—so why don't ya move along." She waved her hand down the sidewalk.

There was a hurt expression on Graham's face, but she was doing the right thing. She didn't have any business with a man like him. The lairds needed to stay up in their castles while her kind stayed down in the streets.

"You…" Graham started.

There was the sound of the bolt sliding on the front doors of the prison.

She turned away from him. "Shag off."

The doors opened and a few prisoners stumbled out. A man Helena didn't recognize had what many would have considered a young face, unblemished and plump, but his eyes were sunken and he carried a look of terror on him, which made him seem much older. A steel-haired man with ghostly white, sun-starved skin and a gaunt frame walked out of the doors behind the age-tarnished young man. The ghostly man shielded his eyes from the bright light of freedom, turning his gaze toward the iron gates.

Helena gasped. Suddenly, the world seemed off. For the old, frail man on the steps *couldn't* be her da. It wasn't possible.

The man made his way down the steps and past the gates. His eyes, blue like the sky, twinkled as he saw her. It was him. It was Da.

Da's lips cracked as they formed a long-forgotten smile. "Come here, Helena, *gra a mo gris*."

He'd called her "love of my heart" since before she could remember, and his sweet words still made her smile.

"Da. I'm so glad you're okay." She threw her arms around

Da and buried her face in his chest as she had done when she was a child. "We've been missing ya somethin' fierce."

"Gra a mo gris, you know what I always said... Loneliness is better than bad company."

When they turned to walk to the car, Graham was nowhere in sight.

CHAPTER TWO

The street lamp flickered, spreading dangerous waves of shadows over the front seat of Graham's car. Hidden in the twisting darkness, he waited for the band of wayward gypsies to arrive.

If he hadn't let Helena's sweet, loving eyes break through the ice of his resolve, he could have handled the necessary business at the prison, but Graham had missed the opportunity, and now what he needed to say couldn't wait any longer—tonight might be his last chance to have a quick meeting with Helena's father. And maybe, if everything played right, he could get Seamus to listen to his offer.

His phone rang. It was the manor.

"Aye, this is Graham."

"Graham? I'm sorry to call and bother you, sir, but I thought you needed to know that Herb went missing this afternoon," the nurse said.

"Has he been found?"

"Yes, sir. He was up in the kitchens again. He was talking

nonsense. However, we've gotten him back and have given him some sedatives to make him more comfortable."

"Is everyone else okay? Danny? Rose?"

"The rest of them are fine. Rose is just now doing a little physical therapy. And Danny… well… you know how Danny is."

He cringed. "Good. And good job finding Herb."

"You're welcome, sir. And don't worry, we won't let him out of our sight again."

"I'm sure you won't," he said in a warning tone. He hung up the phone.

Everything rested on this. Danny waited.

A car pulled up to the side of the bar, and Helena and her father stepped out.

Nine o'clock. Right on time.

Travellers were notorious for being undependable, but Helena had done exactly what he had expected. If she continued being this malleable, every pound he'd given the warden to get Seamus O'Driscoll released had been well spent.

The emerald green sequins of her dress glistened, sending shards of light across the tarmac like broken glass. Her rainbow-colored aura radiated from her as several men poured out of the bar and waved at the guest of honor and the beautiful woman at his side.

It was hard to believe that this Helena was the clairsentient they'd been looking for, but unlike people, auras never lied.

The door clicked as Graham pushed it open and stepped out of the car. He held onto the cold steel edge of the door and watched as a bevy of Travellers, all wanting to receive Seamus O'Driscoll, flooded from the bar's doorway. The noise of the gypsy mob echoed out into the street, filling the quiet night with their loud Gaelic jargon and laughter as they welcomed the old man. Graham held no hope they would treat him with even a degree of the same acceptance.

• • •

Moments like these were one of the reasons Helena loved being a Pavee. Live music bounced off the walls and reverberated through her body as she sat at the head table and watched Da perform a jig in the middle of the pub's small dance floor. The sight brought a smile to her lips—a smile she hadn't had in what, five, six years? This was how it should be—families, friends, and her people together. Always.

She couldn't imagine being alone—without this... huge, all-encompassing family and way of life.

Mam flopped down in the chair a few down from her, her eyes glassy with drink. "Why aren't ya out there dancin'? Are ya too good for it?" She hiccupped.

"Just takin' a break, Mam."

"If ya knew what was good for ya, ya'd be out there lookin' for a good man. Ya need to start thinkin' about movin' on. Now that your da's back, you're only another mouth to feed." Mam took a long drink from her plastic champagne flute. "It's time you were somebody else's problem."

She tried to ignore Mam's drunken rambling and turned away from the ruddy-faced wolf. Tonight wasn't the night to have a row. Nothing good would come of a fight.

There was a flash of red out of the corner of her eye—nothing more than a swirling skirt as her aunt danced over toward their table—and her mind jumped to the Manchester-United-loving Graham. He had acted so cocky, so headstrong, and yet—Helena glanced around the room—none of the men were anything compared to the brown-eyed gorger who had smiled at her earlier that day.

"Your da is a right fine man," her aunt said as she drew near. "You're one lucky lass to have such a man to protect you."

"Aye, I'm mighty lucky," Helena answered only half paying attention.

"I can't believe how many came out to support your da…"

"Everyone used to think the world revolved around him." Helena gave her a weak smile.

"It must be real tough on you all now that it's all changed." The skinny woman pulled at the strapless red evening dress, raising it dangerously close to her nether regions.

Helena didn't hear anything beyond the pitch of her words as her aunt continued prattling. After a moment of chatter, her aunt stopped, looking for a response. Helena gave her a numb nod. With a disgruntled sigh, almost as if she were upset she wasn't going to get any fresh gossip, her aunt spun on her spiked heel and pranced away into the bustling crowd.

Across the room, a group of her cousins sat around visiting. A man in a mud-brown suit leaned over and said something behind a cupped hand. The man he was speaking to looked over toward Helena and started laughing.

She didn't have to hear their words—they were passing judgment on her fam. They were probably telling each other they would never let one of their daughters do as Helena's sister Angel had done as they drank the booze and ate the food she and Rionna had prepared.

Most of the people in this room might have been family, but not all were their friends. Some had only come to see what had become of her da and to laugh at the disastrous mess that was their family. Many of the guests were friends, but when the liquor ran dry and the food grew cold, the rest would fall away like dying flies and only their true allies would remain.

A new song blared from the big black speakers that stood at the front of the room. A line of women filed through the dance floor, their arms in the air. The group looked like a picture she had seen of women at the Carnival in Rio de Janeiro, with their gold, sequins, and tight-fitting corsets. The queen of them all had to be her cousin, Lydia— who wore a dress that was a perfect replica of a flamingo, pink feathers and all. The crown atop her head was shaped like a diamond-encrusted beak. The effect was breathtaking.

Rionna twirled with a few of her friends amidst the women while the crowds of unmarried boys stood around and whispered. The night had the feeling of a wedding; the only thing missing was the tall wedding cake and the happy couple.

Da's laughter floated around her as he slipped into the chair beside her. "Mighty fine night, *gra*. Mighty fine," he said, breathless from his dancing.

Helena relaxed into her unyielding chair. At least she didn't have to dance. The matching heels she had picked for Rionna and herself were beautiful, with red beads and diamonds on them, but they pinched the bejeezus out of her toes. It even hurt to watch as Rionna jiggled out on the dance floor, teetering precariously on her six-inch spikes.

Concealed by the long white tablecloth that adorned the head table, Helena wiggled a foot out of its shoe and stretched her sore toes. She sighed with relief as it escaped its confinement.

"*Maa'ths*, Mr. O'Driscoll." A young man, whom Helena recognized as another of her many cousins, stepped up to pay his respects. Swaying a bit, his hand firmly clutching a pint of dark ale, he continued. "I can't thank ye enough. Ya had every right to belt that ball-of-shite gorger. Angel had no business shacking up with him… And then getting *knocked up*." He laughed like a braying mule. "I hope other Traveller women will learn from what happened. They go to messing around, they gotta pay."

Da's smile disappeared and he cleared his throat. "That was an awful hard lesson for everybody. And Angel paid a real high price."

"Where's the brasser anyway? I told me boys she wouldn't have the guts to show her face."

Helena bristled. "Shut your mouth, you damned eejit. You don't know what you're talking about."

Her cousin reddened, and he raised his hand as if he were going to pummel her for her outburst.

"Now, now, Helena," Da said as he patted her hand. "He didn't mean nothin'. It's only the booze talking." He turned back to the young man, his voice taking a dangerous edge. "Isn't that right, boy? And there ain't no sense in bringin' up the past, is there?"

The boy looked over and glared at Helena with his tiny black eyes, but she felt nothing but the desire to slug the bugger in the face. He was the kind of man who gave Travellers a nasty image.

"The past and our fam makes us who we are." The boy paused to take a sip of his ale. "If we go against our fam… we might as well not even call ourselves Pavee. Don't forget it—you don't want to end up alone, like your sister." He turned and stomped away.

Mam reached over and grabbed Helena's hand with her bony fingers. "What do ya think you're doin'? You have no business talkin' back to your cousin like that." She squeezed Helena's fingers together so hard they began to throb, but Helena didn't budge. "What's wrong with ye, girl? Don't you know we're tryin' to look better, not worse?"

She wanted to yell at Mam that she was the only thing making them look like shite—Mam was the one who had brought this all upon them. She only cared about herself and what was best for her reputation—regardless of the effect on their family. But nothing was ever going to change. There was no point in being upset. Helena dropped her gaze to the crisp white tablecloth. "Sorry, Mam. I know."

"Where *is* Angel tonight? Did you tell her about your da's release?" Mam released her grip on Helena's fingers.

"She sends her best."

Mam tsked. They both knew the truth: Angel, her gorger husband, and her half-gorger baby weren't welcome—and Angel knew it.

It had been a month since Helena had spoken with her sister. Last she heard Angel had moved out into a house in Rathkeale, close to other Travellers. But no matter where she went, her scarlet letter followed her. She'd never truly be welcome in either culture.

Sadness tugged at Helena's heart, but Angel had chosen her path. There was no point dwelling on it. Pavee girls were expected to marry and get out from under their parents' care. For Angel, that choice had entailed leaving her people behind, while she started a life with a gorger. And for Helena… for Helena it meant that, at twenty, she should have been married years ago. The thought gripped her. She didn't want to be married, but she didn't want to be a burden either. Reaching into her purse, she felt the smooth cover of her studier. Education was her only way out of a forced marriage. If she did well on her tests, she wouldn't need a man. She could make her own living and get her own trailer. She wouldn't have to be some man's slave—or worse, be stuck in a marriage like her parents'.

In that way, she was different than the rest of the Traveller girls. For many of them, their biggest goal was to find a man as soon as they could. Perhaps they were on to something; if they got married, they got to escape.

Yet some prices were too high. No matter how angry she was at her mam, flying into the arms of a man who might hold her back was just running from one bad life to the next.

A shadow passed over her, and she looked up to see a stocky man in a blue button-up shirt and white collar standing before her. His hair was slicked back with too much gel, and in his hand was a half-empty pint.

"Ya wanna dance?" He directed his pint toward Helena.

Mam smiled. The edge of her red lipstick was smeared slightly. "Answer him, girl."

"Um, well, I…" Helena stammered. She hadn't planned on dancing, or even being invited to.

In her culture, it was fine for a woman to dance amongst their friends, but if a man and a woman danced together it would be scandalous if they didn't get married. It was all part of the strict rules everyone followed when it came to courting, the most important rule being that Traveller girls didn't date around. They were expected to date one and only one man—the man they would marry.

Helena's stomach clenched tight and sweat pooled in her fisted hands. "I was just about to go for a stroll. I need some fresh air." She stood up, forgetting about the shoe that rested on the floor next to her bare foot.

Mam covered her face in embarrassment as Helena teetered on one heel.

"Sorry. I just gotta…" Helena leaned over and slipped her foot into her shoe.

Mam huffed.

"Ya want me to go with ya?" the man grumbled. "I can get my cousin to tag along."

At least he wasn't completely oblivious to the custom—which also meant he must've known what he was asking her. Her stomach dropped. This wasn't what she wanted, some rat-arsed man to pick her up. Nothing good would come from it except marriage, which was exactly what Mam wanted.

Feeling her mother's glare, Helena turned her decision over in her head. Going for a stroll was dangerous, but it was also the best way to get out of an uncomfortable situation without disgracing her family by rejecting the poor drunk. And maybe she would get a chance to steer the man away from her once they were out of sight. Mam wouldn't be any the wiser.

Helena scanned the room until she saw her cousin, Lydia, on the dance floor. Waving until she got her attention, Helena motioned her over, and then turned to her potential suitor. "Lydia'll come with us. Aye?"

The man lifted his chin slightly as he looked over to the hot pink bird fluttering their way.

Helena held her breath. If there were two girls, the chances of not being grabbed were a little more in her favor.

Grabbing was an infamous tradition. If a man really wanted a girl, he could make himself known by pulling the girl into the shadows and going in for a kiss. When it worked, it was a guarantee that the boy would have the girl as his wife, but if the girl got away, the boy would have to go after another. It was a ridiculous game, though Helena often heard Rionna talking excitedly about it. All Helena could think of were the stories of the boys who had gone too far, leaving the girls with rips in their fancy dresses and tears in their eyes. Helena looked down at her emerald green dress, covered in drifter's diamonds. That was no way to start a life together, with tears and broken things.

"Hiya, Helena. Who's this fine-looking stranger?" Lydia appeared at the table, eying the stocky brunette.

"I'm James, but you fine ladies can call me Jimmy." The man straightened his posture and smiled for the first time since Helena had seen him. He stuck his thumb under the edge of one of the buttons that ran up the center of his shirt.

Maybe the problem would go about handling itself.

Helena followed the two out the door as the boy rambled on and on about football and family and how much money he was going to make working for his family's tarmac business.

Lydia's eyes gleamed, and her teeth reflected the blue light from the pub's sign. At least someone was enjoying herself.

"Helena?"

She recognized the brusque voice. *Graham.*

"What?" She glanced around frantically for the man who wouldn't get out of her thoughts, but he was nowhere to be seen.

"Ya all right?" Lydia asked, sounding annoyed that Helena had interrupted her chat.

Helena nodded as she gazed down the sidewalk, but saw no one except a few men who looked to be up to no good as they lurked beneath the flickering light of a lamppost. Following Lydia and the boy in the opposite direction, Helena glanced over at the pub across the street. A golden neon sign in the shape of a horseshoe hung in the window next to a set of black wooden doors, and parked in front was a white Mercedes with its windows tinted an inky black.

The car's door opened, and a brunette man stepped out. Even from across the street Helena could make out the handsome grin on his lips. Graham was still wearing his red Manchester United jersey, and it looked even gaudier and out-of-place than it had at the prison. He dipped his head in acknowledgment, but his eyes never strayed from hers.

"Whatcha doin', Helena? You comin' with us?" Jimmy asked.

She turned, afraid that if she kept looking she wouldn't be able to walk away. "Aye, I'm comin'."

Lydia pulled on Jimmy's arm, giggling as they made their way to the end of the block. As they turned the corner, Helena let herself look back in Graham's direction. In a secret compartment of her soul she held hope that he had followed, but he was nowhere to be seen.

Helena trudged behind the gabbing couple, but she couldn't stop thinking of Graham and why he had once again shown up at the edge of her life. She tried to push away her thoughts.

"A blonde, a brunette, and a redhead walk into a bar..." Jimmy's voice droned on and on as Lydia's laughter grew louder with each of his asinine jokes.

Helena's thoughts went back to Graham's reappearance. There were hundreds of pubs in Limerick. It had to be more than a simple coincidence that Graham had been at this one, at this time.

They made their way around the block and back to the front entrance of the bar. The white Mercedes was still parked in front of the bar across the street. Graham was close.

Almost as if on cue, the pub doors flew open and a pair of men tumbled out onto the sidewalk. Helena gasped as the other man's arm drew back and his fist smashed into Graham's chin. Men poured from the bar's entrance, cheering and rooting for a victor, as Graham and his opponent rolled around on the ground, their limbs a blur of movement.

"No! Stop, don't hit Graham!" Helena screamed, but her voice was swallowed by the roar of the onlookers.

Lydia turned and gave her a questioning stare.

Blue and red flashing lights illuminated the scene as the guards arrived in their squad cars. The gypsies grouped together, a force united against the guards. The men with records silently drifted to the back and away from the crowd, careful to remain unseen.

Lydia and Jimmy were whispering with another couple, but her cousin kept glancing over at her.

Trying to blend in, Helena pushed into the crowd and away from Lydia's judging gaze.

It didn't work; instead, Lydia followed, grabbed her by the arm, and dragged her into the empty pub.

"How in the hell do ya know that damned man? Why in the bloody hell did he walk into your da's party uninvited? Did ye tell him to come?"

"Nah… I never…"

Lydia glared at her. "Apparently he was saying all kinds of things to your da. He even offered him a job. Are you behind this?"

"I've never seen him before in my life," Helena lied.

The police lights flashed through the bar's windows and cast an odd glow on her friend's face.

"Bollocks. Do I look like some kind of eejit?" Lydia's beak-shaped tiara tilted in her hair like it was about to swoop in for the kill. "What was he doing here?"

"I don't know."

Lydia's eyebrows arched dangerously high. "You don't have no business cozyin' up with no gorger."

"Don't worry, Lyd. It's nothing. I barely know him."

"Don't make me tell your mam that yer walkin' about with a gorger. Ye know I wouldn't want to do that to you, but I'm the only one you got in your corner. Ya need to listen."

"I know." Helena shifted her weight from one painfully confined foot to the other. "And I'm not seein' him. We talked. Just for a second. 'Twas nothing, and I don't care to see him again." As the words left her lips, she felt the weight of her lie.

CHAPTER THREE

"This ain't no way a Traveller woman should be livin'... takin' care of her good-for-nothing husband who can't keep his arse out of the clink." Mam's voice carried from the other end of the trailer. "You shoulda taken the job the gorger offered; it'd give us the money that we need, but no... not you, Mister Too-fancy-for-a-good-payin'-job. Who in the bloody hell do you think you are? The Earl of Limerick?"

Helena blinked away the image of Graham tumbling back as the man's fist connected with his chin. It had been a long, fight-filled week since the party, and the gorger's beating. The memory of him being belted had started to fade, but the strange, unwelcome desire to see him again remained.

Sprawled on the foldout bed with her siblings, Helena pulled the copper-haired Gavin closer to her. His curls framed his cherubic face as he looked up at her. "Is everything gonna be okay?"

"Aye, Gav." She tried to sound positive.

Her thoughts drifted back to when she and Angel had

been young and traveling around Ireland with Mam and Da. In those days, they had spent many a night sitting around the fires with Da while Mam caused a ruckus in the trailer, throwing and cussing as she looked for another bottle. To keep them from being afraid, he would sip on a cup of hot tea and tell them tales of fairies, trolls, gnomes, nature sprites, and the gold-fearing phantom of death, the Dullahan. After a bit, when Mam had found the bottle and sunk comfortably into its depths, Da would carry them into the quiet trailer and tuck them into bed right next to one other.

Before they fell asleep they would each make a wish for the night. Most times they wished for practical things—that Mam would get better, that Da would get a new lorry. But once in a while they would wish for silly things—dreams that would never come true.

Angel's silly wish was always the same; she wanted a pink wedding cake with yellow birds made of frosting. On and on she would talk about her wedding, and all the pretty dresses she would select for her cousins and sisters, and the fancy country shoes, and Helena would listen until finally they fell into the trap of sleep.

Helena's stomach ached thinking of how Angel never got that pink cake with the yellow birds. She probably never would.

The day Helena found out about Duncan's relationship with Angel had been the day Da had been arrested. Her father had followed the unwritten laws of their clan and taken his anger out on the gorger. Duncan had needed more than a hundred stitches and a set of wires in his jaw when Da had finished. When Helena heard about his actions, for the first time, she feared her da.

Then again, Angel had known better than to turn her back on the Traveller code by bedding a gorger. To this day, Helena couldn't wrap her brain around the idea of Angel abandoning her whole world to be with a man she hardly knew. Angel had given up everything, travelling around the countryside, the nights around the fire, the stories, the family, her culture, and worst of all she had given up Helena.

A bottle shattered against the wall.

Helena stared at the thin particle-board divider that ran between their parents' bedroom and the main living area of the trailer. Like so many times before, she wished it were thicker.

"Have you guys ever heard the saying, *'Ki shan i Romani—Adoi san'I chov'hani'?*" she asked as she ran her hair through Gavin's curls.

Gavin shook his head, and Rionna rolled her eyes and turned her back toward her.

"It means, 'Wherever the gypsies go, there the witches are, we know.'"

"Really?" Gavin asked in his curious, high-pitched voice.

"Ah, there ain't no thing as witches," Rionna grumbled.

An image of the crone flashed through her mind. "That's a right awful thing to say, Rionna. Of course there be witches," Helena whispered. "Do ya have questions that ya can't answer? Are there things that ya just can't explain, no matter how hard ye try?"

Rionna seemed to ignore her, but Gavin nodded.

"There're a lot of things that can't be explained. Why, Da once told me a tale—"

"Ya stupid bastard!" Mam yelled at Da from the other room, making Gavin tense in her arms.

"Shhhh…" she urged Gavin, giving him a squeeze. "Now, Da used to tell me that when he was just a wee lad, he got lost in the woods. The mist rolled in all round him. He said it was so thick it sat on him like a bag of wet wool. Even as a youngster, he knew that unless he found his way out back to the camp or built himself a strong fire, he would die long before morn."

Gavin laid his head on Helena's chest; his warm breath tickled her skin and made her smile.

"Night quickly fell as he went to building himself a fire. As he was making his last trip with a handful of kindling, somethin' ran in front of him in the fog."

"Was it a stag?" Gavin asked.

Helena smiled. "The bushes in front of him rattled, and being the tough, strong boy Da was, he ran toward them. When he reached the bushes, no one was there, and when he called out, no answer came."

She ran her fingers through Gavin's fine hair. "Da put down his sticks, and got on his hands and knees—thinking maybe it was a rabbit he'd happened upon, and perhaps he would have a fresh supper. Da pushed aside a low-lying branch and *whap*!" Helena grabbed Gavin's fingers. The boy let out a muted squeal, and they giggled with excitement. "A wee little bugger laid into Da's finger."

"What was it? What was it?" Gavin squeaked.

"Da swears 'twas a tiny little goblin. With black eyes and wispy red hair, the color of the morning sunrise, with green warty skin. The wee man wouldn't let go of Da's finger no matter how hard Da tried."

Gavin covered his mouth as an excited giggle escaped. "What happened?"

"Well, finally the beast let go and muttered what Da said sounded like a curse. Then it ran straight back under the tree." She looked down into Gavin's eyes. "The next morning his ol' da followed the trail of smoke from Da's fire right to where Da slept under the stars. When Da told Ol' Da about the strange redheaded beast that had bit him, Ol' Da took him straight away to the camp healer—the one that everyone said had *the gift*."

Gavin sucked in a quivering breath.

"She took one look at the tooth marks on his finger and almost fainted. She'd never seen nothin' like it—she'd only ever heard of it from the old-time healers. When he asked her about the redheaded man, she told Da about the myth of goblins. It was said that once a man was bitten he would be of two spirits—one of which would roam the world forever."

"Da's gonna be a ghost?" Gavin snuggled in closer.

Helena laughed, but goose pimples rose on her arms. "Nah, lad. It's just a story now. Don't fret. Da's gonna go to heaven, just like the Pope says."

"What's it mean then? If he ain't gonna be a ghost?"

"I don't rightly know. It's just an old fairy tale anyhow. The healer may have been razzin' him. You know how those old crones can be." Helena thought back to the woman she'd met outside of the prison. "Some healers think it's a right gas to play tricks. They're just like them old goblins.

"Now ya need to get your rest. Ya don't know what tomorrow'll bring. And who knows, maybe we can find some goblins of our own?"

Gavin wiggled down deeper under the blanket, and before long all but Helena were asleep. The fighting between

Mam and Da had quieted, but she could still hear their muffled voices.

So much time had passed since Da had last been around that Helena had forgotten this part of her da being home. Or maybe it was never this bad before. She couldn't quite decide, but either way it made her cringe to hear them bickering. Some thing marriage was, if it made people so cruel.

• • •

The morning fire sputtered and spit to life like a hacking old man outside the trailer. Peering out the tiny window, Helena watched the smoke curl up from the feeble flames, begging the world around it to help it along.

It was her favorite time of the day: no squabbling, no cold shoulder from her mam, and there was something about the morning air. Maybe it was the promise of a fresh start the breeze carried that brought her such excitement, or it could have been the way yesterday's problems seemed to have disappeared with the shadows of the night.

It seemed so impossible that she would ever have anything besides her Traveller life. Not that she minded everything. She was gypsy through and through. She loved that they were never strapped down to one place. They travelled on the winds, letting only their whims, or maybe the next job, be their guide. It was a life of freedom.

Leaning down, she opened her drawer and pulled out her studier.

The book's curled pages gripped her finger like a baby's hand as she sat the book on the counter and flipped it open. She turned to the section on the Irish language—a subject required in the Post Leaving Certificate exam, but one she felt comfortable with… so long as she could keep it all straight in her head.

A clang of metal on metal sounded from the side of the trailer. Helena flinched at the familiar sound of an upcoming move. Where they would be moving to she could only imagine. Perhaps her da wanted to find an escape from the memories of the prison which must have swirled around their campsite. Or it could have been the subtle breeze that whipped the campfire's flames, stirring them up and begging Helena's family to move forward. Whatever the reason, it was time. Time to travel. To make a fresh go of things.

She was squinting at the book's page, trying to clear her head and focus, when the door to the back bedroom opened and Mam stumbled out, deep bags under her eyes. She looked over at Helena, standing at the counter. "Studying again?"

Helena nodded.

"Did ya muck out the trailer yet?"

"Aye," Helena whispered as she motioned to the sleeping kids.

"Well, that studying be a waste of time. You're as dumb as an old rusty knife and about as much use as one too."

Helena cringed, but she closed the book and stashed it in the small drawer filled with her clothes—the only space that was hers.

Mam stepped beside her and stared out the kitchen window, as if nothing were wrong. Pulling a ciggy from the packet on the counter, she lit the round tip. A curl of smoke twisted toward the ceiling.

Helena set about with breakfast until the distinct aroma of sausage and eggs crackled up from the cooker, spoiled by the tarry scent of Mam's ciggy. Helena dabbed her hands on a towel, then pushed the kids from the bed. As they washed their faces, she turned the small bed back into their dining table in a few well-practiced motions. Spitting in her palm, Mam drowned her ciggy and pushed it behind her ear. With a grunt, she plopped down beside the children while Helena dished out portions of the fry-up.

Their chewing was interrupted by a thump when Da closed a door on the outside of the trailer.

"Where're we goin'?" Gavin asked between bites of egg.

Mam stabbed a sausage and lifted it up for inspection. "Your da finally is gonna do what's best for him." She took a bite.

"Whatcha mean?" Gavin asked as he grabbed a struggling bit of egg with his pudgy fingers.

"He's gonna be taking the job the eejit gorger offered him." Mam grabbed the wet ciggy from behind her ear as she dug around in her pocket for a lighter. "Girl, eat your food." She motioned to Helena's half-eaten fry-up.

Helena pushed her plate over to Gavin, who took it eagerly. The boy couldn't get enough to eat, and after what little sleep Helena had gotten, she didn't feel much like breakfast. Dreams of numbers, and words, and equations... and Graham and his chocolate-colored eyes had plagued her.

"I'm gonna go help Da." She walked out of the trailer before Mam could start grumbling. Standing in the dust, Da twisted a rope around his arm in a tight figure eight.

"Breakfast's ready," Helena said, glad to be out of the smoky trailer.

"That's grand." Da's lips flickered into a weak smile,

but his eyes looked deeply troubled. "How'd ya sleep, gra a mo gris?"

"Just fine, Da," she said, trying to reassure him, as if he were one of the children.

"So ya heard us fighting did ya?"

Helena looked away.

"Well, you don't need to worry, gra. I got in touch with the gorger from the party and got me a job—but there's a bit of a catch."

"What?"

Da's gaze fixed on the rope round his arm. "I need you to go with me. They want us both."

"But, Da…" she said, trying to calm the butterflies that awakened in her stomach at the thought of being so close to Graham. "I can't, Da… What about my exams?"

"Look, gra a mo gris, I know ya want to finish your school and put it all behind you, but I need you. They won't hire me if you don't come along."

"But—"

"I know 'tis a lot to ask," Da interrupted as he moved toward the corner of the trailer, where the door was open to expose the guts of the metal box. "You heard your mam; we need the money."

Her exams were two weeks away. She needed every second of the time to concentrate on her learning, and if she went with Da, the work and her proximity to Graham would only get in the way of her studies. Yet family and home came first—and if her actions could help put a stop to Mam and Da's fighting, then her sacrifice would be for the greater good.

The door slammed, and Mam marched out of the trailer.

Da stepped behind the corner of the trailer and pulled Helena after him, out of Mam's sights. "Don't you be telling your mam our plan," he whispered. "She won't take it well that you are plannin' on going to work with me... You know how she can be about these things."

Helena had received more than her fair share of jabs from her mother for lesser things. "Who'll take care of Gav and Rionna if I'm helping ye?"

Da frowned and looked toward Mam and sighed. "Your brother and sister'll be all right, lass. She can handle those lil' heathens. Besides, hopefully I won't need ya round real long. I just need ya to help me get started."

A memory of Mam with a bottle in her hand fluttered into her mind. When Helena had been a wee girl, Angel had been there to help raise her up. Rain or shine, most days they had spent away from the trailer, investigating the woods or the markets near where they had parked, not coming back until Mam had passed out from the drink and Da had found his familiar place at the fire after a long day of work laying tarmac.

Da was right. Gavin and Rionna would be fine. They were hard-raised, just as Helena and Angel had been, but the thought of leaving them filled her with dread. She'd been there since each of their first breaths, only leaving them when forced. Leaving them would be as dangerous as leaving a fox alone with chicks—it would only end in disaster.

Mam stomped over, her face in a tight frown. "What are you two up to now? Thinking of ways ya can go and get my life all banjaxed?"

"Cora, be quiet," Da said in a voice that made it clear he meant business.

"It must be nice for you two, now that ya can gang up against me, ain't it?" Mam glared at Helena with the power of hellfire. "Well, did your little gra tell ya 'bout what happened the other night? At your party?"

"Cora, I told ya to be quiet…"

Mam waved him off. "Did Helena go and tell ya she knew that man? One of the women even said she called out his name."

Da glanced over at Helena. "How do you know that gorger?"

"He was outside the prison… 'twas nothing," she lied, thinking about the way his eyes had caressed her like a wanting hand. "I was just surprised to see him at the party was all."

"I think it's time we start thinking 'bout finding her a husband." Mam pointed at her like she was some kind of livestock. "Before somethin' happens."

Da looked over at her with pity in his eyes. "You're all right, lass? Aren't ya?"

"I only met him for a second Da I swear. It didn't mean nothin'."

Da turned back to Mam. "If she says t'wasn't nothing, I believe her. You need to have a lil' more faith in Helena. She's the best girl of the bunch."

Mam's face pulled into a tight snarl. "You don' need to tell me who ya love the most. It's never been no secret."

"Ya need to get your head on straight, Cora. I've only been back a week, and already you ain't done nothing but complain. Ya need to stop worryin' about me and Helena and start worryin' about your other kids. You don't want the womenfolk to know what a shitty-arse mam ya really are."

Mam's jaw dropped, and she stepped back as if Da had punched her square in the gut. "I never…"

"*You never*, all right… You've never been there for those kids. They need you, and yet you're out here, badgering us. Get in the trailer and be a mam. 'Tis your last chance."

Mam stomped away and threw open the door. "Ya shoulda stayed behind those bars. You'll never change, always a little rat who don't care about nobody but his self. We were better off without ya."

The door slammed shut.

"You don't believe that do you, gra?" Da asked.

"Nah, Da," Helena stepped closer and took his weathered hand. "Everything will be as right as rain… We'll go take the job. Mam will get better. You'll see."

For a moment, she felt like she had as a child, lying in bed and wishing on dreams.

CHAPTER FOUR

Every time Graham saw his stepfather, John Shane, all he could think of was an American cowboy: tall, moody, and dangerous. His well-groomed dark brown hair was dappled with gray, the same color as the moustache which wrapped around his mouth in a sharp curve. His eyes were angry as he tapped his fingers against the top of his desk. No matter how long they'd been what most considered family, when it came right down to it, they were little more than business partners. If they hadn't shared mutual interests in the people they loved, they would have fallen away from one another years ago.

"You're sure they have decided to come?" Mr. Shane growled.

"Yes. They should be here anytime."

"You've been saying that all week." Mr. Shane stared up at him from under his furrowed brow. "I don't want any more *incidents*. You aren't to be involved in any more fights."

Graham licked the cut on his lip where the gypsy had

split it with a well-placed punch. "That was an accident, sir. I went in with the intention of offering Seamus the job and getting out of there, but they got the drop on me. It wasn't Seamus's fault."

Mr. Shane shook his head with disgust. "Did you at least get the information I requested?"

"Yes. It doesn't sound like all of Seamus's children have supernatural abilities."

"That's fine." Mr. Shane leaned across his desk and pulled a cigar from his black humidor. "One Traveller and her father are more than enough to get what we need."

• • •

On the outskirts of Adare Village, the sun-bleached gates marked the spread of land which would serve as Helena's home for the foreseeable future. Across the government-owned square, the tall weeds leaned like broken men, their heads low and their arms limp. Overgrown trees surrounded the small camp, keeping them out of sight of the road and the judging eyes of the townspeople.

Helena moved around the square, picking up dead branches and bits of discarded lumber and anything that would build a suitable cooking fire. The door to the trailer banged as Mam threw it open and walked outside. She grabbed a folding chair and sat it next to the fire pit facing Da, who was working on the propane lines under the trailer.

"So you're going to go to Adare Manor?" Mam flopped down in her chair like she was a judge taking her seat at court. "Just gonna up and leave? I shoulda known."

Da wiggled out from under the trailer and stood up.

"First you wanted me to get a job, and now ya don't want me to be leaving? Make up your fecking mind, woman."

"All you seem to be good at is leavin' this family."

Helena moved toward them, careful to stay out of Mam's range of vision.

Da wiped his brow with a handkerchief. "I got better things to do than listen to your ramblings. Why don't you run along and find a bottle?"

"You arse. You don't got no room to be judgin' me."

Rionna opened the door and stared outside as Gavin scampered out from underneath her arm. The teen sneered at them as if she were Mam's bailiff, ready to take down anyone who went against the magistrate.

"By the way," Da said, undeterred by the petulant Rionna, "I'll be takin' Helena with me."

He was answered with an unintelligible mix of profanity. Rionna grabbed a bottle of caramel-colored whiskey and carried it to Mam. She unscrewed the lid and took a long swig.

Helena tried to stay unnoticed as she dumped the wood into the pit and started the fire in the ash-filled ring at the camp's heart. While she struggled, Gavin ran through the weeds, letting them tear at his pants but never letting them slow him down. She envied those days, when Mam's outbursts were frightening and loud, but forgotten by the end of the night.

"I hope you got everything set up inside," Da said, jamming his kerchief into his back pocket.

"Helena can do it. She needs to be makin' herself of some use before she runs off to be your *wee helper*." Mam ran her hand under her bloodshot nose. "I don't know why that little brat has to go with ya. She'd be of more use helpin' round here, learnin' how to be a proper wife while keepin' after Rionna and Gavin." Mam took another gulp. "I don't know how ya expect me to keep after them all the time. They're like fleas."

"Cora, our kids ain't no fleas. They're free spirits. And, for the most part, I'm proud of the little buggers. They've made do when things have been tough." Da shook his head. "Rionna can help with Gavin. She's old enough."

Mam snickered as she lifted her fingers from the bottle and licked the spilled booze off. "She's got better things to do. Rionna's got *prospects*." She gave Helena a sideways glance.

"Cora, did anyone ever tell ya that ya got a way of lookin' at the world that couldn't be more wrong than if it came out a dog's arse?" Da motioned to Helena. "Let's go, gra."

• • •

Da drove the lorry out of the square and down the road, his eyes reflecting the storm that loomed overhead. They passed shop after shop on their way to the manor. On the side of the road was a sign which read "Welcome to Adare, Voted Ireland's Most Picturesque Village."

On most days, Helena imagined the sign was bang on. The thatch-roofed cottages and shops in varying shades of blues and pinks were cheery and bright, but today the heavy clouds seemed to have smothered any joy the village hoped to create.

A fat raindrop landed on the windshield, and the few remaining people in the streets retreated.

"Heck of a day," Da offered. "You know what they say: Rain on a big day is good luck."

"It was only a drop, Da."

No matter what Da said, they didn't have any luck. Nothing good had come about—except Da's job. Yet Helena couldn't bring herself to trust the offer. It didn't seem right, a manor looking to hire a Traveller. If she had to guess, by now the owner must have found out more about them, and she and Da would be turned away at the door. It had to have been an oversight that Da, a good man but a convict nonetheless, had been offered a job anywhere, let alone the prestigious Adare Manor.

Perhaps this was all some sick joke.

The lorry slowed as Da turned down the road leading to the gates. On the left stood a stone abbey, its steeple reaching up to the sky as if it waited for God's blessing. On the right stood an unwelcoming stone wall; behind it were tall ash trees. Through their camouflaging leaves, bits of the granite manor flashed by.

Coming to the gates, Da stopped the lorry and a security guard in a black suit stepped to the window and tapped the glass.

Da hesitated for a moment. With a deep breath, he twisted the crank and opened the window.

"Hello, sir," the guard said. "May I ask why you are visiting the manor today?"

Da's fingers curled tightly around the steering wheel. "We've come about a spot of work."

"Really?" The guard stared at them. "Do you expect me to believe that? Why don't you be moving along. This is a place of business, not somewhere you can come for a free spot of lunch."

"We've got an appointment. We're to be seein' Graham Kelly," Da growled.

The guard pushed a button on a walkie-talkie clipped to his lapel. Turning his back to them, he whispered something. After a moment, he walked to the granite wall and punched a code into the keypad. The gates swung open, and the man waved them through. When they drove by, he wouldn't look them in the eye.

"Da, are you sure you want to do this?"

"Do what, gra?"

"Work here." Helena shifted in her seat. They didn't belong there. The guard had made it clear; no one would ever see them for anything but untrustworthy gypsies. "Do you really want to work at this place?"

"Lass, we have debts that need to be paid."

"What debts?"

"Your mam had to borrow a lot of money from the O'Donoghues when I was away. If I know them, they'll be comin' to call. You know how those people can be."

Helena nodded. The O'Donoghues were amongst the foulest people of the Traveller community. They were known for their shady construction. It seemed they always were one step ahead of the guards.

"Isn't there something else you could be doing? Isn't there a Traveller family who'd give you a construction job?"

Da gave her a weak smile. "You know how those jobs can be—I'd have to be careful about who I went to work with. I can't be riskin' anything. I need somethin' that will keep me out of the clink."

"But Da, there has to be somebody who'd be willin' to help us get back on our feet."

"Gra, you know how it is. Don't ya?" He looked over at her. "The world isn't always kind to people like us. We have to fight to prove 'em wrong, lass. And takin' this job is the best way I can see how. I get real wages at a job that won't be under the guards' microscope, and we can show these lairds what it really means to be gypsy—what it means to have a good heart... and to be free."

By God, she had missed her da.

Helena sucked in a breath as they approached the granite citadel. It was immense and impressive, with tall green and red vines weaving up the stone surface and around the arched gothic windows. Each stone of the manor's surface was smooth and unblemished, scarcely showing the ravages of time.

On each side of the lorry were large gardens of salvia whose red, bobbing flowers seemed to be turned away from them, as if even they knew that she and Da shouldn't have entered this place. Next to the unwelcoming flowers were long, weaving labyrinths of thorn-filled bushes. It was easy to imagine ladies in fine dresses walking through the gardens, reminiscent of days long past. Da pulled the lorry into the car park at the side of the manor and next to a gold-accented Rolls Royce.

Along the top of the house, on the parapet, the stone was cut into letters and arranged to read, "Except The Lord Build The House Their Labour Is But Lost That Build It."

Helena recognized the words from Psalms, but what they meant she didn't know. Was it a thank you to those who had built the house? Or a call to supremacy made by the laird? She looked over to Da, but knew she couldn't ask him. He would be just as confused.

Throughout her life, Helena had spent many a day begging for pocket change, or selling trinkets she and the children had made. She'd stood outside pubs and prisons, but never in her life had she felt more out of place—or unwelcome. Yet now was the time to stand up and walk proudly.

On the left side of the manor, the door opened, and a man wearing a red tartan kilt stepped out. He smiled and brushed his dark chestnut-colored hair out of his face, exposing the yellow-and-brown edges of a healing bruise under his eye. Even marred from his fight, Graham was more handsome than she remembered.

"Hello, and welcome to Adare Manor, Hotel, and Golf Course," Graham said robotically. His gaze darted over to her, but quickly flashed back to Da. "I'm glad you've decided to take me up on my job offer—especially after the other night. I'm sorry for disrupting your party."

Da gave Graham's hand a strong shake. "I must apologize for my clan. They get a bit rowdy—'specially when they think their toes are bein' stepped on." Da glanced at Graham's face. "I always thought a split lip and a good shiner was the mark of a night well spent. I hope ya feel the same."

Graham licked the healing line on his lip and smiled. "It was a night to remember."

"What can I say? We Travellers like to have a good time in a bad way!" Da led the way to the castle, stopping by the door. "We are born and bred free and wild as the River Shannon. Or should I say the River Maigue?" He chuckled and motioned in the direction of the gurgling river that ran just north of where they stood.

"Aye, yes... I've heard that before." Graham glanced over at Helena.

"I hope you don't mind that my gra came along. She wanted to see the manor while the rest of the fam went about settin' up camp."

"That's fine," Graham said, giving her a sly wink. She dropped her gaze to the ground. "So you know, you're welcome to take up residence in one of our cottages at the edge of Adare Village. We have several that are currently vacant. It's not a long walk, should you choose to live there."

Da looked over at Helena and smiled. "I think we'll be fine in our trailer. Don't want to be giving ya more work than ya already got. Where do you live?" he asked Graham.

"Right now I'm staying behind the manor, in the groundskeeper's old house. He passed last fall, and since then I've been trying to do some of his duties."

"I'm sorry to hear of his passing," Helena offered.

"He was a good man." Graham turned to Da. "And I was hoping that you, Seamus, would be willing to take over his position as groundskeeper. What level of experience do you have?" His gaze moved over to Helena as if he were hoping she would have the answer he wanted.

"I've done a bit of construction and a bit of hunting. Don't tell the guards, but I'm damn fine at rustlin' up fresh meat for Helena here." He patted her arm. "And I got a bit of experience when it comes to layin' tarmac."

"Would you be interested in working as our head groundskeeper?" Graham motioned toward the great house. "There is always something in this place that needs to be fixed. Think you'd be up to the task?"

Da nodded. "Aye, but I won't be askin' when and where I can take a piss."

Helena flushed as Graham shook with laughter. "That's good, because I don't want to hold it for you."

Graham looked over and must have noticed her blushing. He reached over and touched her shoulder reassuringly. The second his fingers brushed against her it was as if a bomb had exploded inside of her. Visions and memories swirled, overtaking her and forcing her to close her eyes. Once again, she was outside of the prison, watching as Graham made his way down the concrete steps.

Graham jerked away his hand as Helena opened her eyes. The world seemed to swirl around her like roiling water, and her legs wobbled like they were threatening to give out. She put her hand against the wall for support, trying to blink away the strange dream that had overtaken reality.

A sense of weariness shrouded her, weighing her down.

"Helena?" Graham moved toward her as if to take her arm to help support her, but he stopped and looked down at his hands.

Had he felt the charge between them? Had he had a vision as well?

Da stared at her, a look of worry on his face. "You okay, gra?"

She dropped her hand from the wall, willing her body to regain its strength. "Aye, just fine, Da."

Graham stepped back. "You don't have to stay. You can both come back tomorrow. I can go over your duties then."

Da stepped between them, blocking her from seeing Graham. "Don't be worrying about Helena any. She's tougher than she looks. This job's important to me... to both of us."

"I'm sure you're right. As you know, we'd like to keep you both on staff as long as possible." There was a touch of excitement in Graham's voice, but Helena could have gotten it wrong. Maybe it was merely her imagination.

Da glanced over at her nervously. "Aye, that's kind of ya, Mr. Kelly, but Helena here is plannin' on goin' to university after she takes her exams."

Graham frowned, and darkness washed over his features. "When are your tests?"

"Not long from now," Helena replied. "I... I do appreciate what you're doin' for my fam and all, but—"

"Education is a valuable thing," he said, cutting her off. "Yet, sometimes the best thing in life, and the best way to learn, is by doing something that you can be passionate about. I believe, here at Adare Manor, we can provide you with an experience that will be both rich and fulfilling."

Da nodded with approval. "I tried to tell her the same thing—you learn by doin', not by talkin'."

She bit her tongue. Her desire to go to university had little to do with book learning; rather, it was the only way for her to break from the grip of tradition. Da didn't understand, and as *rich and fulfilling* as her work at the manor might be, she doubted that it would provide her with the escape that she needed.

Graham sent her a thin smile, almost as if he could tell that she was holding back.

She looked away from his gaze. Above the door, carved in the granite, were ancient-looking symbols of triangular family crests with stags, horses, swords, hammers, and runes. The markings reminded her of the druids.

"'Tis a beautiful manor. When was it built?" Da asked, as if he too were embarrassed by the direction the conversation had taken.

Graham stepped to the wooden bench beside the door, only a few steps from Helena. His scent, the familiar aroma of sweet grass and fresh air, wafted toward her. "This house was built in the 1700s, but the second Earl of Dunraven took over in the 1830s and turned the manor into what you see today. All the stone and wood in this castle has been handcrafted—and all are shrouded in a bit of mystery and symbolism." Graham motioned toward the entrance.

"Some people believe the Earl of Dunraven and his heirs had a special connection to the old gods as well as the new. In fact, they were one of the only families in the Irish aristocracy of true Gaelic origins. If you pay attention, there are many secrets held within the manor's walls."

"Hey," Da said, not paying attention to Graham. "You want me to fix that?"

"What?" Graham asked.

"There's a crack." Da walked over to the sleigh-backed bench and crouched down. "See? Right here." He pointed at one of the claw-footed legs. A thin crack ran up its length.

"Oh, that can't be fixed."

"Ho, ho, there you're wrong. Just wait here a sec." Da stood up with a broad grin on his face. He looked over at Helena, then back at Graham. "Helena, you okay if I run to the lorry? I need to get my tools."

Helena nodded.

He looked back and forth between her and Graham.

"Graham, I need ya to promise me somethin'; if we're gonna work here I need to know you'll look after me daughter like she's blood of yer blood. Can I trust ya?"

Graham gave Da a confident, if not overly excited, smile. "Seamus, you have my word."

Helena stepped back, her back pushed against the cold stone. "Da... I'm fine."

Da waved her off. "Good. That's a good man." Da turned and raced off to the lorry.

She and Graham stood alone.

She wanted to ask him so much, but she was already running a risk by being this close to him—Mam would have a right fit if she found out that Da had left her unchaperoned. Sweat collected in her palms.

Graham cleared his throat. "I'm sorry about the party. I didn't mean to ruin your night—and I know I didn't say the right thing at the prison. I shouldn't have called you a gypo. I owe you an apology. I just didn't realize..."

She tried, but no matter how hard she attempted it, she couldn't hold her tongue. "That I was a pikey?" Her nerves mixed with the anger in her gut. "Why did you talk to me at all?"

"I guess I thought we could be friends, or maybe—"

"You thought you would make friends with a gypo standing outside of Limerick Prison?" she interrupted. "What's your angle?"

"I don't... there's no..." Graham's mouth opened and closed like a fish gasping for air, but she didn't wait for him to finish.

"You people always think you can *buy* whatever you want. But you got another thing comin' if you think that's the kind of woman I am." She looked up at the castle and some of the air left her argument.

"I never said anything like that." He reached out for her, but she moved away from him.

"Why did you give Da this job? Were you tryin' to get in my knickers? Or is this just some happy coincidence?"

"Your *knickers* have nothing to do with why I offered your father the job." The softness in Graham's features hardened.

"Then why are we here? Were you tryin' to get my father to take the fall for something?"

"Don't you trust anyone? Can't someone just want to help you? I hate to squash your conspiracy theory, but I wanted to hire you and your father because I thought you would be valuable additions to our staff." Graham shook his head in disgust, but there was something in his eyes, some shadow, that made her second-guess his motivation. "What kind of man do you think I am?"

"I don't know what kind of person you are. You speak of trust, but there's something wrong... I can feel it. You ain't tellin' me somethin'."

Graham opened the door and stepped inside. He turned back to face her. "Think what you want. You'll come to see that I'm not a monster."

CHAPTER FIVE

"I don't know what they did around this place before I got here," Da said to Helena as they arrived back at the manor the next morning. "Did you see the look on Graham's face when I fixed the bench? Just a lil' crushed pecan shell and that bugger was good as new."

Helena nodded as the gates of the manor passed by. She'd spent the previous night trying to tell Da that she didn't trust Graham and that he should find another job, but the words just wouldn't come. Now they'd be back in Graham's presence within minutes.

Sighing, she leaned her head against the lorry door. Maybe it *was* best that Da stayed. Settling down for a little while would be good for the family. The kids could finish the school year. The family could pay off debts. She could focus on her studies in the evening—at least when Mam and Da weren't fighting—and show the world that she had the power to create her own path. She could escape.

Her opinion of the handsome-but-off-putting Graham

didn't matter. She needed to accept their situation and focus on the family and the greater good.

"You okay, gra a mo gris?"

She faked a smile. "I'm fine. Just a bit tired."

"Sorry about the fighting again last night. I hoped your mam would be better since my new job, but those kids ran her ragged. I dunno know if she'll be able to get on alone with 'em."

"Does that mean ya want me to stay at the trailer?"

"Nah lass. She's gotta learn how to handle the kids if we're gonna make any money. Did you get that paperwork filled out?"

Helena patted her purse. "With all the right details."

She had made sure to give them a fake name and address. No one in the government needed to know anything about their family—they didn't need to be tracked like sheep.

"Good, and don't worry about the family. Rionna's old enough to take control."

"I hope so…"

Da pulled the lorry into the employee car park. Graham was working on the manor's town car and, as he spotted them, he stood up and closed the hood. Today he wore a crisp white shirt, unbuttoned just enough for Helena to spot the subtle curves of his tanned, muscular chest, but the same impractical red kilt. Very few men wore kilts. He probably did so in an effort to get the tourist girls running to him, but no matter how hard he tried, she'd never fall for his attempts to be sexy.

"Hi, Helena," he said as they got out of the lorry, his voice carrying an edge of overly friendly warmth. "Morning, Seamus."

Da nodded.

"This week the village is going to be celebrating *Feile na Maighe*," Graham said with a wide smile. "The festival will be in the village's square, but there'll be some big names staying here at the manor. We need to make sure we have everything in order when they arrive."

He turned to Da. "I was hoping that you and I could start going over more of what I will expect, as far as your daily duties are concerned. Will that work for you, Mr. O'Driscoll?"

"Aye, but what about Helena? She'll be workin' alongside me, ain't she?"

Graham's smile never wavered. "I'm afraid not, Seamus. I've arranged for another position for her."

Da's face darkened as he glanced over at her. "Why don't you wait here, gra? I think me and Mr. Kelly got a bit o' talkin' to do."

A thousand thoughts raced through her mind, only worsening as she watched the two men walk away toward the gardens.

Graham turned back. "Helena? Why don't you go inside and take a look. The house staff will gladly show you around. Just let them know that I sent you."

"We'll only be a minute," Da grumbled as he frowned at Graham.

Helena lifted her purse higher on her arm and thought of Ogak Beoir. Had the old crone known this was coming? The woman had been right when she had told her things weren't as they seemed. If she had been watching now, the crone would probably have been laughing away in her onion-scented shawl.

As she made her way into the entrance hall, Helena's

shoes clicked on the white marble floors. In the center of the room stood an enormous golden vase filled with antique pink roses and greenery. Its soft floral scent filled the air, melting away some of the hard edges of her thoughts.

She continued down the hall, taking in the wainscoted walls, the black marble doorways, and the antique wood ceiling. The effect was breathtaking, and though it was only a large entranceway, Helena had never been in a more lovely room. That was, until she walked into the main parlor. The parlor walls were filled with oil paintings of ancient-looking men, most accompanied by their hounds. A large, intricately carved staircase rose from behind the front desk, where a receptionist sat dressed in a black pinstriped suit. She looked up from a computer. "Hello, may I help you?"

"I... I'm here to help my—" Helena stammered.

"Oh, you must be the new girl Graham hired," the woman interrupted. She stood up and walked around the desk. "Follow me. I'll take you back to the kitchens."

"I'm not—"

The receptionist waved her hand. "I know you're nervous, lass, but you'll fit in in no time. The women back there are nice, though strict. Make sure you're on time each day for your shift, and you won't have any problems."

"I don't think you have the right person."

"Nonsense. He described you perfectly." The receptionist smiled and led her through a service door and down a maze of wood-paneled halls.

Helena's face burned. How exactly would a man like Graham describe a Traveller such as herself? Before she could ask, the woman pushed open a swinging door and led her into the kitchen. The kitchen staff moved through the stainless steel prep tables and stoves carrying trays of roasted meats, steaming pies, and sizzling veg like they were members of a well-choreographed ballet.

"Here you go, lass. Best of luck." The receptionist turned and rushed out before Helena had the chance to thank her.

Helena sucked in a breath. The place was everything she expected and more from a professional kitchen. People stood in front of prep tables, calling out orders as they stirred and chopped. Some of the staff worked behind long rows of cookers as they flipped and scraped. Others kneaded dough, and a few washed and scrubbed and cleaned. The place was so busy, so frightening, and so absolutely incredible.

A stout woman with mushroom-colored hair, a thin gold wedding band, and a crisp white apron stomped toward her. She had a crooked nose and a large mole beneath her left nostril. "Are you the new girl?" she asked in a strong Dubliner accent.

Helena nodded.

"What's your name, girl?"

"Helena." She tried to cover her Cant Traveller accent, but the woman's eyebrows rose.

"Well *Helena*, I'm Mrs. Mary Margaret. You can call me Mary. We're gonna need you to be here on time each and every day." The woman looked down at her clothes and scowled. She waved at Helena's tight white top and shorts. "Ach... You can't be wearing none of that around here. We have strict standards. You hear me?"

Helena nodded.

"Good. Before you start, I need to know what you're made of. Can you cook?"

"Aye." Helena had been cooking for her brother and sisters for as long as she could remember. It had never been anything beyond what they could catch or trap or what was cheap at the shop, but she could put together a meal like nobody's business.

The woman led her through the kitchen, sidestepping people dressed in white aprons, black ties, and tall toques. A few of them smiled, but most looked at her with mistrust.

The scent of the meat mixed with the aroma of cinnamon and cloves as they passed the row of cookers. Helena stopped and closed her eyes to enjoy the rich mix of scents, but when she opened them, the world had transformed. The kitchen was motionless. Mary Margaret, the staff—everyone was missing.

She stepped forward, and her foot made a wet, sucking sound.

She looked down. On the floor, surrounding her feet, was a pool of crimson blood.

At the base of the stainless-steel table lay a man. He was on his back and his white chef's jacket was speckled with blood. His dappled gray hair and bushy sideburns stuck out from under a crooked toque. He stared into nothingness.

Helena rushed toward the man, but stopped. The kitchen, so busy with activity only moments before, was silent. This couldn't be real. This all had to be some crazy dream...

Helena closed her eyes and took a deep breath. The scraping of spatulas, the scratching of whisks, and the laughter of a chef flooded her senses. She blinked and stared down at the pristine white-and-black-tiled floor.

The blood was gone, and so was the dead man.

What in fecking hell is going on?

"Helena? I asked you a question. I thought my Herbert was bad at listening..."

"Your Herbert? Huh?"

"Yes, my husband." Mary Margaret waved her hands in frustration. "But never mind him. I was just asking if you've ever been in a professional kitchen before."

Helena shook her head, but she couldn't stop staring at the spot on the floor—the spot where the body had been.

"Well, you're gonna have a lot to learn then. First thing is, don't be standing in the way."

A big man with gray bushy sideburns stood next to her, carrying a large copper pot.

It was the man. The dead man.

She gasped.

"Out of the way, lass. Some of us are tryin' to work round here." He pushed by her.

The man moved through the room, working away, oblivious to the fact that she had just seen his death. She made to follow him, but Mary stopped her.

"Come along, we don't have all day." Mary led her toward the back of the kitchen.

A wave of exhaustion passed through her, nearly forcing her to sit down and rest, but Helena forced herself to keep walking after Mary. She must just be tired. This was nothing. She wasn't losing her mind. She couldn't be losing her mind. Her family depended on her.

They stopped in front of a long, stainless-steel prep table in the back of the kitchen. "I want you to mince these mushrooms and chop the onion." She pointed at the boxes of veg that sat at the end of the counter. "We'll start you here and see how things go."

A stack of aprons sat on the shelves next to a bin for laundry. Mary reached up and handed one down to Helena. "You need to put this on." She turned to walk away, then stopped and turned back. "And here in the kitchens you can't be *manky*." She spat the word and looked Helena up and down. "I know about you and your kind. Know that I'm taking a chance on a gypo like you. Don't make me regret it." Mary turned around and stomped off.

Helena's cheeks flushed. She tried focusing on the piles of papery onions and earthy mushrooms, but couldn't bring herself to work. Was this her future? Would she never be able to escape her stereotype? It was hard to imagine that things would be different even with a university education. No one would care that she had a paper that said she was educated; they would only see where she had come from.

Helena pushed her heavy, book-laden purse under the counter and washed her hands, making sure to scrub until her skin was shiny and red. She tied the apron around her waist and set to work washing the mushrooms.

Pulling a mushroom from the bin, she grabbed a knife from the block and started to mince. Maybe she could get by at a place like this. Save some money. Run away to England. Go see Manchester United and see if Graham was right about them being God's gift to man.

She sat the knife down. *Graham.* If she had to lay a wager, that man damned near thought *he* was God's gift to womankind. She grabbed the box of onions, slammed it down on the table next to her, and started slicing.

The onions' stinging scent made her nose prickle, and tears welled in her eyes, but she bit them back. She could feel the gazes of the other cooks in the kitchen. Keeping her head down, she continued on, working hard like Da had taught her, all the while trying to forget about Graham and his irksome red jersey and even more irksome red kilt.

Before long the boxes sat empty, and the chopped veg were stacked in the industrial cooler.

Mary stomped over and looked down at her watch. Her eyebrows rose, and she peered over at the fridge. "There's no way you got done that fast."

Helena wiped her hands on her apron. "Aye, ma'am, I finished."

Mary walked over to the cooler and opened the door. "All right, lass. If you want the job, it's yours."

Helena paused. Did she really have a choice? If she said no, she could go back to studying, but Graham had made it sound like she and Da were a package deal. If that was the case, she couldn't bear the thought of how Mam would react if she heard they'd both lost their jobs because she didn't take the job.

"Aye, ma'am. This job would be grand. Thank ye."

"Ach... Don't be thankin' me yet." Mary crossed her arms over her ample chest like she was trying to look tough, but there was softness around her eyes that made Helena smile. Maybe this was where she was meant to be—tucked away in the kitchens, away from the prying eyes of her mam, with a place to study for the days to come.

"Get going, lass, but be back tomorrow no later than six o'clock. Got that? No later than six."

"Okay," Helena said, almost in a whisper. She turned to go.

"And lass?"

Helena looked back over her shoulder. "Aye?"

"Good job."

CHAPTER SIX

Graham couldn't look away from the aura that pulsated around Helena. She looked like she was sitting in the middle of a rainbow. Perhaps she was his pot of gold.

It had been a hard sell to get Seamus O'Driscoll to agree to let his daughter work for the manor, but in the end, Graham had won when he suggested Helena could work in a place out of the public eye. That had seemed to calm some of the Traveller's fears.

Helena stuffed a thick book into her purse as she made her way out of the manor and into the bright afternoon sun. When their gazes met, a whisper of a smile played over her lips. She turned away, but it was too late. Her expression had already made his heart sputter.

Seamus waved at his daughter. "Where've ya been, gra? We've been lookin' all over for ya."

"Sorry, Da."

Da leaned in and sniffed. "You stink to high heavens. What were ya doing, rollin' in onions?"

Helena laughed. "I was just in the kitchens. They showed me about."

"Well, gra, Graham and I've been talkin'. He's agreed to keep an eye on you while you're here working. But you gotta promise that your mam ain't to find out that you're working on your own. Are we square?"

"Aye, Da." She turned to him and her body grew rigid. "Thank you for the job, Graham."

"You're welcome. You'll like Mary." An image of Herb flashed through his mind. Hopefully with another hand in the kitchen, Mary could find more time to visit the infirmary. "Besides, she could really use the help. You know… with the cooking and all."

Every time she was around him, he couldn't seem to get his words right—and he needed to focus. The manor needed him. His family needed him. He couldn't be worried about a woman—even if she was the most beautiful woman he had ever seen.

"So what kinda job is this that ya already found yourself?" Seamus asked as they walked toward the car park and their waiting lorry.

"It's just kitchen work, Da. Today Mary had me choppin' veg, but you should see the space they have, Da. And the stuff they got. They got everything you'd ever need to make whatever you want." She talked faster and faster, and her eyes grew wide with excitement. "Plus, Mrs. Mary Margaret said I did a good job. She invited me to come back."

Graham nodded his approval. "Mary's a hard one to impress. You must have done a damn fine job."

Helena's smile widened, and her teeth sparkled in the afternoon light. He'd thought her beautiful from the moment he'd first seen her picture, but now, standing beside her in the hazy afternoon, beautiful didn't seem to fit. She was beyond beautiful, the way her black hair contrasted with the rich olive color of her skin, and the way her eyes seemed to change from a rich walnut color to that of warm honey. She radiated magnificence like it was a color in her rainbow aura.

"Ummm..." Graham forced his mind back to the task at hand, but he couldn't stop staring at Helena and the soft tendril of hair that had broken free and haloed her face. "Before you go... Mr. Shane likes to meet all new employees. Do you think you're up for meeting him?"

"I must smell, like Da said, but..." Helena glanced over at her father.

Seamus nodded. "That'd be fine. I'd like ta know the man who'll be signin' my... I mean our... checks."

They followed behind Graham as he turned and led them back into the manor.

"Good job, lass," Seamus whispered. "Maybe Mr. Kelly was right about lettin' ya work here. I think ya'll do me proud."

"Of course, Da..."

Hopefully Graham's stepfather would be just as proud of him for getting them to stay—most importantly, for getting *Helena* to stay. Everything hinged on her ability. Hopefully she would be as pliable when he told her the truth... Hopefully she would forgive him for deceiving her. But if he told her the truth now, she would think him crazy and undoubtedly run from this place. He couldn't risk losing her.

The receptionist didn't look up from her computer as

they passed by. She didn't notice too much around her—which was likely why Mr. Shane had put her there.

Graham led them past the red-hued drawing room. The scent of oolong and honey cakes wafted out of the room, where several couples sat chatting. At the table nearest the window with a view of the River Maigue, a woman wore a purple fascinator that looked like a bird had perched on the side of her head. The bird-shaped hat bobbed as she swirled her tea, careful not to clink the spoon against the gold-encrusted china. Each week it was a different woman and a different fascinator, but it was always the same: wealthy tourists coming and going.

"This is the formal dining room and restaurant," Graham whispered, trying not to draw their patrons' attention.

Helena was wide-eyed as she took in the room of people. It wasn't too busy this time of year; next weekend, and the festival, marked the beginning of the tourist season. Then she would see busy.

Graham continued down the hallway toward the stairs.

"I've never seen anything like this in all my life." She hurried after him.

"You should see the formal dinners—ladies and gentlemen dressed in gowns and tuxes. Now that's a sight." Graham led them up the immense double-winder staircase. He paused for a heartbeat as his eyes caught the mysterious carving in the top stair's kickboard. The carving was like the trinity, with three interlocking loops, but at its center was a small thistle. The artist had done a fine job blending it into the wood, but Graham never missed the special marking.

Stopping at a pair of hand-carved teak doors, Graham

knocked. "Mr. Shane? I've brought the new employees for you to meet."

From the other side came the sound of a sliding desk drawer and the jingle of keys. "Please, come in."

The door swung open, revealing Mr. Shane's large office and the back of his black leather chair.

• • •

Helena stifled a gasp as she walked into the immense office. Red, brown, and green books lined the outside walls in testament to the owner's intelligence. The walls that weren't covered in bookshelves were skirted with wainscoting and decorated with one-of-a-kind oil paintings of picnics and meandering creeks. A large, arched window looked out onto the gardens and the gurgling river.

At the center of the room stood a glass-covered desk with a laptop computer and a trio of gold-plated pens. The chair behind the desk slowly turned.

The man, whom Graham had addressed as Mr. Shane, sat with his fingers tented in front of his face. He looked to be about sixty—old by Traveller standards—but still strikingly handsome. A well-trimmed mustache curled around his lips and ended right at the corners of his mouth.

"Hello, I'm John Shane." His American accent was like something straight off the telly. He stood up and extended his hand.

Helena was happy to wait for Da to make the first move. When he stepped forward and shook their new boss's hand, Mr. Shane continued, "And you are?"

"This is—" Graham started, but Da cut him off.

"I'm Seamus O'Driscoll. This here's me daughter Helena."

Mr. Shane extended his hand to her. Da tilted his head, encouraging her to do as the man wished. Obliging, she stepped forward. The man stared at her as he shook her hand. His lingered a moment too long, and she pulled back.

"I'm sorry," Mr. Shane said. "You look like someone I once knew. Strange world."

"Aye, strange." She pushed her hand behind her back, away from his reach.

Mr. Shane sat down and motioned for them to sit in three large chairs that faced his desk. "So how has Graham been treating you? Fairly, I presume?"

"Aye, yes. He's been mighty grand." Da teetered on the edge of the seat, as if he didn't want to dirty the white cloth with his clothes. "'Twas real great of ya to give us these jobs. We were needin' 'em."

"Is that right? And why is that exactly?" Mr. Shane asked.

They were done. No American businessman was going to allow a convicted Traveller and his underdressed daughter to work at such a fine place.

"Well, to tell ya the God's honest truth, I was in the clink for protectin' me daughter's honor."

Helena's cheeks flamed as Mr. Shane looked over at her.

"Do you have a wee daughter, Mr. Shane?" Da asked.

Mr. Shane laughed, the sound deep and rich. "No, I'm afraid not, but I can understand the need to protect one. It wasn't Helena you were protecting, was it?"

"Nah, 'twas another. Only have one boy. 'Tis a cryin' shame; the boy's gettin' to be more spoiled than a little prince. Causes gra a mo gris here a fair bit o' trouble. Then again, he always keeps her on her toes."

Helena silently prayed for the meeting to end, for Mr. Shane to let her leave with the little dignity she had left.

Graham reached over to pat her arm, almost as if he could see how mortified she felt. His touch was soft, but the heat that radiated from his fingertips felt like flames that nibbled at her skin and raced toward her heart. She closed her eyes.

Her thoughts grew muddled, and bright lights flashed until images started to float through her mind.

A young boy ran alongside the red salvia gardens in front of the manor. The boy stopped at the edge of the river and teetered on the bank. In the distance, a woman stepped out of the side door and yelled something Helena couldn't understand.

Graham let go of her arm. The images stopped, and reality swirled back into place.

She gripped the chair's armrests so hard her fingers ached, and her nails threatened to tear away. She had to be going crazy. That was twice... twice in one day that she had seen... *something*. What was happening?

"Are you okay, Helena?" Mr. Shane asked. "You look a bit pale." Mr. Shane motioned for Graham to get her a drink from a pitcher of water on the bar in the far corner of the room.

"I'm... I'm fine... I think I'm just a bit wiped. Been a long day."

Graham handed her a glass.

"Thank you." She took a sip, letting the ice-cold water slip down her throat. The exhaustion she'd felt in the kitchens returned, and her body ached for sleep.

She wrapped her hand around the sweating glass, and the cold nipped at her skin, forcing her to stay awake.

"Welcome." Graham walked to the window behind Mr. Shane and cracked it open. A flood of fresh air wafted against her sweat-dampened skin, further chilling her.

Did she look so bad that he was worried for her? She set the glass on a coaster on Mr. Shane's desk and ran the back of her hand over her forehead. Her skin felt hot; perhaps she was running a fever. Maybe that was what was causing these... these hallucinations.

"This all must be overwhelming for you," Mr. Shane said, his lips trembling as he attempted to console her with a rusty smile.

Da patted her hand. "It'll be okay, lass. Won't it?"

"Yes... You're right. I'll be fine. 'Tis nothin'." She felt like an invalid what with everyone hovering over her as if a simple breeze would bring her to her knees. The vision had been nothing, maybe something she had seen on the telly or a glitch in her overworked mind. She was stronger than they were treating her. She sat up straighter. "So, about the job?"

"Yes." Mr. Shane flipped open a ledger that sat on his desk, grabbed a pair of reading glasses from his pocket, and put them on. "Graham has told me you will be working in the kitchens. Did Mary Margaret give you a uniform?" He looked up at her over the edges of his glasses.

"Not yet."

"Well, remind her that you will need one. She should know these things by now." Mr. Shane wrote something down on his ledger. "I will cover the price of your uniform this time, but should you need another, it will come out of your paycheck."

"How much will she be making?" Da put his hands on the edge of the desk as if readying himself for negotiation.

"Well, she'll be on salary. Forty hours a week and extra as needed during the main season. How does twenty thousand sound?"

Helena tried to cover her shock. She had never earned so much as a euro in her entire life. Da had given her a few notes here and there for clothes and such, but *twenty thousand…* That would be plenty. Plenty to build herself a life.

Da whistled through his teeth and dropped his hands from the desk. "Away with ya… Ya gotta be kidding."

"Okay. Twenty-five." Mr. Shane smiled, as if fully aware that he had overpaid at twenty. "You drive a hard bargain. Deal?"

Da stuck out his hand. "I think ya got yourself a deal."

Mr. Shane chuckled as he shook Da's hand.

Graham looked over at her and gave her a smile that seemed to erase all of the things she'd been holding against him. Maybe he had been telling the truth; maybe he wasn't out to use her and throw her away.

"Congratulations." He reached over and touched her skin.

A woman's scream echoed up from the courtyard and through the open window. "Get away from there!" she yelled.

"What's going on?" Mr. Shane stood and stepped to the window. "Graham—"

"Charlie! No!"

Graham's hand fell to hers and the energy buzzed between them. He stood up and pulled her to the window, where she peered around his shoulder out into the gardens.

The vision that had played out in her mind only

moments before was unfolding in slow-motion on the estate grounds below.

The young boy with the blond hair, the boy she had seen in her mind, teetered on the edge of the riverbank. The boy's footing gave out, and he pitched backward into the water. For a split second, Helena could have sworn she saw a green hand coming out of the river to grab the boy's ankle.

She must have been going mad.

The woman who had screamed, the boy's mother, weaved through the maze of bushes, her long blond hair fanning out in the wind as she sprinted toward her drowning son.

Helena let go of Graham's hand and rushed out of Mr. Shane's office, through the corridors, and outside. Breathless, she reached the bank as the mother began flailing around in the water, trying to lift the boy, who was no bigger than Gavin, onto shore.

The boy's hair was stuck to his skin and his clothes pasted against his tiny frame, giving him the look of an angelic doll that a child had carelessly thrown into the river.

Helena grabbed the boy under the arms and heaved him up onto the grass.

His eyes were closed and his body motionless. His lips had turned a faint blue. Helena pressed her hands onto his chest over and over, trying to do CPR, but the boy didn't respond.

The mother waded out of the water and dropped to the ground beside the boy. As she looked down upon her child, a choked cry escaped her.

Helena lifted the boy's chin and pressed her lips to his. A faint charge, like static electricity, snapped between them. Energy moved between them as she breathed into his body.

His lips warmed beneath hers, and a muscle in his cheek twitched with life.

She sat back. Some of his color had returned, but his chest remained still. "Come on, Charlie... Take a breath, gra."

She bent down again. A surge of energy, stronger this time, moved through her and spread into the small boy. In her mind, it was almost as if she could feel the energy seeping into the boy's cooling body, spreading to his lungs and capturing the water within them. Pain rose in her own lungs, as if she were fighting for her own life instead of the young boy's. She pulled back.

One, two, three, four, five times she compressed his chest. She leaned in and pinched his nose. Another breath. The pain in her lungs lessened as her energy grew stronger.

Please Lord, save this boy.

One, two, three, four...

An overwhelming sense of fear surged up from the boy and spread through her fingers. She dropped her tingling hands from his chest, and the sensation stopped.

The boy spewed water from his mouth. Helena drew back and shook out her hands. Nothing made sense, but it didn't matter—she had saved the boy.

Water trickled down from his lips as he started to cough.

His mother lifted him into her lap and rested his head against her chest. "Charlie, oh my god, Charlie. I love you." Tears slipped down her cheeks as she rocked back and forth with her baby.

A hand touched Helena's shoulder. She looked up, into Graham's eyes. He helped her to stand. Her knees were weak, and she choked back tears. She had no power to resist as he pulled her into his arms.

The little boy could have been Gavin, playing too close to a dangerous river... In another second he would have been gone, slipping into the greedy hands of death.

She pressed her face into Graham's warm chest.

The boy had come so close to dying—and she had seen it all play out before it happened. Was she causing these awful things to occur? Or was there something more? Something she didn't dare whisper?

CHAPTER SEVEN

The feeling of Graham's arms around her was something Helena would never forget. He had held her so tightly that she heard the beat of his heart. After a moment, her own heartbeat matched his, as if they had become one—if only for a single moment.

A piece of her had fallen away when she forced her body to step out of his arms, whose hold had seemed made for her alone.

Why did she have to feel this... desire? He was out of bounds, off-limits on every front. The attraction could be nothing more than a fleeting thought, just like the moment she'd spent in his muscular arms.

Helena stirred the lamb stew that simmered on the cooker as she glanced out the window of the trailer. Mam hadn't moved from her seat by the campfire all evening. Da sat next to her. Mam's face was contorted with rage as she spoke to him.

The door to the trailer slammed open, and Gavin ran

inside, followed by the more sluggish Rionna. Her fingers tapped away on her mobile as she looked up. "What's for dinner?"

"Stew and soda bread. Sound good?" Helena sliced a carrot and slid it into the pot.

Rionna shrugged and flopped down on the couch.

Gavin latched onto Helena's leg. "I missed you! Did Da like his new job? What's it like? Did they have puppies?"

"It's grand. Lots of flowers and a garden. There's even a pretty river, but I didn't see a pup."

He let go of her leg. "A river? I wanna go swimmin'."

"Nah, not in that river…" Helena's thoughts drifted to Charlie as she went back to stirring the stew. His mother had rushed him to the hospital, but no one had heard anything else.

Da stepped into the trailer. "Gavin and Rionna, run along. I need to talk to your sister."

Gavin scampered past Da and headed straight for the woods, but Rionna sighed as she stood up and stuffed her mobile into her pocket, as if Da had interfered with her ever-important social schedule. She slammed the door as she stomped out.

"I'm sorry about today, gra a mo gris. 'Twas a bit of a bugger, but you did real fine with that boy. You did me proud. But 'tis not what I came to ask you about." Da moved to the table and sat down. "Is there somethin' ya need to tell me, gra?"

"What do ya mean, Da?"

"I mean…" He ran his hands over his chin. "That Graham… He seems to know ya real well. And when he touched ya… You didn't look *right*. Did he do somethin'…

somethin' ya need to tell me 'bout? You've been a little chilly with him. Did somethin' happen outside the prison?"

"What? No." Helena stopped stirring. That wasn't entirely true. She had thought he was making a pass at her, but something more had happened… Something she had forgotten to tell Da. "Wait."

"What?"

"The day ya were released, I met a woman. She told me to send you her regards…"

"Who was she?" Da frowned.

Helena let the wooden spoon drop against the side of the pot as she turned to face Da. "She said her name was Ogak Beoir."

Da stood up and grabbed her by the arms. "How in the bloody hell did ya meet her? What did she say t'ya?"

"Not much… She just said to tell you 'ello. She laughed when I met Graham and told me that things weren't as they seemed."

"Not as they seemed? Did she tell ya what in the bloody hell that meant?" Da asked, so rapidly that the sentence sounded like a single word.

She shook her head. "She said something about how great it was to be Pavee, and that I—" She paused. Based on the way Da was taking the news of the woman, the last thing she needed to tell him was that the woman had said she had the forshaw. "I think she was off her rocker, Da. Don't worry. Really…"

Da let go of her arms and stepped back, but he looked troubled. "Have you seen her again?"

"Nah, Da."

"Stay away from her. We don't need none of her black

magic in our house. Why didn't ya tell me about her earlier?" Da asked. "You shoulda never been around that fecking woman. Did she tell you anything else?"

"I don't remember," she lied. "I'm sorry Da, I... I didn't know that you didn't like her. She seemed to know ya."

"Ya did nothin' wrong, gra, but I don't want you to be talkin' to the likes of her. You need to stay away from that kind of trouble." His face grew a shade lighter as he turned and walked out of the door.

It was already too late. She couldn't avoid that kind of trouble—she *was* that kind of trouble.

The woman had been right.

She had the forshaw.

Helena turned off the stove and leaned against the counter as the full impact of the realization hit her.

Dropping her hands to the sharp edge of the counter, Helena forced herself to breathe.

If she had the forshaw... that meant everything she saw would come true. Or not. The man she'd seen in the kitchens, the bushy-haired man, hadn't died. That had to mean her visions weren't always accurate, didn't it?

Maybe her vision was flawed. Maybe something had happened to change the future. Maybe the man had escaped his fate.

• • •

The night was long and filled with dark thoughts, but when Helena rose the next morning, she knew what she needed to do. She needed to pass her tests. The sooner she did, the sooner she could run away. If she ran, no one would know

about her forshaw. There would be no one to judge her…
no one to condemn her for a curse that she couldn't control.

She looked in her purse. Her book wasn't there. She
rushed to her drawer and pulled it open. Aside from her
clothes, there was nothing.

Helena stepped to the thin door that ran between the
living area and her parents' room. "Mam?" she called quietly,
so as not to wake Rionna and Gav.

Mam pulled open the door. She wore a baggy pair of
sweats and a white shirt dotted with ash. "Whatcha want?"

"Have ya seen my studier? I can't find it." Helena pushed
back a strand of hair that had fallen from her band. "I need
to work."

"Girls don't need to be studying. Ya need ta get married
and get outta me and your da's hair."

Helena turned back to her open drawer and started to
dig through her clothes. "What happened to my book? Was
Gavin playin' with it?"

"Nah, girl." Mam walked out to the counter and stopped
by the window. "I burned it. Needed something to start this
morning's fire." Mam pointed toward the fire pit. "Ya left
the damn thing out. I thought ya didn't need it no more."

Helena slid her drawer shut and sank to the ground.

There was no way she could buy a new one, or even
a used one—not until she got paid from the manor. That
would be at least another week, which would leave her with
less than a week to study. She would lose so much time.

Helena stood up and faced Mam. She wanted to yell,
to tell the world what a god-forsaken creature her wretched
mother was, but she glanced over at her sleeping brother.

His thumb was in his mouth and his sweet ginger curls hung down in his face.

A tear threatened to spill down her cheek, but she blinked it away. She turned her back so Mam wouldn't see.

"I thought now that you were done wit your teenage demons you'd be done with this daydreaming, but *no*... Won't you just get it through your thick skull that ya shouldn't be wantin' for things that ain't ever going to come to pass?" Mam picked up a packet of ciggys and pulled one out. "You're about as dumb as that cubby if you think you've got a chance of passin' that damned test." She pushed a ciggy into her mouth, letting it dangle from her lip. "You shoulda gotten married years ago. But no—you were too good for that."

Helena bit her lip in an attempt to stop the tears. Her teeth sank into her flesh until the bitter taste of blood filled her mouth. Maybe Mam was right. Maybe marriage would have been smarter than sticking around here—maybe it still could be. She could finally escape this place and the rancid temper of the beast who had borne her—but she'd never give in that easily. Mam could throw all the fits she wanted, but Helena couldn't throw herself on the mercy of a man.

Mam's hands lifted like two vultures coming down on their prey. "It must be *daughters*. Ya can never do nothing right by 'em. I'm just tryin' to take care of the fam, clean up the clutter, but *no*. Some fecking book is more important."

Helena turned her back to Mam. "Do ya want me to get the kids ready for school?"

"Those fecking kids don't need no school. Look at me." She jabbed her thumb against her chest. "I turned out just fine. Just give 'em a whippin'. That'll learn 'em." Mam walked over to the fridge, grabbed a beer, and twisted the lid off. She took a long draw from the bottle. "Look at ya. Thinkin' you're all high and mighty. Betcha think just cause ya got some schoolin' that you're better than your mam, don't ya?"

Helena shook her head.

Mam took another long pull from the bottle. "You and your da are nothing. Ya ain't no better than me."

Mam stumbled out the door and stood by the fire.

Helena reached into her purse and fished out her mobile. Only one other person knew how to escape this place, this life, and *that* woman. Her fingers found the number for her sister, Angel. Helena moved to the front of the trailer and cupped her hand over her mouth.

She waited as the phone rang.

It was early; maybe Angel was asleep.

The phone rang again.

"What the *craic*?" Angel's foggy voice answered.

Helena smiled. She forgot how much she missed her sister's voice. "Angel?"

"Helena?" Some of the sleep in her sister's voice fell away. "What's wrong? Why are you calling? Is everything okay?"

Helena hesitated. "Everything's fine. We're staying in Adare, but… can you come and get the kids and make sure they get to school in Limerick? Mam won't let me take them, and I don't think they should be stayin' alone with her."

"What? Why?"

"I'll tell you more later, but right now I can't talk. I have to go to work with Da. Will you please come get the kids and take them to school?"

"Fine." Angel sighed. "But what am I gonna do about

Mam? She won't just let me walk back into your camp and take the kids."

"I'll have them waitin' for you near the road. Trust me. Mam's been drinkin' again. By the time you get here, she'll never know they're gone."

. . .

Graham held the pane of glass for one of the manor's cracked windows and grabbed his blade. Nothing in the place was standard-sized. Everything had to be specially made or specially ordered, but at least one of their special acquisitions was turning out to be exactly what they needed.

Helena was the clairsentient that they had been hoping for. The minute she had touched that boy, Charlie, beside the river, her aura had changed from its normal rainbow of colors to the turquoise shade of a healer.

This morning, when Helena had arrived to work, she hadn't so much as looked at him before she'd rushed off to the kitchens.

He had been relieved. He'd gone too far when he'd pulled her into his arms. No matter how hard he tried, he could still smell the floral aroma of her hair and the slight scent of campfire on her skin. His arms ached to hold her again, even if only for a moment. Something about her being close to him felt so right.

The glass squeaked as he ran the blade down, scoring its surface.

The cutter slipped, and the glass cracked.

"Shite," he grumbled. Throwing the blade down, he slid the broken glass into the bin.

ONCE A GYPSY

He couldn't stop thinking of the way Helena's dark hair glistened in the light or the way her body had fit so well against his own. He closed his eyes, imagining what it would be like to kiss her luscious pink lips.

He opened his eyes. *I'm acting like an eejit, dreaming about some woman. There are plenty of girls in Ireland. Why do I have to be stuck on the one I can't have?*

He pulled off his work gloves and dropped them on the table. The glass could wait.

The employees' dining hall, behind the kitchen, was deserted when he walked in. He made his way to the fridge and grabbed his sack lunch and a cup of coffee from the stained pot on the counter. Sitting down, he opened his lunch and took out his pasty. He had bought the little meat-filled pastry from a shop, and it was cold but it was better than anything he could have made himself, and a nice break from the corned beef sandwiches he normally brought.

The noise from the kitchen swelled and then quieted as the door opened and closed. Helena walked into the hall. She looked breathtaking in her new uniform. Her black pants stretched across her hips, and a white jacket pulled against her chest. Seeing her made his arms ache to hold her again.

She sucked in a breath as their gazes met. With a nervous nibble on her lip, she glanced over her shoulder toward the kitchen door, then turned.

"Wait."

She stopped, but kept her back to him. "What?"

"If you want to go... fine. But I just wanna talk. And we don't have to talk about what happened between us yesterday."

She turned. "You promise?" She sounded tired.

He wondered if she'd spent the night like he had, tossing and turning with the thoughts of her in his arms.

"Aye. I'll even share my pasty with you." He motioned at his lunch. "You gotta be hungry." He stood up and grabbed a plate and a fork from the cupboard beside the fridge. "You like coffee?"

"Nah, but thanks." She moved to the table and sat across from where he had been.

Graham halved the pasty and placed part on the extra plate, then set it before her.

"Thanks. I forgot to bring our lunches. Da's gonna be as weak as a salmon in a sandpit." Helena took a bite.

"I can get Mary to whip him up something."

"Nah, he'll be fine. He wouldn't wanna be puttin' anyone out."

"I'll bring him something later."

Helena smiled, and the faint flowery scent of her hair wafted toward him. He looked at her, but she never glanced up from her plate, and her aura was a dark, pulsing red—the color of stress and emotional upheaval.

"Are you okay?" he asked.

"I'm fine. It's just a lot. You know with the boy and the job and…"

"I'm sorry." His breath caught in his throat as he stared into her almond-shaped eyes. "It has to be a lot to handle."

Helena looked back down. "I'll be okay. It's just that on top of everything, I lost my studier and I think I'm losin' my mind."

"What do you mean?" His gut tightened.

"Nothing," she sighed. "I just had a shite mornin'. I've

been tryin' to study for my exams and my mam threw my book in the fire. I don't know what I'm going to do."

He dropped his hand next to hers, his fingers trembling. He longed to touch her, but now wasn't the time. "Can I help?"

"No." She took a bite, carefully avoiding his gaze. "I'll just have to make do without it. If I pass, I pass."

"What made you decide to take the tests?"

Helena looked at him like she wanted to say something but held back. "I wanna finish my schoolin' and do somethin' that'll change my life."

"Well, then you can't risk failing the tests."

"It's not that simple. My fam needs me." She stabbed a piece of meat.

"If you wanted, you could keep working here. Maybe work your way up in the kitchens."

"I don't want to cook all my life. I want to help people. And if I stay, I know my mam will just marry me off. I don't want nothin' to do with marriage—not right now." Her cheeks flamed and she looked up at him. "I mean... I appreciate this job and all... and it's not that I don't want to get married someday. It's just that—"

"Don't worry. I get it," he said. "I want you to stay, but if your exams mean this much to you, maybe I can find a studier."

She pushed her food around the plate. "I won't be takin' any handouts—not even a free meal." She stabbed the last bite of the pasty. "So tomorrow I'll bring you lunch. I'll put it in the cooler for ya for whenever ya want it."

He pushed his fingers closer to hers. "Well, if you like, I

could meet you again. That way I can tell you whether I like your cooking."

"I'm a fine cook. Just wait and see." She glanced down at his advancing fingers and drew back her hand. "But I don't think it's a good idea that we're alone."

CHAPTER EIGHT

Helena hadn't been able to stop thinking about her vision ever since lunch. She'd been so absorbed in her thoughts that, while mincing, she almost chopped off the tip of her finger. Mary Margaret would have been furious if there had been blood on her turnips.

She washed her hands, dropped her knife in the sink, and lifted the trays of prepped veg. The cooler made goose bumps rise on her skin as she put them away amongst the rows of plastic bins full of peppers and lettuce.

Back in the kitchen, she stared at the black-and-white-tiled floor where she had seen the man lying in a pool of blood.

She looked up at the bushy-sideburned man who stood at the cookers, grilling several thickly cut steaks. He turned to the counter behind him, grabbed a handful of mushrooms and tossed them on the grill. He glanced over at her and, catching her eye, sneered. "Damned Travellers. And no good, none of them…"

Helena made her way across the kitchen, ignoring the sting of his words. She had to tell him, no matter how vile a man he was. She had to tell him what she'd seen.

Mary grabbed her arm as she passed. "What are you doing, lass?"

"I was just—" She motioned toward the man.

"Don't be bothering Chester," Mary said, stopping her. "Did you clean your station?" Mary pulled her back to her work area. "You can't be going anywhere with a mess like this." She motioned to the scraps of veg and juice that puddled on the counter.

"Aye, Mary. I wasn't done, I just—"

"Before you find yourself in trouble, you need to be getting back to work." Mary waited for Helena to grab a sanitized rag before she turned and walked to Chester, the chef. Touching his arm, she whispered something into his ear. The man laughed.

There was something about the way Chester leaned into Mary—the way he laughed, the way he seemed to melt under her touch. But Mary was married to Herb… wasn't she?

Helena turned back to the mess on her prep table. They weren't the first people to ever have an affair, or the last, but it was in her best interest to mind her own business. She had no time to dwell on other people's lives—hers was already a big enough mess.

Grabbing a bucket from under the sink, she dropped an extra capful of bleach into it and filled it with water. She scrubbed and swirled until every surface shone.

Mary stomped back over. "Do you do everything this fast?"

Helena shrugged. "I guess there's somethin' to growin' up a gypsy."

Mary ran her hand along the top edge of the backsplash. "I can see that." She rubbed her fingers together. "Why don't you head home?"

Helena took off the white jacket Mary had given her and threw it into the staff's laundry hamper. "Thanks."

"Aye." Mary smiled, and the mole under her nostril wiggled as if fighting to break free. "And Helena?"

"Yes, ma'am?"

"We're all real impressed. I'm glad you took the job." Mary turned away.

Helena smiled. She liked it here—Mary checking on her, Da close by, a thousand things to learn and do. Da was sitting in the lorry waiting for her when she reached the car park. She got in and shut the door.

"How was your day, gra? Are ye likin' yer job?"

"Aye, Da." She rested her tired head against the cool glass of the window.

"Graham told me about your mam and the book. I'm real sorry, gra."

Helena's stomach tightened. Why had Graham told Da? He didn't need to know; there wasn't anything he could do.

"It's all right. I'll make it work," she said.

"Your mam doesn't want you to be takin' those tests. Come hell or high water she ain't gonna let ya."

"But I need to, Da. I've never finished anythin'. I never even spent a full year in a single school. We were always up and leavin' before I had the chance to make a go of it. I want to finish something. I want to do something for myself. I need to prove that I can do this. Then I don't know what I wanna do. University would be grand, but more than that I wanna follow my heart. I want the chance to be my own woman. I don't wanna depend on some good-for-nothin' man."

"Gra… I wanna do right by ya. I want ye to follow yer heart, but sometimes the heart leads us astray." He put the lorry in gear and gave a long sigh. "I don't think you takin' the tests is a good idea. I know why ye wanna be doin' it, I do… but we can't afford ye takin' any time off from your job just now. And I don't want you gettin' into any trouble. At that school you'll be surrounded by gorgers, alone."

"I'm surrounded by gorgers here, Da."

"But I'm never too far away. If you needed me, I could get to you. In Limerick, ya ain't got nobody to watch yer back."

"Da, I'm fine. It's just for a few days. I did all right when you were away."

He cringed. "I shoulda never gone and done what I did. I made a mistake, and I left you alone. I can never let that happen again."

"But Da… You were the one who said we needed to take this job so we could show the gorgers what we're really like. And now you're judgin' them? Da…"

"I'm not judgin' all them, gra. There's nothing wrong with a gorger, but look at Angel. She fell in love, got married, left the fam. No matter where she lands, that girl will never have a full life. You can't go forgettin' your past. It has just as much to do with your life as the present."

"Da, I'm not Angel."

"Nah, gra. But if you take these tests… I know you; you'll run. You'll run from your mam… fine. But if you leave her, you leave me. And I don't want to lose you again."

He continued down the drive. "Once we get back on our feet, you can go back to life at the trailer and then we can arrange a marriage and you can get to startin' your own life. A life near me. Do you want that, gra?"

"Da…" She wanted to insist, but it didn't seem right after he'd poured out his heart to her. She could understand how he was feeling. A person's life was short, but family was forever.

A fog had rolled in off the river, filling the estate with shadows. Its darkness was heavy and thick, like nothing she'd seen before, and she couldn't resist the desire to look back as they drove out the gate. She closed her eyes.

Let me see the future. Will I only be a Traveller woman, taking care of a husband, being his brood mare? Or will I get a chance at something… more? Will I get to follow my dreams?

She opened her eyes as the lorry slammed into a pothole.

"Da, do ya think I can borrow the lorry?"

"Why, gra?"

"I had Angel pick up the kids and take them to Limerick so they could go to school. They only got a couple of weeks left… I didn't want them to be missin' out."

Da tapped his fingers on the steering wheel and let out a long exhale. "What did you tell Angel about your mam?"

"Only that Mam wasn't in no condition to be watchin' the young ones."

"Did Angel say anything?" His voice carried a tone of sadness. "About me?"

"Ya know she loves ya, Da. She's never forgiven herself for what happened."

"She's a good girl. I'm real sorry about… well, everything."

"The boy had it comin', Da. You had to do what you did. Angel's honor was at stake."

"I don't like the boy. Never have." He stared out the window. "But that boy musta really loved her to take the beltin' I gave him and still go back. And love... love is a rare thing in this world."

• • •

The kids were standing outside the school when Helena arrived. Gavin smiled and waved, but Rionna looked around cautiously, making sure none of her friends saw that she was getting into a manky lorry with her gypsy sister.

There was a knock on the driver's side window. Standing outside the lorry was her cousin Lydia.

Helena rolled down the window and smiled. "Hiya! Not wearing your flamingo dress today?"

Lydia's laughter filled the air. "It was in the wash. I'm picking up the kids for me mam and noticed that Gav and Rionna were still here. Thought I'd keep an eye on 'em 'til you got here."

"Thanks." Helena smiled as she pulled her purse over her uniform pants.

"To tell ya the truth, I wanted to talk to ya, too. You remember the boy from the other night? Jimmy?"

There was no way she could forget the boy who had made a pass at her at Da's party. "Aye, what happened? Did he ring you up after the party?"

Lydia pulled her mobile from her bedazzled purse. "Look." She scrolled down so Helena could see the word-filled screen. "We've been texting nonstop. He says he really likes me."

"And?" Helena smirked. "Does this mean what I think it does?"

Lydia covered her mouth as she giggled. "I can't say for sure, but I've got my fingers crossed that he'll ask. I want a summer wedding."

"You're lucky he didn't have time to grab you the other night."

Lydia's cheeks flamed. "Well..."

"You didn't let him, did you?"

The kids scrambled into the lorry, bickering the entire time.

Lydia ignored the question and looked past Helena to the kids. "Gavin, talk nice to your sister."

"Answer me, Lyd. Did you get grabbed?"

Lydia looked back at her and flashed a guilty smile. She leaned in close to Helena's ear. "He's a real good snogger. He told me I was better than any other girl."

"How many girls has he been snoggin'?"

Lydia waved her off. "Don't matter. He's gonna pick me. And we're gonna get married."

Lydia needed support—even if Helena's heart wasn't in it. "That's great. I'm real happy for ya."

Lydia straightened her tight pink top. "Ya got some time? I wanna show you his trailer—he's at the Limerick camp."

Rionna let out a yawn and dug through her bag as Helena peered at them in the rearview mirror. "You guys wanna stop real quick? We can't stay long."

"I don't give a shite," Rionna grumbled.

"I guess I have the okay." Helena smiled, trying to ignore her sister.

"Follow us. It's nice there. There's even a few havaris."

Helena hadn't seen a havari since the last Banlasloe horse fair. The covered wagons were kept more out of nostalgia than anything else and, like most things Pavee, they were revered as a sacred part of their past.

"Jimmy told me to getcha to go with me so I could come over. I haven't gotten to see him since the party. He's gonna be so excited."

"You know, if you needed a chaperone all you had to do was tell me."

Lydia pulled up her bedazzled purse. "Don't ruin the fun."

"Lydia, do you have a studier for the Post Leaving Certificate exam?"

"I don't think so. I ain't got no use for something like that—not once I'm married. Jimmy promised he would take care of me."

"What does Jimmy do?"

"He works with tarmac, and he does real good."

"If you get married, what're ya gonna do?"

"Well, I'm gonna have a big white dress. With hearts. And diamonds. Maybe I'll come to the ceremony in a horse-drawn carriage or a Mercedes. I always wanted to ride in a Mercedes."

"But what are you going to do after the wedding?"

"Have a big party, with a deejay and a cake with five tiers, and lots of lights and flowers—"

"I meant after the wedding day. What are you and Jimmy gonna do?"

"Well, I'm gonna have some babies and take care of Jimmy." She said it as though it were the most obvious thing in the world.

Helena forced a smile. "That's great."

"When are you gonna find a man and get married?" Lydia teased. "You and me, we ain't getting any younger. Pretty soon our sisters are gonna be gettin' married. If you don't hurry up, your sister's gonna beat you to the altar."

Rionna's eyes widened in the mirror. "Really? Ya think I'm gonna get married before her?"

Helena reached back and touched the young teen's fingers. "You don't have to be in a rush to get married. The most important thing is that you find someone you love."

Rionna stared at her. "Are you going to find love?"

The memory of Graham holding her in his arms flashed through her mind.

"Someday I might think about love, but right now I need to do what's right for me."

CHAPTER NINE

The caravan of trailers was set up according to how and when the Travellers had arrived. A makeshift road had been created that weaved around the vehicles like a man after too much drink. Helena was careful to keep the lorry close behind Lydia's truck as she maneuvered through the tight spaces.

Mothers tended the outdoor fires. Fathers napped or fixed up their trailers. Kids ran through the streets, carrying sticks that they swung like swords. Gavin pressed his face to the window, almost licking his lips at the prospect of joining them out in the dusty road.

Lydia pulled over and parked by a long, white trailer with mauve striping and a Celtic cross sticker in the back window. Two teenage brunette girls stood at the hitch end and stared at them.

Gavin bailed out of the lorry, Rionna following, and they headed straight over to the girls.

"Stay close. We ain't stayin' long!" Helena called after them.

Gavin waved as he disappeared into the camp.

Lydia's brother and sisters rushed out of the car, scrambling to catch up to Rionna and Gavin as Lydia stepped out of her lorry. Sucking in a breath, Helena reached down for the car's door handle, but she stopped as a haze filled her mind. She closed her eyes.

The world had formed a foggy cloud around her when she opened her eyes. She stood inside a havari, the air thick with the scent of burning sage. Across the table sat a woman. Her gray hair was long and matted with blue beads and red and white feathers throughout, and it fell past her shoulders.

"I knew you would be comin' to see me, lass. My friend, Ogak Beoir, is a woman with clear sight..."

Helena forced her eyes open, and reality collapsed back over her. Lydia stood outside the door, her hands on her hips.

Please don't be a vision. Please don't—

The door of the lorry opened. "You okay? You look a bit flush. I ain't that bad of a driver, am I?" Lydia asked.

"No... I'm fine."

Jimmy stepped out of the white trailer. "Hey, ladies!"

An older woman with spiraling black curls peeked out of the trailer's window. Helena nodded to her, and the woman frowned and pushed the curtain closed. Helena got out of the lorry and followed Lydia, who was already arm-in-arm with Jimmy.

"You all want to go for a walk? 'Tis a fine evening." He tipped his head toward the storm clouds that rested on the horizon.

"We'd love to. Wouldn't we, Helena?" Lydia said.

Helena would have preferred not be the third wheel in their little stroll, but if nothing else, it would give her time to think about her visions. "'Tis fine."

Jimmy gave her an apologetic smile. "I'm sorry I tried to chat you up. Me and the boys were off our faces—too much of the Arthur Guinness."

"Don't worry about it, happens all the time," she joked.

"I bet." Jimmy smiled as he led them away from the stares of his overly protective mother, who was at the trailer window once again. "I'm just glad you brought my Lydia down to see me."

Lydia giggled and rubbed her hand over Jimmy's stout chest. He walked tall as more people peeped out their windows. For a moment, Helena wondered what it felt like to be so in love with a man. It must be easy for Lydia. Jimmy was a Traveller boy. Their path would be one that many generations of Travellers had walked before—and that meant security. Lydia would know exactly what to expect from her man, and from her life.

Children's laughter echoed through the caravan, followed by the screams of a grisly faux-pirate death. Jimmy led them around a corner. He stopped as they came into view of a round-topped havari, which stood at the end of the path nestled between patches of thorny bushes. The wagon's sun-bleached red paint was chipping away in spots, revealing aged gray boards beneath. What had once been an intricate exterior was now in the autumn of its time, flaking away and disappearing in the dirt beneath.

"I dare you to go knock on the door," Jimmy said, an edge of fear in his voice.

A single, rickety-looking step led up to a red door, the

universal symbol for "all welcome." It was a sharp contrast to the foreboding ache that seeped into Helena's core.

"No, thanks. I'm not goin'." Helena spun on her heel, but Jimmy stopped her.

"What are you, some kind of chicken? There ain't nothin' to be afraid of." Jimmy laughed, trepidation in his eyes.

"I didn't say I was afraid. I said I ain't goin'."

Lydia stepped between them and turned to Jimmy. "She don't have to do nothin'."

Helena held her breath. Lydia was putting herself in a precarious situation. Going against her potential husband was asking for trouble.

Jimmy glared at Lydia. "Get out of my way."

He pushed her away.

"Don't be treating her like that. She didn't do nothin' wrong," Helena said.

"I try to show you both a good time and this is how you act? Like two spoiled little girls? Why don't you go running back to your daddies."

Lydia looked at her with fear in her eyes. *Please*, she mouthed.

"Fine…" Helena stepped past Jimmy toward the havari. Her heartbeat thundered in her ears. She turned to face Lydia and Jimmy. "I don't know why you needed to make us—"

The door hinges squeaked behind her, stopping her midsentence.

"You don't have to fear me, lass. It ain't my intention to hurt you."

Helena recognized the voice.

When she turned, the gypsy woman from her vision stood before her. Her hair was matted with blue beads, and red and white feathers stuck out haphazardly from her locks. Her eyes were steely gray and her lips pale, giving her the appearance of an otherworldly creature.

"Hello, ma'am. I didn't know ya were in there," Jimmy said. "We didn't mean to be interrupt ya. We were just havin' a little disagreement, nothin' serious." Jimmy took Lydia by the hand and turned to leave.

"I know, James. I didn't come out here to speak to ya. Not that you don't need a stern talkin' to, but I got better ways to waste my time."

Helena smiled. Maybe the woman wasn't so bad.

The woman stuck out her hand and motioned for Helena to come closer. "Don't be afraid now, lass. There ain't nothing about me that's gonna cause ya more trouble than what you're already in."

"How do you know about my... trouble?" Helena stepped toward the havari.

Lydia moved to stop Helena, but Jimmy stuck out his arm, stopping her. "You ain't going nowhere."

Lydia's shoulders fell, but she obeyed.

Helena turned back to the strange woman. She was on her own.

The woman smiled invitingly. "You can trust me, lass." She extended her hand.

A wave of calm swept over her. Helena slipped her hand into the woman's dry, bony fingers and followed the woman inside the havari.

"We... we'll wait out here for ya," Jimmy called after her, his voice trembling.

The door squeaked shut behind her. The scent of sage washed over her in a thick cloud.

The woman uttered a Cant incantation: "*Gwili dil uwi. Slocka dil gloyday. Smay a lugil. Swunni nalk!*"

Chills ran through Helena as she repeated the woman's words in English, "Rest in your grave. Rot in your dirt. Spit and tears. Washed away!"

Helena peered into the darkness as her eyes adjusted to the dim light of the small wagon. Strewn across the floor were threadbare velvet pillows with thin gold piping. In the center of the mess of pillows stood a low table with a dainty white teacup on it. Inside the cup was a collection of small bones. Across the top of the china cup rested a brass key.

Along the walls of the arched roof, shelves overflowed with brown, green, and clear liquor bottles. Some of the bottles had tops dipped in red wax, others had ripped paper seals and were half-emptied of their contents.

Rows of neatly organized plants, in various stages of drying, dangled from the ceiling. Between the rows of plants hung metal idols and symbols, some cut out of what looked to be bits of discarded fizzy drink cans.

"I knew you would be coming to see me, lass. Ogak Beoir is a woman with clear sight... as am I."

The woman motioned for her to sit down on one of the worn pillows. Helena obeyed, careful to not disturb the table.

"There are some of us in this world who have the gift. Others fear us, some revere us, but most—wisely—avoid us. It is a terrible and wonderful thing, this gift we have."

"That *we* have?"

The woman nodded. "There's no need for you to hide your ability from me. I can feel your energy like a faint pulse. I know exactly who and what you are."

Helena moved to stand up.

"Stop, lass." The woman grabbed Helena's hand and pulled her down again. "You know that you want to learn. You are hungry for knowledge. Don't run away because you fear yourself."

"I don't fear myself. I fear you."

The woman's laughter filled the havari. "I'm only here to help you, lass. If it makes you feel better, you can call me Ayre."

Ayre picked up the brass key and sat it down on the table, in between a set of deep, long scratches. She lifted the dainty teacup and poured the bones out into her hand. "Do you want to know what your future may bring?"

Helena shook her head. A glimpse of what was to come could do nothing to help her. Or would it?

Ayre smiled at her knowingly. "Why do you say no, lass?"

"I... I got no questions."

"Now we both know that you aren't speakin' true. You have many questions, or you would've never entered this place." Ayre pointed to the door. "Just take a look at your cousin and her lover. They wanted no part."

"How do you know who they are?"

"My friend, do I need to show you who I am before you'll believe me? Are our souls not the same? Do you not feel what I feel when we're together?"

Helena stopped. The woman walked her fingertips across the table and brought them down upon Helena's skin. Helena's arm hairs stood on end, as if an electrical current had passed from Ayre's touch. Ayre looked up at her from between matted strands of hair as an orange flame flickered in her sky-blue eyes.

"There are very few like us—that truly have this uncommon gift."

Helena drew her hand back from the woman's touch. Chills swept through her. "Are you puttin' me on?"

"I know you have many questions. I'll always be here for you." Ayre shook the bones that rested in her hand. From under the table, she pulled out a white rabbit's pelt and smoothed it out on the table. "First, let me read the bones for you. Perhaps not for the future, but instead for your character—they will likely show you have little to fear. At the very least, they will tell us much of what you will need to know for the days to come.

"Let me begin by saying that most of us who have the forshaw have a tool that we use for interpreting the signs. Some of us use bones, as I do, some numbers or books, others use oracle cards, and others have the gift of the true sight—the sight that needs no tool for divination." Ayre's gaze bore into her. "You, Helena, have the true sight."

"What do you mean? The true sight?" Helena had to ask. "Do I have no power over the forshaw? Will I be plagued with visions of doom and death forever?"

Ayre smiled a reassuring smile. "You simply need to learn your craft, and things will get easier for you. Did Ogak tell you nothing?"

Helena shook her head. "She didn't tell me much. Only that things weren't as they seemed."

Ayre's eyes sparkled with thoughtful curiosity. "'Tis strange... But if Ogak said such a thing, it must be true."

"Do you know what she was talking about? What she meant?"

Ayre shook her head. "Let me read your character, we

will learn more. And remember this is your character, not your future, so be brave, my friend."

The bones rattled in Ayre's hands, sounding like macabre glass. She cast some of the bones, and they landed haphazardly upon the pelt. There were strange markings on each of the porcelain-colored pieces: harsh black lines, straight and unwavering. The marks of the ancient runes.

"Aye…" Ayre mumbled as she poured the rest of the bones back into the dainty tea cup. She kissed her fingers and raised her hand reverently to the sky. "*Mala nu sedi.*"

Helena recognized the prayer: "To the hands that heal." When Mam had been healthy, she had said it often.

"This one here." Ayre pointed at a bone that was engraved with a mark that looked almost like an *n*. "This is the Uruz, the ox. You are coming into a time in your life where there is great strength, freedom, and courage. There is untamed potential within you." Ayre grinned like a child with a secret. "It can also mean sexual desire."

Helena's cheeks burned as her thoughts went to Graham.

Ayre's fingers moved to the next bone, which carried a mark like a sideways *v*. "Kenaz. The vital fire of life and transformation—you have the power to create your own path."

Ayre took Helena's hand. The same electrical current ran through her touch as before, but Helena resisted the urge to pull away. "Why do you think people come to see those with the gift?"

"I don't know."

"They come to people like us because they want a change. They want to see hope, light at the end of the tunnel." Ayre pulled her hand back and motioned to the Uruz bone. "It's empowering to know that you have strength. Isn't it?"

"I suppose." Helena twisted the edge of the pillow between her fingers.

"Most people who come here are at odds with their lives. They are without jobs, going through break-ups, or have lost a loved one. No one who is truly happy steps within these walls." Ayre motioned up at the rows of liquor. "We have a responsibility to promote goodwill, to bring happiness into their lives. However, as you well know, there are times when there is no light, no happy ending. Sometimes we see things that they may not want to hear."

Ayre pointed at the last bone that lay on the rabbit pelt. The bone had a line and a sideways *v*, the mark almost like a lowercase *b*. "This is Thurisaz, the thorn. This is an omen of things to come... This is your darkness."

Fear blew through Helena like a biting winter wind.

"Do you want to hear what it means?"

"Will it change me? Or my future?"

Ayre smiled. "You're a smart woman. I can see why the goblins picked your father for the gift."

"What?" Helena asked. "Da has the forshaw?"

"He does, but he doesn't know. He has a very weak gift— it's more of what people call déjà vu... a bit of a feeling he gets, rather than a clear message. He passed you the gift, and you were very blessed—you have a strong essence."

"What... what of the other children? Will they have the forshaw too?"

"It's hard to say. They may or may not have the gift. It's selective." Ayre traced her finger around the bone with the *b*. "My friend, there are things in this world you cannot change.

We only see the future as it may be, but we have little power to change the fates. Usually what will be shall be."

If she couldn't change the future, then at least she could know what was in store, for good or bad. "What does the bone mean?"

"This last bone, Thurisaz, is a reactive force, a force for destruction and conflict. It is reversed, which is more ominous. There will be a compulsion, betrayal, hatred, torment, spite, and lies."

As the words tumbled from Ayre's lips, Helena moved back from the table. "You said this was a character reading… not my future."

"I know, lass. This is a force that you will have to control, a force that lives inside of you. Only you can control your inner darkness." Ayre dug in the pockets of her skirt and pulled out a card. Its edges were curled and soft with age. "You'll have many questions in the coming days. If you need me, this is how you can reach me. Day or night, don't hesitate."

CHAPTER TEN

The sunrise broke over the tree tops as Helena walked toward the fire ring. The antique percolating coffee pot jingled in her hand. The children were nestled tightly in their beds, dreaming of all the wonderful things that would happen in the days to come. She wished she had their innocence in sleep, but since meeting Ayre, Helena's dreams had failed to bring anything but nightmares.

Droplets of water slipped down the side of the tin coffee pot as she sat it upon the ground near the fire pit. Yesterday's flames had ebbed, leaving only a few glowing coals in their wake. She set a cluster of dried grass on the coals and blew until she had coaxed the tired flames to life. When the fire was ready, she lifted a bit of kindling and placed it on the hungry flames. Their orange forked tongues licked up the kindling and reached toward the sky, looking for more to consume. Pulling the grate over the fire, she set the coffee pot on top.

As she waited for the coffee to boil, Helena's mind filled

with thoughts of what the forshaw would mean for her and her family. The gift could bring much if she used it as Ayre had advised—she could be altruistic, giving hope to those who needed it the most, and it could give her another way to provide for her family. With her new job and the gift, she and Da could quickly pay back what was owed.

Heavy footsteps sounded from the trailer. The door squeaked and Da popped his head out. "I thought I heard ya. Whatcha doing, gra?"

She brushed the dirt from her fingers and stood up. "Nothing, Da. Just started the morning fire and gettin' some coffee goin'. You sleep okay?"

He stepped out and gently clicked the door shut. "I didn't find much rest. I got to thinkin' 'bout the new job." He stepped to the trailer window and pressed his face to the glass, as if checking to see if the others were asleep. "Are ya happy, gra? Is this something ya really want to be doin'? I know you're a bit different from the other girls, but I feel like I forced this job upon you, tellin' ya we needed the money and all."

"Nah, Da. I'm real happy. I like the job."

"You know you don't have to work if you don't wanna. You can get married and start your life. You don't have to be sticking around to help your mam and me. It ain't right for you to be holding back from living just to keep us all in line. We'd go on without ya."

Envisioning a future where she stood behind a sink, washing the dishes with a wee one scrambling up her legs while another squirmed in her belly, made her shudder. She was already living that life. She had already raised children. To think this was all life offered filled her with a profound, gut-wrenching sadness. There had to be more than breeding and hand-to-mouth living—like Graham said, the best thing to have was passion.

"Don't be daft, Da. There ain't no reason for me to be movin' on. I like it here, I like helpin' the fam." She rubbed the last bit of dust from her fingers. "I like this... the simplicity. I just don't like the thought that this is all there is."

Da gave her a weak, depressed smile. "Did I tell ya about when I was in the clink?"

Helena shook her head as Da picked up a few pieces of kindling and pushed them into the growing flames. "I had a lot of time to think when I was trapped in there." His eyes gleamed with unspent tears. "I want you to know that I believe in ya, gra a mo gris. You've always been real special to me. And you're a smart one. I know it would make your mam happy to marry ya off, but I want ya to do what is right for ya."

"Da, but I don't wanna get married. I want to take the exams so I'll have a choice and to find out who *I* am. I want a chance to be on my own and help people—maybe be a nurse or somethin' someday."

"I know, gra..." Da picked up a stick and poked it into the fire, sending up sparks.

"But you don't want that for me... do ya."

"It's not that. I want ya to follow your heart, but ya can see where that led your sister. Now she's got no fam... She's got nothin'."

"Times are changing, Da. We can change."

"No one can have it all, gra." He stabbed the fire again. "But if this is what you want, I can talk to your mam. Maybe with a little coaxing I can get her to agree to let you take those blasted exams. If nothin' else, at least ya can do 'em. I can't promise that even if ya pass, you'll get to go to university."

"Just gettin' to take the exams would mean the world to me, Da."

He smiled weakly. "Just remember, gra, with good grass a foal can outrun its mare."

. . .

The crisp paper lunch bag hung at Helena's side as she made her way into the manor. The scent of freshly fried sausage and onions seeped through the thin paper. Hopefully Graham would like the Dublin coddle she had prepared for him. For dessert she had whipped together a simple gooseberry crumble from fresh berries she had picked near their camp. It was early in the season, but she had found just enough of the plump little green berries to make a dessert for two.

It felt strange to cook for someone outside her family, but in an odd way it felt good. Was this what new wives felt? A sense of pride in creating something her husband would enjoy?

Mary and the receptionist stood by the front desk chatting as she made her way into the entrance hall. Mary's black summer jacket hung over her arm as if she had just arrived.

Helena waved at the pair. "Ladies."

"Helena," they answered in unison and then returned to their conversation.

Helena walked around the corner and sent a glance back at the women. A pair of hands grabbed her shoulders, and she gave a surprised squeak as she reached up to push the offender away. Her fingertips brushed against the strong muscles of his chest and, even before she looked up, she knew the man was Graham. "Ach... Excuse me, I was..." The warmth of his skin seeped into her fingers and moved down into her core.

Graham smiled. "Good morning, Helena."

"Aye." She struggled to find words as she dropped her hand. She couldn't draw her gaze away from the thin line of flesh that peeked out above his slightly undone white linen shirt.

"Is that my lunch?" He motioned to the bag in her hands.

She looked down at her hands, the simple action breaking the spell he had unintentionally cast. "Aye. I hope you're hungry."

Helena pushed the bag at him.

"I am." Graham smiled wickedly and took the bag. "I hope you're going to eat it with me." He opened the door to the servants' hall that led to the kitchen. "I have to admit I've been thinking about you... and your cooking all night."

Helena's cheeks flushed. "There's a gooseberry crumble—"

A high-pitched woman's scream pierced the air.

"What the bloody hell?" Graham put his hand up protectively. "Stay here."

"No." Helena moved toward the scream, which had come from the kitchen.

The swinging door squeaked as she walked in, Graham at her side. He pushed ahead of her and moved around the massive stainless steel tables. When he turned back to her, his face was a ghostly white, and he blocked her view of the rest of the kitchen. "You don't need to see this."

"See what?" Helena stepped around Graham. A brunette woman, one of the kitchen staff, stood by the counter, her hands over her mouth and tears streaming down her cheeks. On the floor at her feet was a gray-haired man with bushy sideburns, surrounded by a pool of dark red blood. Chester's toque sat crookedly on his head. His eyes were open, and his mouth was shaped in a surprised *o*, like he was trying to say something that would never come.

The woman's whimpers filled the kitchen as she drew her hands over her face, blocking her view of the carnage.

Graham brushed his hand reassuringly over Helena's arm. "I think he's gone."

Her feet scraped on the tile floor as she moved back from his touch. The cold stainless steel counter stopped her. "Oh, *shite*. It's really happened. It's come true."

"What's come true? Are you okay, Helena?"

She couldn't bear to look at Graham—to let him see how sick she felt.

She should have said something to Chester. She should have warned him. Instead he lay dead at her feet.

Her fingers trembled as she made the sign of the cross. *"Ain dha moniker o Gaater, dha Kam, ain dha Mun'ia Gradum, staish amen."*

Graham followed her lead. "In the name of the Father, the Son, and the Holy Spirit, amen."

The woman looked out from behind her hands. "Why? Why would someone want to hurt Chester? He ain't done nothing to no one." Her breathing quickened, and she started to hyperventilate as she stared down at the man on the floor.

"Let's get you both out of here." Graham motioned for Helena.

"No, I'm staying." Helena stood immobile as she tried to make some sense of what had happened in the room. "You need to take her out."

"I'll be right back." He led the hysterical woman from the kitchen, leaving Helena alone with the dead Chester.

She felt a faint breeze against her skin in the confined kitchen, and chills rose on her arms.

"*You did nothing...*" a man's ghostly voice said.

Helena's jerked with surprise. "What? Who's there?"

"*You knew...*"

Helena carefully stepped around the body and looked around the kitchen, under the cabinets and prep tables. No one was there.

"*You said nothing...*"

She turned and dropped to her knees next to the dead man. "Rest in your grave. Rot in your dirt. Spit and tears. Washed away!"

Just in case the ghost was gypsy, Helena whispered the same prayer in Cant. "*Gwili dil uwi. Slocka dil gloyday. Smay a lugil. Swunni nalk!* Begone, foul spirit. You are not welcome!" she said.

Above her, the metal spoons trembled.

From the far recesses of the kitchen, bells jingled, the sound growing closer and closer. A horse snorted. Helena stood up and ran toward the door. She turned the corner of the counter.

In front of her, between two prep counters, a coach driven by a headless fairy stormed to a stop. Six black horses, all with blood-red eyes, drew in wheezing breaths. Candles burned along the coach-a-bower's length, each one mounted in a human skull—surely the heads of the fairy's victims.

It was the phantom from her childhood ghost stories. It was the Dullahan.

The death carriage squeaked as the headless phantom stowed his whip, which was made of a human spine. The black steeds stomped and shifted impatiently, and droplets of blood dripped from their heaving sides.

The Dullahan stepped down from the driver's seat. Under one of his arms, the macabre phantom held his ghostly green head. The beady, fly-like eyes flickered around the room and settled upon the man who lay upon the floor.

The phantom's empty hand lifted, exposing gnarled bony fingers. He opened his fingers, exposing his fleshless, skeletal palm, and whispered an eerie incantation.

A shadow oozed from Chester's body and slid across the floor. The soul's dark fingers clawed at the black and white tiles, frantically searching for something to hold, but Death called, and the soul was forced to answer.

Helena pressed her back against the wall.

The Dullahan won't take me. He won't take me. She repeated the mantra over and over.

The door to the devilish carriage opened as the Dullahan chanted a spell, drawing the writhing soul into the black beyond. The head smiled, and its beady eyes sparkled with malice.

She struggled to recall the stories of her youth. The Dullahan was afraid of something... but what was it?

She scanned the kitchen for something that would stop the phantom. Next to her on the edge of the counter was a golden-plated serving spoon. Gold. The phantom hated gold.

She grabbed the spoon and shoved it out in front of her.

The phantom peered down at her. Its head shifted in its arm like a confused dog's. The green head's lips quivered and it released an ear-splitting squeal. The Dullahan stumbled backward, bumping into a counter. The face under his arm cringed and hissed as he backed up to the coach-a-bower. Lifting the head by its putrid white hair, the Dullahan stepped up into the driver's seat. Without a backward look, it pulled away.

The world spun around her.

She had faced down the phantom of death. The kitchen blurred and, as if she were looking through a tunnel, all she could see was the red blood.

She tried to force herself to breathe.

There was blood everywhere. The floor. The ceiling. Her hands. Everything was covered with blood.

The world went black.

CHAPTER ELEVEN

Graham would need to tread softly; they had entered dangerous ground. Mr. Shane had warned him that this day would come. The day of enlightenment.

There was a strong knock on the door. "Graham?" Seamus's voice called.

Graham opened the door of the tool shed and walked outside. Seamus had his back turned and he stared out into the distance, making Graham fear the worst. "Hi, Seamus. How's Helena doing?"

"She's restin' in the dinin' hall. Mary's keeping an eye on her. She's shaken up, but she'll be all right." Seamus rubbed his hands together. "I need to thank you... for getting' Helena outta there. She don't need to be round no guards."

"I understand."

"Did you hear the guards are thinkin' the man offed himself?"

"Aye." Chills ran down Graham's spine. Chester wasn't the kind to do something like that.

"It's hard to tell what someone may or may not do… I've found that people are always surprisin' me." Seamus looked at him.

A wave of relief washed over Graham.

"You've proven to be a good choice. You've done a fine job." Graham paused.

"Is there anythin' else you need me to be doin' before I round her up and take her home?"

"Actually, I need you to check the irrigation lines on the south quadrant of the golf course. When you're done, you can head out."

"I'll head right over there," Seamus said. "Anything else?"

There were a lot of things he needed—help, courage, and the strength to do what needed to be done. Yet Seamus couldn't provide the inner strength Graham required. The only thing he could give him was time with Helena.

"If you don't mind, I might take Helena into town with me. I have a few errands to run. It would be easiest if I just dropped her off when we're done."

The air between them buzzed with tension.

"I promise Helena'll be in good hands," Graham said.

"Aye. I have no doubt." Seamus's face tightened. "But I don't know about ya dropping her off. I don't know if Helena's told ya, but her mam ain't going to be real pleased if she sees you two together. It would look real strange for a gorger to be dropping her off."

"Oh."

"If ya didn't drop her off right at the campsite maybe you could take her with ya. Just be careful no one sees ya." Seamus ran his hand over the stubble on his chin. "Are ye sure ye want to be takin' her along? I mean, she's a real good help, but she's had a bit of a long week with Chester's death and all."

"Don't worry, Seamus," Graham said. "I won't keep her long. Just a few stops."

• • •

A lump rose in Graham's throat as he opened the door to the dining hall. The time had come to tell Helena the truth. It couldn't be avoided any longer. He could only hope she was ready.

If things didn't go as he planned, it would be hard to convince her to stay on at the manor. If Graham lost her, there would be no getting her back. And if she left, he'd be letting everyone down. No, more than that. His brother's life would be at stake.

The door drifted close behind him. Helena sat at the table, her head on her arms. Her long black eyelashes were closed in sleep. He'd never noticed the faint pink hue of her lips, nor the tiny freckles splashed across her thin nose. There was something about her that made him want to touch her, to feel her in his arms, but holding her again was an impossible dream.

He hated himself for what he was going to have to do. This enlightenment would only bring more stress and discord to her life, but if he did everything right he could make her understand why the secrecy had been so vital.

He moved toward her and accidently banged his toe against the table leg.

Helena stirred. "Oh…" She lifted her head from her arms. "Graham? Where's Mary?"

"In the kitchen." Graham smiled softly.

Helena sat up and readjusted her hair. "I don't know what happened. I was just taking a little break. I must've been more tired than I thought." She looked up at him with her buttery brown eyes. "It's been one hell of a day."

And it was only going to get worse.

"I'm sorry about everything that's gone on here the last few days," Graham said as he sat down across from her. "But I'm glad I caught you. I was hoping we could talk a bit."

Helena ran her fingers under her eyes, whisking away a little smear of her black eye makeup. "What happened to... to Chester?"

"I think you already know."

"It wasn't all just a horrible dream?"

He shook his head.

"It seemed like Mary and Chester were real close. Did they have some kind of relationship?"

"She's always been good friends with him, but she's married to Herbert."

Her eyes darkened.

Graham's hands shook as he stared at Helena's fingers. He longed to reach out and touch her, to console her after all she had been through. "Can I ask you a question?"

Helena nodded.

"Why did you faint?"

"There was..." She paused.

"What?"

She dropped her gaze to her hands. "There was... just so much blood."

"Really? With the emergency with the little boy you just

jumped right in. But when a man you didn't know well was killed, you... shut down. It doesn't make sense to me."

Her fingers trembled, and he couldn't hold back any longer. Reaching over, he took her fingers in his, letting her warmth soak into him like a beam of sunshine breaking through a storm. "You know you can tell me anything. You can trust me. If you *saw* something in there—*anything*—you can tell me." He let his meaning sink in.

Helena scowled and pulled her hand from his. "What in the bloody hell are you talking about?" She glowered. "He was dead when I got there. I'm a Traveller, but I didn't have nothin' to do with his death."

"I know you didn't have anything to do with his death. That's not what I meant."

She looked toward the door.

"Something happened. I'm no fool." He paused, searching her face for answers. "I know there are things that go on in the manor that can't be explained. I want to know what you saw."

She flushed. "I saw exactly what you saw."

He extended his hand. "Come with me. I wanna show you something."

She slipped her hand into his, and they made their way out of the kitchen.

The manor was filled with meandering tourists. Most clicked away with their cameras as they stared slack-jawed at the cathedral seats and marble busts which filled the halls. High tea would be starting soon, and the halls would empty as the people rushed to the drawing room to feast on their fancy little sandwiches and cookies—all of them unaware of the death and mayhem that had filled the staff's hidden lives.

Helena ran her hand over her hair, nervously pushing down the loose ends.

"You look great." Graham led her past the front desk. "Don't worry."

She looked down at their hands and gently pulled her fingers from his.

He tried to focus on his task instead of the soft sound of her breath as they made their way to the deserted hallway near the south end of the manor. He came to a stop at the end of the hall.

The only evidence of the door in front of them was a thin line that ran down the wainscoting. Adorning the wall was an oil painting of a group of men standing under threatening gray clouds as they mended a skiff's nets. Around the picture was a subdued black frame, which made the painting seem bland in comparison to the priceless art that filled the rest of the manor.

Graham ran his hands down the sides of the dusty frame.

"What are you doin'? Should you be touchin' that?" Helena stepped back and looked over her shoulder. "What if someone sees us?"

"Don't worry. I'm not stealing it." Graham found the tiny brass button hidden in the frame's carved folds.

A man and a woman walked by, their arms wrapped lovingly together. The woman giggled at a joke that Graham couldn't hear. He glanced at Helena. Even if everything went right, and she decided to stay here and help him, they could never be like that enamored couple.

Graham reached out for Helena, but he stopped himself from touching her. "You need to be quiet when we go down."

Helena nodded.

Graham pressed the cold button. The door clicked open, and the dank, earthy cellar air washed over him. Though he'd been going down to the basement every day, the sickening scent of decay still gave him chills.

"You ready?" A tiny part of him wanted her to say no, to turn around and escape the manor's hold and never look back, but if she left here, not only would she leave him, she'd also take away any spark of hope he still had for Danny.

"What's down there?" Helena asked, sounding apprehensive.

Graham flicked a switch, and dim yellow lights flickered to life. He moved to the top step. "Down here, I hope you can find your future."

She moved onto the top stair. The door clicked shut behind them. "I hope this place is filled with gold."

"I can say with the utmost certainty that it's not." Graham laughed, and some of his nerves slipped away.

Dusty bottles of wine filled the racks on each side of the steps. In most ways, the cellar appeared to be nothing more than a cobweb-filled underworld, but it held secrets and more than one family's tragedy. The bottom stair creaked as they stepped onto the dirt floor.

"At one time, this was the manor's dungeon. It was never really used; it was merely built as a show of power."

"And now you use it as a wine cellar?" Helena glanced at the bottles that surrounded them.

Graham laughed, but the musty air deadened the sound. He led her around a rack of wine bottles to what appeared to be the back of the cellar. A worn gray stone the color of a grave marker jutted from the wall. He pushed it in with a click.

A woman's cough broke the silence as the door slid open.

• • •

Helena gasped. Her knees threatened to give out as she stared at the hospital beds lining the walls. One of the many IV pumps beeped. Bed after bed was filled with gaunt, pale men and women. There must have been at least thirty sickly people that she could see, although she guessed there could be more around the room's far corner.

One nurse was helping a man walk at the end of the hall, while another was talking to a patient. Everything in the room was shiny and clean, and the IV pumps and beds looked like they were top of the line, but everything was out of place. Why was there a hospital ward in the manor's basement?

"What're all these people doing down here? What's goin' on? Who are they? Why are they here?" All of her questions spilled out in a mess of syllables.

Graham put his hand to the small of her back. "It's okay, Helena," he said softly. "They're all here by necessity or choice. I promise you."

There was an older man to their right. His eyes were closed, but his lips moved like he was talking in his sleep. She walked over to the bed and ran her hand over the footboard.

"That's Herbert. He's Mary's husband."

"Does Mary know he's down here?"

"Aye." Graham led her farther down the corridor, to a bed where a boy lay with his eyes closed. The boy's hair was silver, and his face was the pale white of the long-sick. In fact, the only color upon his skin was the pale pink of his thin lips.

Something about him made Helena think of Rionna.

"How old is he?" Helena whispered.

The bed squeaked as Graham sat down on the edge and ran his hand over the boy's forehead, pushing back a strand of the boy's silvery hair. "Danny's almost sixteen. He was the first to come to the infirmary."

She looked around at the lonely lines of beds—there were no visitors. "Who is he? Doesn't his family care that he's here?"

"Yes. Mr. Shane and I care very much that he's stuck in this place."

"Danny's your brother?"

"And that woman there." Graham pointed to the next bed over where a haggard, smoky-haired woman lay fast asleep. "That's my mother, Rose."

Her stomach clenched. What had happened to force both his brother and mother to live in a subterranean ward?

A nurse turned the corner and rushed down the hallway toward them. Graham gave her a stoic nod, and the woman stopped and stared, wide-eyed, at Helena. "Who... I... I mean..." The woman took Graham by the arm. "Can you give us a minute, miss?"

"Aye." Helena wandered down the corridor between the rows of beds. Some patients were fast asleep, while others writhed and pitched violently, letting out raspy wails, as if they were fighting off demons only they could see.

A monitor beeped from behind her, and she glanced back, catching sight of the smoky-haired Rose.

She had wondered about his mother, but never in all her life would she have expected anything like this.

The nurse talking to Graham circled something on her clipboard. Graham nodded, but there was a worried expression on his face.

Helena stopped next to Graham as the monitor beeped again. "Is Danny okay?"

"Excuse me, miss." The woman in the white lab coat squeezed by her and pushed buttons on the boy's IV pump.

"There." The monotonous beeping stopped. "Graham, I would appreciate if you would mention getting more staff to your stepfather." The nurse glanced around at the filled beds. "I would hate for anything like what happened earlier this week to happen again."

Graham's eyes darkened. "Aye."

The nurse pushed the clipboard under her arm and smiled. "See you soon." She made her way out of the hall.

Helena turned to Graham. "Why are all these people here? Why aren't they in a *real* hospital?"

He let out a long, tired exhale. "These people are all here because they need our help. *Real* hospitals would stuff them away in psych wards, out of sight and out of mind. Here, we can help them."

"What are you talking about? What's wrong with them?"

"Would you please sit?" Graham asked, patting the bed next to Danny.

Helena gazed at the boy as she sat down next to him. Rionna looked so much like him when she slept, peaceful and innocent.

She ran her thumb over the young man's hand. A charge

ran between them, just like what she had felt with Ayre. She jumped up, knocking into Graham.

"Are you okay?" He stared at her, a sly smile on his lips.

"I'm... I'm fine." She crossed her arms over her chest.

"No. You're not. You felt something when you touched him, didn't you?"

"I... I don't know what you're talkin' 'bout."

The next bed over, Rose jerked in her sleep. Her white lips opened. "Never... No... Ghost... go away!"

Helena took a step back.

"It's okay. She's fine." Graham put his hand to her arm, stopping her. "What happened when you touched Danny?"

Helena looked back at the boy. "Nothing, just a small current." She sounded madder than the old crone at the prison. "It ain't anythin'."

"You and I both know that isn't true." He grabbed her shoulder and turned her to face him. "I know about your gift. If you wanted to, you could help all the people in the infirmary. You could heal them. You could change so many people's lives."

She stared at the patients surrounding her. "What are you talkin' about, Graham?"

"You're a clairsentient... It's okay..."

"What in the bloody hell is a clairsentient?"

"It's someone who can harness energy. Some can see the future, some get a sense of foreboding when things are happening, and the more powerful clairsentients can heal—like you."

It was impossible. She'd never healed anyone.

Except the boy in the river.

But that had been a fluke.

"I can't do anything to help these people."

"Yes you can," Graham said, his voice so low it almost sounded as if he were begging.

"Graham, I don't know what's going on with me... I don't know if I'm a healer, or mad, or if I'm just living in some sick, twisted dream. In any case, I'm not who you think I am."

"That's not true. You saved that boy."

"I did CPR. It didn't have anything to do with *healing*," she said, spitting the word.

His eyebrow rose. "So you're telling me you felt nothing when you helped him?"

She looked down at her hands. Her lungs ached as she thought back to the boy.

"I know you did, Helena. And I know you can help here. You have a gift. You may not have control yet, but someday... someday you might." He reached out to touch her, but she didn't move forward to meet him. "You're our only hope."

"How do you know so much about all of this... this stuff?" She motioned around her.

"Danny's a clairvoyant." He slowly dropped his hand. "We've tried everything to help bring him back, but nothing has worked. The only thing we haven't tried is a lobotomy. It's barbaric and it would be irreversible. He would never be the same—yet Mr. Shane's threatening to have it done if you leave us."

"A lobotomy?" she asked, shuddering at the word.

"He wouldn't want to use it just on Danny... he'd want to try it with my mother as well."

She didn't know what to say. Was Mr. Shane really

that awful? If so, it was no wonder Graham had been so desperate to bring her into this strange reality.

"You're their last hope. Please, Helena. Please try. Just touch him again. See what happens. See if you can heal him."

It broke her heart to hear Graham beg. She couldn't do what he wanted. She was no one, nothing special.

All she could do was show him that she wasn't the woman he needed.

Helena stepped closer to the boy.

The boy's chest rose and fell with shallow breaths as she placed her hand upon his cool forehead. A wave of weak energy pulsed between them. His body seemed to absorb the current, but he didn't move.

She looked down at Danny as the energy ebbed and flowed between them. Unlike her experience with the little boy, the energy didn't seem to go deeper or expand. She felt nothing but warmth—there was no pain.

"I don't know what to do. I'm telling you, I'm not a healer."

"That can't be true." Graham collapsed against the wall of the infirmary. "You just need more practice."

She shook her head. He was giving her far too much credit. Just because there was some—some energy that ran between her and Danny didn't mean that she could heal. For all she knew, she was merely imagining the feeling.

Graham ran his hands over his stubble and took a long breath. "Danny and I were always close as kids. When I first got my driver's license, he and I had a special day. We went everywhere he wanted to go. We started at the sweets shops." He laughed weakly. "He ate so many chocolates I thought he was going to be sick, but he held it together. By the end of the day we found ourselves at a football match between our two favorite teams—Manchester and the Republic of Ireland. I always promised him we'd go to another game, but then he got sick."

"He sounds like a lad after my own heart." She smiled. "I love the Boys in Green."

Graham took her hands in his and looked deep into her eyes. "Just try to help him. Do whatever it is you need. Take whatever time you need. I want my brother and my mother back."

Graham let go of her hands.

Helena knew the desperation he felt—she would feel the same way if any of her siblings fell ill like this.

She had to try again.

Closing her eyes, she imagined Charlie as he lay upon the river bank. She tried to recall the fear and adrenaline of watching the boy's life slip away.

Using the time-dampened fear, she pressed her hands to both sides of Danny's face. A slight current flickered through her. She tried to imagine the fear and confusion Charlie must have felt as he fell toward the water, but she felt only whispers of swirling energy. She squeezed her eyes shut and forced herself to recall all the memories she had of the boy.

Nothing happened. The flicker of energy faded. She stayed motionless and waited for something to happen.

Guilt drove through her like a well-honed knife.

She couldn't help Danny.

Helena glanced up at Graham. His eyes were filled with hope. "I'm so sorry, Graham. I don't know anything about helping people."

She dropped her hands from Danny's face.

Graham stepped closer and she let him lift her chin. "Helena, you can help people. I know you can. It's the reason Mr. Shane and I were so adamant in getting you and your father to the manor. It's why we paid the warden to release him. I know you can help—but you must *want* to."

"You paid off the warden?" Helena pulled away from his touch.

"We had to have you here." He looked down at his brother. "Don't you realize how much convincing it took to get you and your father here? It's not like having your kind work here is something we normally do."

"My *kind?*" Helena sucked in a breath.

"You know, gypsies," he said.

"That's shite." She recoiled from him. "Is that why you brought me here? Because you think you can manipulate me? Do you think that I'm stupid? That you can flash some money in my face and buy me?"

He stood up and moved toward her, but she stopped him with a wave of her hand. "Helena... I didn't mean—"

"You lied to me. You manipulated me. You manipulated my da. And now you bring me to a boy's sickbed to pull at my heartstrings."

Helena pushed his hands away from her and stormed out of the makeshift hospital, letting the door slam behind her.

Graham had the wrong woman.

If he had wanted her to do something, he should have been honest from the beginning. If he had wanted her to be a nurse, he should have told her.

He didn't have to play the cloak-and-dagger game.

Helena stopped and pressed her body against the wall.

Next to her was an oak cask, and stenciled on the end were the words "Jameson, Special Reserve." A part of her yearned to open the barrel of whiskey and breathe in the scents of almonds, vanilla, wood, and pepper. She ran her fingers over the rough wood.

The door cracked open, and Graham stepped into the cellar.

"I'm sorry, Helena."

She rubbed her dusty fingers together. "How often do you bring new clairsentients here?"

"I've never—"

"I tried to tell you the truth. Now you should try and do the same."

"You are the first clairsentient we've had."

"Bullshite. Is that what happened to all those people?" She pointed toward the infirmary. "You tried to have others like me help him, and they go mad?"

"What? What are you talking about, Helena?"

"This doesn't make sense… Why would you have all these people in your basement if you weren't trying to hide them?"

"They're all here because we can help them. We *have* helped them. We have a book." Graham stepped closer to her, and the smell of sharp antiseptic wafted from his skin. He moved his hands down his kilt, nervously smoothing it. "You'll be nothing like any of those people in there."

"Then what happened? Tell me the truth. How do I know I won't end up like Danny if I help you?"

"Danny doesn't have the gift of clairsentience, only the gift of sight. When the visions started, he couldn't deal with all that he saw. He knew he needed help, but before we could do anything, he fell victim to his visions."

Helena could understand the boy's fears, the thoughts that had driven him to madness. If someone hadn't experienced the darker side of living, it would be easy to fall into the chaotic fear created by the forshaw. Even for her it was a mental battle between what was real and what wasn't, between memories of the past and thoughts of a future that brought her no comfort.

"Did he see the Dullahan too?"

Graham's gaze dropped, and he shook his head. "You saw him, did you? I saw the gold in your hand, but I was hoping—"

"That you could keep the secrets of this place away from me a little longer?" Helena interrupted. "If you want me to stay here and keep workin', or helpin', or whatever it is that you want me to do, you need to tell me what is really goin' on."

He opened his mouth and paused, as if unsure of where to begin. "The Earl of Dunraven built this manor to be a... spiritual portal."

"He built this place for ghosts? For the Dullahan?"

"No, he built it to be as close to the paranormal as a human could be. The druids and the Celts all used this place as a threshold to connect with the spirits and to facilitate healing. Dunraven realized its potential to help those who were stuck between two worlds, like Danny, so he built the manor. Nothing and no one was more important to him than this place."

"How can bein' closer to the spirits help with healing?"

"There are good and bad spirits. They all effect energy.

Some draw it out and some give it away. And for those like you, this is a place where you have extra power. It's like an amplifier. Whatever powers you have outside the village are multiplied as you near the manor."

Helena's head swam. "What else do you know?"

"There are secrets that we're still learning about this place. Mysterious things happen, and the unexplained is a regular guest."

She had said she would stay if he told her the truth, but now that she knew what surrounded them, and the danger it posed to her, she wondered if she had made a mistake. Perhaps some truths were better left unknown.

CHAPTER TWELVE

There was nothing worse than not knowing what was going on—at least Helena had thought so, until she learned that Adare Manor served as an amplifier for the spiritual world. The door of knowledge had opened, and Helena had passed through. There was no going back.

Helena had tried to phone Da, but he hadn't answered. He must have assumed that she would be fine in Graham's company. How wrong he'd been.

The door to the manor slammed behind her as she made her way out into the English-style garden. She weaved through the hedges and made her way toward the riverbank where she had rescued the boy until she reached a secluded bench. Black lichen twisted skeletal tendrils over the seat's cracked and aged surface. When she sat down, the cold cement drew the warmth from her skin like the boy had drawn her energy.

Did everything and everyone in this place want something from her?

It all seemed to come with a price. She wanted freedom, and she had found her way to the manor. She was given a job that was supposed to solve her family's financial problems, but the chance had turned into something she had never expected.

Helena rested her head in her hands and tried to stop the tired tears that threatened to sneak out.

"I'm sorry." Graham's voice broke through her wall of self-pity. He sat down on the other end of the bench and dropped his hands between his knees.

"Where did you come from?" Helena moved away from him, teetering on the bench's worn edge.

"I know you said you need time to think. But I didn't want you to think you have to deal with this alone. Even if we just sit here and don't speak, that's fine." He stared out at the river. "But if you want to talk or if you have questions, I'm here."

She should have been angry that he'd followed her. She should have berated him, but instead she found herself feeling glad that he cared enough to reach out.

"Where's my da?"

"I sent him home. I told him I would bring you back to the campsite. If you want I'll get someone else to run you back to your place."

She didn't answer.

The silence rested between them. The only sound was the river as it washed past on its way to something bigger.

Her mind raced. She wanted to run away, to go back to the camp and never look back at this crazy place. Yet beneath her selfish desire to escape, the need to help was stronger. If she left this place, if she left Graham, there would be no coming back. She would have to live with the guilt that she had rejected the chance to help those who really needed her.

For a moment she imagined Charlie on the river's edge, his little blue lips motionless as he lay limply at her feet. Droplets of water slipped down his face. Helena blinked the memory away.

"What happened to Charlie?" she asked.

"What?"

"I never heard what happened to him."

Graham peered down at his hands. "He only had a few bruises and a terrible fright."

She nodded limply. At least she had helped one person. Saved one life.

Graham moved toward her on the bench. "I know you've probably had enough of the supernatural for one day, but... do you know why his mother couldn't pull him from the water and you could?"

Helena thought back to the frail woman. "I thought he was just too big for her."

"No. Not quite." Graham looked up at her with a tired sadness in his eyes. "We try to be careful about everything that happens here, but it's impossible to keep watch all the time. Normally the water spirits are innocuous, and usually they aren't out during the day, but for some reason the Glashtyn wanted that boy."

"The Glashtyn?"

"You know... the little goblin that lures small children into the water and drowns them."

"I know what the Glashtyn is." Helena paused. "But what about the boy, was he some kind of..." What was she to call the thing she was? Supernatural? A freak?

"Charlie was just an innocent victim." He moved his hand closer to her, but stopped and dropped it on the black edge of the bench. "Are you okay? I know this is a lot to take in. After what you saw in the kitchen I'm impressed you didn't end up in the infirmary. You're strong."

"I'm a Traveller. There ain't no room for the weak."

"That's why we chose to bring you here." Graham reached up and pushed her hair behind her ear.

The action came so suddenly that Helena let his fingertips caress her skin. His touch was soft and caring, and it shook her to her core. No man had ever touched her in such a way. The Traveller code said she should slap him for the touch, but another part of her, a deeper part, wanted to feel his hand on her.

He dropped his hand. Helena couldn't look away from his strong, work-callused fingers.

"Is that the only reason you want me here, for my abilities and my strength?" Helena wished she hadn't said the words. She didn't know if she could stand the pain if he said yes.

Graham sucked in a breath, but didn't reply.

"I shouldn't have said that. Don't answer," Helena said quickly. "Look, I don't think I can help you. I haven't even finished my exams—I'm not close to being of any use."

"What do your exams have to do with anything?" Graham forced a smile, and his teeth sparkled in the late afternoon sun. "I don't care if you know geometry or literature."

"I'm not much of a nurse. I know you think I can heal, but I have no idea how to do that. About all I can do is cook and take care of children. In the infirmary I'd be about as much help as a rotten potato."

Graham's smile grew. "That's not true. I've seen how hard you work in the kitchen. You'd be a great help."

Helena stared out at the river. "Yeah. I'd be a great *maid*."

"There's nothing wrong with being a maid." Graham tried to reassure her, but the words struck her as infuriating.

"That's not what I want," Helena snapped. "I don't want to be a maid. I don't want to work in the kitchens forever. I don't want…"

There were so many things she didn't want, but she couldn't tell Graham about them. He had already given her more pity than she wanted.

"I need to take my exams."

The edge of Graham's warm hand brushed against hers. "Don't let anything stop you. If you think that's what you need to do, then do it."

A lump rose in her throat. "I don't know if I can."

"Just because you are a Traveller doesn't mean that you don't have the right to take the fecking test. You can do whatever it is you want to do."

Helena let his hand keep touching hers. The heat radiated off him, warming her skin. Her whole body begged to move closer to him; she willed him to touch her face. For his fingers to linger on her cheek like a lover's touch. For him to move in and kiss her yearning lips.

"When is this test?" Graham stood up.

The place where his hand had been grew cool. "It's in a week and a half." She stood up and followed him from the garden and toward the car park.

"Have you been studying?"

She shook her head. "I've tried, but not lately."

"Is Mary working you that hard?" He smirked.

"No." A wave of embarrassment rose within her as she thought of her moneyless purse. "I haven't found another studier."

"Well, you're in luck. I just happen to be running into town. You can go with me. I need to run to a shop. Then maybe we can find a library or something."

Helena smiled. "Okay, but we can't be too long. Aye?"

"Aye." He walked with her across the gardens to his white Mercedes. The door squeaked as he opened it and motioned for her to get in.

Helena hesitated as she looked at the passenger seat. Da had given his permission, but it still felt strange being alone with a man—especially if they were out at the shops. Yet, her desire for a studier outweighed her apprehension. As long as no one saw them, she would be okay.

Graham closed the door behind her. A rebellious, giddy excitement filled her.

Her exhilaration was cut short as her mobile vibrated. A text message popped up. It was from Angel, wondering when Helena would come by to see her.

She couldn't see Angel—not today.

The sun sat low over Adare Village as they made their way out of town and toward Limerick. The radio crackled with static, and Graham pushed a button, putting a stop to the abrasive sound.

"Graham?" she asked, breaking the silence.

"Hmm?"

"Do you have an ability, ya know, like Danny?"

His hands tightened on the steering wheel. "There are many different types of abilities. If you're asking if I can see the future like Danny—no, I can't."

"But you do have some kinda gift?" She bit her lip.

"I can read people's auras."

"What does that mean?"

"I don't know how to explain it." He gave her a modest smile. "I guess the best way is to say that when I meet people I get a feeling for them, and sometimes I can see a glow. I can't read minds, or tell the future, but sometimes I know when a person is going to be a danger, or I can see if they have a particular strength."

"If you can see danger coming, then why couldn't you stop the death in the kitchen?"

"I have to be around the person who means harm. Even then, my sense isn't perfect." The white Mercedes sped up as Graham made his way onto the highway. "All I see is a color. When I met you at the prison, you glowed in rainbow colors—almost like you were standing in the light that passes through a prism. It was the first time I'd seen someone with such a strong saturation." He glanced over at her. "Now you're a dark gold."

Helena looked down at her arms, but there was nothing golden about her, just the perpetual tan that came from being a Traveller. "What does that mean?"

"Gold usually indicates a student, or someone who's trying to learn everything all at once."

"You're putting me on."

"I promise I'm not."

"Then what color is my da?"

Graham shook his head. "Like I said, it depends on the day, and his mood, but lately he's been a purplish-blue."

"Aye… and what does that mean?"

"That he's having deep feelings and that he's on the right path."

"Really?"

"I don't know for certain, though. That's the thing about an aura—it's subjective."

It was hard for her to make sense of what exactly Graham meant. She had heard of aura readers before but, like ghosts, the Dullahan, and the forshaw, until recently she hadn't thought they were real.

They pulled off the highway onto the familiar Limerick streets, past the tree-filled People's Park where a couple sat under the gazebo, enjoying a picnic in the evening sun, blissfully unaware of the supernatural activities Graham was talking about.

In what seemed like no time, they were parking. Graham opened the car door for her. She stepped out in front of big plate-glass windows with bold black lettering that read "Barbara's Books."

"What're you doin' here?"

"I'm getting you a present."

Helena stopped as Graham stepped to the door. "You can't be buyin' me anything."

"You need the book. I want to get it for you." Graham pulled open the glass door to the shop and waited for her to walk in. "I'm paying you back."

She couldn't be indebted to him; it would only be another thing he could use to push her into taking on the infirmary work. "Graham, you can't—"

"Nah..." He waved her off. "Consider the book a thank you gift after all you've done today."

The bell jingled as the door shut behind them. A

brunette woman behind the counter looked up over her round glasses. "May I help you?"

"We are looking for a Post Leaving Certificate studier."

"No," Helena whispered, her cheeks flushed.

"Which one do you need? There are a number of different studiers."

"Which one?" Graham asked Helena.

She had been studying the basic exam, but she had an idea. "Which one will help me if I want to get into a school for nursing?"

Helena glanced up at Graham, who had a proud smile on his face.

"You can get into a good university if you do well on your exams, but you know, you will need to score high, at the honors level." The woman led them to the back of the store and handed Helena the thick book. It looked almost identical to the one Mam had thrown into the fire, except this one had the word "Honors Level Studier" in big black letters across the cover.

A knot formed in Helena's stomach. She wanted to do well, to prove to her fam that she could stand on her own two feet and finish what she'd started. Yet she couldn't imagine herself living on campus, talking to boys, studying all week in the library, and getting scuttered on the weekends. It didn't feel right.

Helena flipped through the book. It fell open to the history section. She read the first question: "Write about ballads and songs as useful historical sources."

Memories of Da sitting around the fire singing *Sean Nos*, traditional Traveller songs, flooded her mind.

She flipped to the next section in the book, economics,

and read the first question: "Outline, with the aid of a diagram, how changes in the level of investments affect the level of national income."

Helena closed the book and stuffed it under her arm. She would need to do more studying.

Graham handed the clerk the money for the book. Helena's face burned.

The clerk handed her a paper bag, and Helena slipped the book inside.

Graham put his hand on the small of Helena's back. His warm touch soaked through the thin fabric of her shirt and made her already fluctuating emotions and desires surge. "I don't know what to say, Graham. Thank you… but ya didn't have to."

"I know, but I wanted to do something nice for you. To let you know how important you are to me. You're something special."

She rolled the top of the paper bag in her hands nervously as they left the store. "Thank you. *Maa'ths.* For everything."

"You're welcome. There's just one thing I'm less than happy about." Graham took her hand and started to walk to the right, away from where the car was parked. "I didn't get to eat any of that gooseberry crumble you promised."

Helena smiled. He had remembered.

Tradition and habit pulled her toward home and the campsite. Yet her desire for Graham made her grip his hand tighter.

Around the corner was a small restaurant. Its green awning flapped in the breeze, waving at them like a welcoming friend. Graham opened the door for her, but didn't let go of her hand as she made her way inside.

The tables were mostly filled. There was a couple seated close to the door; the man was dressed in a suit jacket and trousers, the woman in a fine silk dress. The man stopped stuffing himself on an expensive-looking cut of beef for a second as he stared at her.

Helena pulled at her dress pants. For a second she wished she had something else to wear, something that would have helped her blend into the crowded room.

Graham smiled, and the cleft of his chin pulled tight. "You look beautiful, lass." He ran his free hand down her arm, making her pulse quicken.

He leaned down close, almost as if he was going to kiss her, but at the last second he turned to her ear. "Your aura's glowing red," he whispered. His breath was warm on her skin.

"What do ya mean by that?"

His smile grew wider. "Let's just say, I'm honored that you think I'm handsome."

"I said nothing of the sort." She stared into his sexy, honey-brown eyes. "What color do you see for someone with an ego?"

Graham laughed as they sat down at their table. Helena was careful to pick a large table, and she set the shop bag between them. Graham didn't need to be getting any more ideas—nor did she.

The waitress came, dropped off some waters, and took their order, flaunting her assets in front of Graham like a hen presenting herself to a rooster. He didn't seem to pay her any mind.

The woman swiveled her hips as she walked away.

"So…" Helena tried to control her annoyance as she glanced back at Graham. "Ya know all about me, but I don't know much about you. Where were ya raised?"

Graham ran his finger through the layer of condensation on his glass. "I grew up in the north, around Belfast. My father died when I was young. I don't remember him. I was about five when my mother married Mr. Shane. At the time, he was an investment banker."

Helena reached over and patted Graham's hand.

"I went to university in Belfast, and when I finished Mr. Shane wanted me to take over his business so he could concentrate on developing the manor, but I didn't want to do investing. I tried to tell him, but he didn't take the news well. And then there was an accident. My mother and brother, well, they—"

The door of the restaurant opened so hard it slammed against the wall.

Graham looked up and his eyes grew wide. "Helena. Your father's here."

Da glared at them as he pushed his way through the crowded restaurant.

Mam stepped out from behind him, wearing a self-righteous smirk. "I told ye. That girl's good for nothin'. Can't be trusted. She needs a good beltin'. Just be looking at what a disgrace she be."

Graham stood between Helena and Mam and turned to Da. "You know this isn't what it looks like. We were hungry. That's all."

Da's eyes were dark in the shadowy restaurant, and he gave Graham a slow, tight nod.

"I don't care what this gorger has to say." Mam charged around Graham and pointed at Helena. "You're no good. You're just like your fecking sister."

CHAPTER THIRTEEN

The ride back to the campsite had been filled with stony silence. Helena was embarrassed, angry at Da for not standing up for her, and furious with Mam for barging into the restaurant and causing a scene.

Graham hadn't done anything wrong. He had only been acting the gentleman, offering Helena a little meal after the events of the day. Yet, there was no use in arguing that point to Mam. She had made it plenty clear that Helena was nothing but a disgrace.

Helena glanced in the rearview mirror, at where Gavin and Rionna sat in the backseat. Their faces were pale, and Rionna's eyes were red as if she had been crying. Gavin fingered one of his wayward curls, but his gaze never strayed from Helena until they pulled up to the trailer.

Another group of Travellers had pulled a trailer in next to theirs, and as soon as the back door opened, Gavin ran toward the new place. Helena got out of the car, stuffed the paper bag with her book under her arm, and walked after him.

"Don't ye be getting no ideas. You ain't going nowhere 'til we talk, girl," Mam growled. "You've been runnin' around like some brasser since your da got out. It's comin' to a stop."

Helena bit her tongue. This storm would pass—Mam's mood swings always did. Soon she would find herself back down in the bottom of a bottle, and Helena could escape until the next storm.

When Da had been gone there had been so many days like this. She used to imagine Da would come home, put his foot down, and take away the liquor—but from the state of her mam, he had just as little control over the rabid woman as Helena did.

He walked into the trailer, shoulders slouched and a broken look upon his face. He turned back and waved her in. "Come on. Your mam's right. We need to have a chat."

Her stomach dropped. Da couldn't be taking Mam's side. Helena hadn't done anything wrong. Da had given Graham permission, so why was he acting as if she had done the family an injustice?

The sun had started to set, and the gray dusk felt heavy upon her as she made her way to the trailer. Even the weeds seemed to shirk away from the stagnant little aluminum box, as if they wanted to flee this place as badly as Helena did.

The vertical bars on the screen door reminded her of the spiked gate of the Limerick jail. She could only assume her shame and dread were like what Da had felt when he had entered the prison.

Mam opened the door and pointed at the laminate table. "Go. Sit. Down."

Helena stared in at a bottle of whiskey, which sat uncapped and half-empty next to an empty glass. An extinguished ciggy sat on the edge of a filled ashtray. A red ring from Mam's lipstick stained its yellowed end.

Da sat down at the small table and dropped his head between his hands.

Gavin raced by. He turned and faced Helena as he stood under Mam's arm. "Helena, I'm hungry! Whatcha makin' for supper? Can we have bread and jam?"

Helena stared at Mam and Da. Gavin would be at a loss without her. Da was a good man, but he couldn't properly keep up with the needs of both Gav and Rionna. They would be the ones who paid the price if she left. Blood was thicker than any desires that ran within her veins.

"You go and play. I'll call you when supper is ready." Helena patted Gavin's curls.

"Aye, don't forget to make bread and jam!" Gavin let the door slam shut behind him as he headed out into the gray evening.

Helena avoided the table and opened the refrigerator door instead, looking for something to make for supper. She sat her bag on the bottom shelf. Mam didn't keep any liquor in there; she'd never find the book.

The refrigerator was almost empty, but Helena managed to find a few carrots and a bit of chicken stock. She moved to the cupboard and pulled out some potatoes and an onion. Mam's glare bored into her, but Helena didn't look back. She was here to help the children, not be derided by Mam's ridiculous accusations.

The whiskey sloshed as Mam poured it into her glass. "Get me some ice."

Helena broke out a few cold cubes and handed them to Mam. They dropped into the cup with a splash. A droplet of whiskey slipped down the glass, and Mam licked it off.

"Now tell us, who was that man?" Mam took a long gulp of the amber liquid.

Helena pulled a knife from the drawer and peeled back the mottled brown skin of the potato, revealing the white flesh beneath.

"Answer me, girl."

The tone of Mam's voice made Helena's skin prickle with anger. Mam had always called her "girl," but it was starting to grate on her. Helena was her child, not some stranger she had picked up off the path. This was more than Helena could handle—it had been one hell of a week.

"He's just a friend of mine." Helena glanced over at Da.

He lifted his chin and looked up at her. The purple and red beginnings of a bruise were visible under his left eye.

What had Mam done?

Helena put the potato and the knife down and stepped over to Da. "What happened?"

His gaze drifted back down to the table.

"Your da's just as bad as you. Can't keep his mouth shut. Can't stay outta trouble." Mam drained the last bit of the whiskey in her glass. "Where did ya meet the gorger?"

"I met *Graham* at Da's work. I help him a bit. I needed to run an errand in town today, and he was nice enough to take me."

"You're lying to me. I can feel it in my bones. Angel always tried pullin' the same types of shenanigans. Out all night with her boyfriend, then lyin' to her ole mam... like I was some eejit." Mam spun the lid of the bottle and poured herself another glass. "You must think you're real smart. Lying to your mam... After I took care of you while your good-for-nothing Da was in the clink. Right good it did me. I should let the banshees have ya."

Helena started slicing an onion. The harsh scent wafted up, but her eyes were already filled with tears. Mam droned on and on behind her, but Helena tuned her out.

"Did ya hear me, girl?" Mam slammed her glass down on the table.

Helena dumped the onions in the pot and wiped the tears from her cheeks. "Aye."

Da stared at her, his face strained. "Did you hear your mam, gra?"

Helena shook her head.

"I should've known. You've always had your head in the clouds. I shoulda taken ya out of school when you were twelve, or at least put my foot down about you goin' back. You got your secondary school done. You don't need any more book learnin'—it certainly ain't doin' you no good. That's it. I'm pulling Rionna out of school. She can help me around the trailer. She's got 'nuff learnin'. I won't make the same mistake a third time."

Da's eyes narrowed. "That's enough, woman." His voice had a steely, cold edge Helena had heard only once before. "I'm sick to death of you and your nagging. That's enough. You need to tell Helena and get it over with. I can't stand no more of your prattling."

"If you're so excited, then you tell her the good news. I'm always the hag—always the one coming between you and your little gra." Mam opened the bottle and took a pull.

"Sit down, gra," Da said, and Helena slid into the seat next to him.

"We had a visitor this evening." Da ran his hands over his face and winced as he touched his bruise. "The O'Donoghues came to collect."

"Is that what happened to your eye?"

"Aye, lass." Da sighed. "I didn't have nothin' to give them, so they took a little payment out in flesh."

"Oh, Da. Are ya okay?"

Mam huffed.

Da glared at Mam. "I'm fine. Nothing a little time won't heal."

"Just get it over with, Seamus. Quit *prattling*." Mam let out a drunken giggle.

"Your mam took it upon herself to make an arrangement. I tried to talk the O'Donoghues out of it, but your mam was a real good salesman."

"What are ya sayin, Da?"

He looked down at his hands. "The O'Donoghues have a boy about your age, Brian." He paused. "And he's gonna be takin' you as his wife."

Where her heart had once belonged now rested an orb of agony, radiating pain through every cell in her body. "What... what about the children? Who's going to watch Gavin and Rionna? They need someone."

"What in the bloody hell does that mean, girl?" Mam screeched. "I'm their fecking mother. Not you. I can take care of my own goddamned kids." The black eyeliner around her squinting, angry eyes was smeared, making her look like a tired old hag.

Helena stared at Da as if he would be able to read her barrage of thoughts. Yet Da avoided her gaze.

"I just don't think it's a great idea for me to get married right now," Helena said.

Mam exhaled with a small hiccup. "You ain't getting married for two weeks. That's plenty of time. I already called the dressmaker. I told her you wanted pink with the birds like ya always said."

"That wasn't me. That was Angel."

Da reached over and squeezed her fingers, shaking his head slightly.

Mam acted like she hadn't heard the comment as she blabbed on about the party they would have for Helena's wedding.

Twisting her hand out of Da's, Helena stood up and walked over to the cooker. The soup boiled. Helena stirred a wooden soupspoon in slow, torturous circles through the liquid.

This wasn't right. She would have to fight—even if it was against the people she loved. It might mean she would lose everything—the kids, her family, and her culture, the only life she'd ever really known—but she couldn't stand by and be forced into a marriage.

Helena thought about the book, now concealed safely inside the refrigerator. Graham had shown her a kindness no other country man had done before. He took her in and gave her a job—all to save his family. He had lied to her, yes, but he had wanted *her* at the manor. His determination made her feel wanted for the first time. No one had ever really gone after her the way Graham had. And tonight, when he had taken her hand, for a split second it had seemed as if he wanted to kiss her.

The boiling soup swirled in the pot.

The O'Donoghue boy didn't even have the courtesy to come meet her in person. Instead he had relied on his father—and an unsettled debt—to find a match.

The soup bubbled up and the hot liquid splattered against her skin. She reached over for the sink's tap, and as her hands connected with the metal handle, her eyes closed and a thick fog overtook her senses.

A vision of a girl wearing an enormous white wedding gown filled her mind. The bride stood at the front of the pews in a massive church, her back turned. Her dress was covered in a swirling mass of pink crystals and a tiara the size of a small statue sat on her cascading curls.

The groom stood next to her. The man was tall and tanned, his dark, ashy hair cut short at the sides, but long and spiked on top. Helena squinted as she tried to see the boy more clearly. He kept looking back toward the door of the church, as if at any moment he would stop the services and run, but his face was constantly obscured by shadow.

The vicar stood at the front, Bible in hand, and motioned to the couple. "Please repeat after me: By the power that Christ brought from heaven, mayst thou love me. As the sun follows its course, mayst thou follow me. As light to the eye, as bread to the hungry, as joy to the heart, may thy presence be with me, oh one that I love, 'til death comes to part us asunder."

The bride diligently mumbled the words as her bouquet trembled. The groom took the girl's shaking hand. He placed his hand atop of hers as the vicar took a ribbon and fastened them.

The pain from the burn radiated up Helena's arm as the haze lifted from her vision. Helena opened her eyes and found her hand still resting on the tap. She turned the lever and stuck her burning flesh beneath the cold water.

Whose wedding had she seen? Was it her own? Was the boy Brian O'Donoghue? Was she fated to marry him?

Or was there another choice?

CHAPTER FOURTEEN

Graham climbed the ladder to the roof of the empty cottage. The straw sat like the weight of the world upon his shoulders. He dropped the bundle down and pushed the wire, used to secure the thatching, through to the inside of the house. "Seamus?"

The wire shot back up from under the straw.

"Did you wrap it around the batten?"

A grunt filtered up from below. The house was small, and thatching it wouldn't take too long, but working with Seamus, in the state he was in, was proving to be almost unbearable.

They hadn't spoken a word about what had transpired between them at the restaurant. It shocked him that Helena and her father had even shown up to work the next morning.

Helena had large bags under her eyes, and her hair was uneven, as if she had weathered a tempest. He'd tried to catch her eye, but she had given him an icy glance and then made her way to the kitchens.

The morning had brought fog along with it, and the

dampness pulled on him as he worked. He tied a knot around the straw. "Seamus, can you hand me another?"

The door to the cottage swung open, and Seamus walked out, careful not to step under the ladder. He threw a bundle over his shoulder and carried it to Graham. Graham pitched it onto the batten and cinched it down.

"I think you and I, we need to have a talk." Seamus's voice had a strange edge.

"All right. Just a sec." The ladder creaked as he made his way down. "Let's get this over with."

"Aye." Seamus's aura glowed dark blue, the color of a poorly moonlit night. He feared facing the truth. Seamus pulled out a cigarette and lighter from his pocket. "Did ya know I haven't smoked in more than six years?"

Graham shook his head.

"Aye. Not since before my time in the clink." The lighter clicked as Seamus lifted it up to the end of the cigarette. He inhaled, letting the fire turn the end into a red-hot ember. A puff of smoke poured from the man's mouth.

"I ever tell you why I got arrested?"

Graham had done his research, and knew exactly why the man had been locked up, but he shook his head.

"I got me another girl, Angel. She started seeing a country boy, much like yourself."

Graham's gut tightened.

"One day, Angel didn't come home after school. So I decided to go out and look for her." Seamus took another puff from his cigarette. "As luck had it, another group o' Travellers had run across her and him in a restaurant, much like the one where I found you and Helena. With one big difference. Angel was in the storeroom with the boy, doing things a Traveller girl should know nothin' about."

There was an awkward silence.

"I've never been more ashamed of one of my girls. In a single second, every dream I'd had for her went down the pisser. I thought her mam would never get over the shame." Seamus ran his fingers over his puffy black eye. "In fact, I don't think she has. That was hard on her. Angel had a real special place in Cora's heart."

Seamus dropped the half-smoked fag and smashed it with the heel of his boot. "I had to do somethin'. I couldn't let it go without some type of retribution.

"I put that lad in the hospital. Nearly killed him. Broke his jaw and cheek. Before I was done, I'd slugged Angel too." The stack of bundles shifted as Seamus sat down on top and put his head in his hands. "I ain't never hit one of my kids. It was an accident. She moved to get in the way. She's never forgiven me for what happened that day. I can't say I've forgiven myself."

"It was a mistake… We all make mistakes, Seamus," Graham said, trying to make him feel better.

Seamus shook his head, dismissing the attempt to comfort him. "I shoulda never gone after that boy. Angel made a choice. I shoulda taught her better, or talked to her about what she was doing wrong. Instead, I lost my freedom, my life, and my family all in a few moments."

"Why did you do it?"

Seamus looked up at him, pain in his eyes. "I thought I had to. It was the only way I knew to handle something like that. It's the Traveller way. If I hadn't done what I did, me and my fam would never be able to hold our heads up around other gypsies."

"Is the boy okay?"

"Aye. He and Angel have a place over in Rathkeale." Seamus stood up and lifted a bundle of straw and slung it over his shoulder. "I'm sorry about last night. Cora asked where Helena was, and I let it slip. By the time she was done ranting, she had me thinkin' that I had another mess like Angel. All that anger came rushin' back. I know you didn't have no bad ideas. I just don't want to be losin' my family or my gra. They need me too much. Things went to hell when I was gone."

He walked to the bottom of the ladder and turned back to face Graham. "I gotta do what's right for my fam. Things got to change."

Graham's gut ached. "Does that mean you're going to make Helena quit?"

"Unfortunately, her mam surprised us all a little last night. We had some visitors who want to start havin' a say in Helena's life."

"What do you mean?"

Seamus made his way up the ladder. "Cora arranged for Helena to be married off to another Traveller. A boy named Brian."

Graham sank down upon the stack of straw. "It'll kill her."

"She's a strong girl." Seamus dropped the bundle on the roof. "But you don't think she wants to get married?"

"I don't know what she wants, but I know she doesn't need to be bartered off like a bloody lamb."

"Is that right?" A sly grin appeared on Seamus's face.

"Then what're ya going to do about it? Her mam's already picked out the dress... A real big fancy one, with gems and everything."

"But... you just said you didn't want Helena to see me anymore—that you hated country boys. And now you're telling me to go after her? Are you putting me on?"

"You didn't let me finish what I was saying." The straw crunched as Seamus tied the wire around them. "When I was in prison I learned that just because you got taught something, that didn't make it right. My da and culture always taught me gorgers and Travellers shouldn't have no part of each other, but times are changing. The way of the Traveller needs to change too. Our girls need to get their book learning. And they need to marry the men they love."

Graham stood up. "You think she loves me?"

"I saw the way she was lookin' at ya last night." Seamus smiled. "Unfortunately, her mam has ideas, and to save my marriage and my family, and I can't be going against Cora. But if Helena chases her dreams, I ain't gonna be the one to stop her. Or you. "

"Do you think you can handle this thatching by yourself?"

"Go on. Go after her." Seamus motioned toward the manor.

Graham turned away.

"Wait. One more thing," Seamus called after him.

He looked back.

"Do right by my gra. Don't make me regret trustin' you. Helena's a real smart girl. I want you to treat her like the princess she is. And don't be tellin' her I said nothing."

Graham nodded, and sprinted toward the kitchens.

• • •

Helena pulled the studier out of the paper bag and stood it against the kitchen's stainless steel wall so she could read it as she chopped the veg.

The words on the pages were clear, but as Helena looked at the book, all she could think of was Graham. She was going to have to tell him that her mam had arranged for her to be married. He needed to know she was going to have to quit her job… and that she would never be able to see him again.

When she had seen Graham that morning, she hadn't been able to look at him. There were too many emotions running through her mind after their time together. She wanted to be there for him, to help him, and—above all—be near him.

But it didn't matter what she wanted; it couldn't happen. Mam had made a deal.

Helena pulled a knife from the block, grabbed a carrot, and began to chop. There was nothing better than a little work to help clear the mind. The knife thumped against the board as she slashed at the innocent veg.

"What's going on here? Are you trying to kill the carrot or chop it?" Mary walked up next to her and took the knife from her hands. She started to chop in fine, well-practiced motions. "You've been *off* all day. You upset about Chester?"

"Chester?" How had she forgotten about Chester? She'd gotten so wrapped up in her self-pity she had forgotten the real tragedy that had occurred. "Oh, aye."

"It's okay to be upset, lass." Mary's gaze moved to the

place on the floor that had only recently been covered in the man's blood. "I still can't believe he's gone."

"Is his fam doin' okay?" Helena asked, picking up a new knife and continuing to chop.

"His wife's sick. She doesn't know about what happened. She wouldn't understand."

"Oh. Is she in the infirmary?"

Mary's eyes widened, and she looked around to make sure no one was listening. "We don't talk about that place in public."

"Oh… I'm sorry."

"It's okay."

They chopped in silence.

"So," Helena started, "do the guards have any leads?"

Mary motioned for Helena to come closer. "I heard them talking. They think Chester committed suicide—something about slash marks on his wrists—but if you ask me, it was murder. They didn't even find a knife. Those cops are about as much use as a tit on a bull if you ask me… How can a man commit suicide, and the knife disappear?"

"That doesn't make sense."

"Aye. I know, lass. But they seem to think that he may have hidden the knife. If you ask me, Mr. Shane called the cops off. Don't look good havin' a murder here right before the tourist season. Chester was one hell of a grump, but he wouldn't go offing himself."

"Who do you think would want to have him killed?"

"He and I were real good friends, and as far as I know no one here had a grudge against him. He normally kept to himself. Did a real fine job here in the kitchen. I don't know why anyone would have wanted to hurt him."

Even if Mary was Chester's friend, it didn't mean she knew everything. Everyone Helena had met in this place seemed to have lies in their hearts or secrets on their lips.

Mary pointed at the studier with her knife. "What's this?"

"I'm tryin' to study for my exams. They're comin' up next week."

She wiped her hands on her apron. "Well, best of luck. Just make sure you don't go cutting off a finger when you're reading. I don't want blood on the food." Mary smiled.

"I'll be careful."

The kitchen matron strode off across the room and set to work preparing the sandwiches for high tea. Helena went through a series of grammar questions as she continued to chop.

Before long, the carrots were sliced and she had made her way through the entire grammar test. She flipped the page and looked over the answers. With the exception of cumulative adjectives, she had done well.

She dumped the carrots into a plastic bin and stowed them in the cooler for later. A stack of tomatoes sat on the prep counter, waiting for her when she returned to her station.

Even though it was only carrots, onions, and celery and the like that she chopped each day, the job gave her a sense of fulfillment. She loved completing a task. It had been that way even when she'd been at home, but it felt more important now that she worked for a boss. If she had to get married in a few weeks, at least she knew she had done something for herself.

On to the math problems. Helena pushed the knife down into the soft red flesh of the tomato as she leaned in to read a number on the page. Juice squirted from the tomato, splashing everything around it with sticky juice and seeds.

"Such an eejit," she mumbled under her breath.

Maybe it wasn't such a bad thing Graham hadn't gotten the chance to see her eat at the restaurant. She would have been mortified if he had seen her do something like squirt tomato juice down the front of her jacket. She whirled around to grab a towel to wipe off her jacket.

As she turned, she crashed into someone. "Pardon." She looked up into Graham's sparkling eyes.

"I can see you're busy." He pointed at the little seeds dribbling down her jacket. "But I was hoping we could try again. Maybe lunch?"

Her cheeks burned. "I'm surprised you want to have anythin' to do with me after last night. It's not every day that you get busted in on by a girl's fam."

Graham's smile lessened. "Your dad's protective. If you were mine, I'd be protective too."

The flame of embarrassment that warmed her face grew hotter. "Well, I didn't bring a lunch." Helena grabbed a towel and tried to dab at the stain on her jacket as she tried to hide her growing chagrin.

"That's fine. I can talk to Mary; maybe she'll let us grab a few bits and cut out for an hour. I'll take you out onto the estate and we can find a quiet spot and have a picnic."

First he had talked about her "being his" and now he was asking her on a date? There was no way she could compromise her reputation within the Traveller community any more than she already had. The neighbors must have heard Mam and Da getting after her last night. Without a

DANICA WINTERS

doubt, word was probably starting to spread about Mam finding her in a restaurant with Graham.

"I don't think that's a great idea, Graham. I need to study."

"I can help. We can just have a spot of lunch in the dining hall. I need to talk to you."

She nodded. She needed to speak to him too; and from the hopeful, bright-eyed look on his face, she knew she was probably going to break his heart.

CHAPTER FIFTEEN

Helena sat across from him at the table, her attention on her studier. A tendril of hair flipped down into her face, but Graham resisted the urge to reach over and press it behind her ear. She had agreed to accompany him to lunch on the condition that he sat quietly while she studied. It was a concession he was willing to make, as long as he could sit with her. When she was ready, they could talk about everything that had happened.

Graham couldn't even imagine how she felt. She had so much going on in her life. A new place, a new job, exams—hell, everything in her life, even her understanding of herself, had changed in less than a week. She was lucky she wasn't alongside Danny in the infirmary.

A groan escaped her as she chewed on her lip.

"You need some help? I can quiz you or something."

"This is ridiculous. I'm never gonna pass the bloody exams. What was I thinking?"

Graham leaned over and read the question.

Using a current event as a basis for argument, discuss the importance of economic stimulation in a bear market.

Helena's eyes were bloodshot and darker than he'd ever seen them. "I'm never gonna be ready for these exams," she said. "I mean, I know the blasted answer—at least I think I do—but how am I gonna remember everything? I haven't even made it to biology. This was such a stupid bloody idea. I should be happy just gettin' done with secondary school and forget goin' to university."

The stray strand of hair fluttered down, teasing him as it caressed her full, luscious lips. They had to be as soft as they looked. He wanted to lean over the table and taste those lips, explore them with his tongue.

Graham shifted, the thought making him uncomfortable. She didn't think of him the same way. He rubbed his hand against his kilt, drying the layer of sweat that had risen on his palm. "Helena, you need a break."

He moved his hand over the table and held his palm open, hoping she would slip her fingers into his. "Let's go for a walk. It'll clear your mind and we can talk about..." He leaned over, coyly moving his hand closer to hers. "Bear markets."

She gave him a cute half smile as she took his hand. "I'll go with you on one condition." She moved her hair behind her ear.

"What's that?"

"We say nothing about bears, bulls, exams, my parents, or murder. I'm tired."

"Sounds great. Wait here." Graham got up and walked to the kitchens.

Mary was bellowing at one of the staff as he approached.

"What happened to all my blasted peaches? I bought three crates yesterday and I'm missing one. How am I supposed to make enough peach pie for the guests?"

Graham smiled as he walked in and put his hand on Mary's shoulder. "I couldn't help but overhear your little meltdown."

"Well, *whoever* took my peaches is going to have to answer to me. *I will find* whoever thinks they can get away with stealing from *my* kitchen!" She stomped on the floor just above the infirmary.

"You know they can't hear you from here, right?" Graham said.

Mary crossed her arms over her chest in disgust as her aura pulsed a muddled red color. "I'm sick to death of them taking things without so much as a whisper of permission. All they do is take, take, take. I make them three square meals a day. If that isn't enough, they need to get a kitchen down there that cooks only for them. I'm about fed up."

Graham squeezed her shoulder. "Don't you think you're overreacting? It's just a few peaches."

"A few peaches here, a tray of bacon there. All they have to do is ask so I know how much to make. The guests come first ya know."

"Do you think Herbert would like the way you're acting right now?"

Her gaze snapped to him. "Shhh…" She looked around to make sure no one was listening. "Don't be talking so loud."

"Have you checked on him lately?"

Mary nodded. "The nurses think he's doing better, ever since they started him on the Ativan."

"Is he still channeling?"

Mary cringed. She motioned him into the farthest recesses of the kitchen. "He says he's still hearing the dead, and they're telling him things… awful things… He's even been talking about the codex more and more. I'm hoping that his therapy and his new meds will help, but only time will tell." Mary paused. "Speaking of the infirmary, Helena let it slip."

"She saw Herb. She must have realized that you knew too."

"But what if I didn't?"

"Helena's smart. She can be trusted," Graham said. "She can help."

"Is that right?"

"I introduced her to Danny."

"Aye?" Mary cocked an eyebrow. "That girl's got a lot on her shoulders. Do you really think she'll be able to take it all on?"

"I think so, but I'm trying to bring her in slowly so she doesn't have any *problems*." He gave Mary a knowing look. "I was hoping to talk to her a little bit more about what we need. Do you think you can handle her being gone from the kitchen for the rest of the day?"

"You can take her. She got more done this morning than most of my staff, but I want my Herbert back."

Graham patted her arm. "I'm working on it."

Mary's eyebrow rose. "Is there something else you ain't telling me?"

He tried to control the warmth that spread across his face. "Nah, we're only friends."

"Well, you ought to start thinking about finding yourself a good woman."

"Oh come now, Mary. You're already taken."

"You little flirt," Mary laughed. "Run along, and take Helena with you."

Helena was concentrating on her book when Graham walked into the break room, but she wasn't the only one there. Sitting across the room was one of the nurses from the infirmary. There was a worried expression on her face, and her aura was a bright yellow light. The nurse stood as Graham entered the hall.

"Nurse, what're you doing here? What's wrong?"

"It's about your mother." She glanced across the room at Helena. "Can we talk?"

He gave her a tight nod. "What's going on?"

"Well..." The nurse twisted her hands. "We had Rose sedated. She was having fits this morning. She acted like she had been possessed. We had her restrained; we thought we had her under control, but—"

"She escaped," Graham growled. "How could no one notice her leaving the infirmary? That's two this week!" He slammed his fist against the wall.

Helena jumped, and the nurse recoiled from him.

"Nurse, this is unacceptable. Do you realize what could happen? What if she attacks a guest?" Graham said, trying to control his anger.

"I'm sorry. We were trying to be more careful, but we are low on staff. We tried..."

Graham ran his hands through his hair. "How long has she been missing?"

"Her nurse last checked on her about a half an hour ago."

"That's good." Graham sighed disgustedly. "Have you told Mr. Shane?"

"We haven't. We were hoping you could talk to him."

"You mean you want me to take the fall?"

"We just thought he would take the news better if it came from his son." The nurse shuffled her feet.

"*Step*son." He reached into his leather sporran and took out his mobile. He punched in the numbers and waited as the phone rang.

Why did everything have to go to shite today? All he had wanted was to have a little time alone with Helena.

"Hello?" Mr. Shane sounded annoyed.

"There's been a breach."

"Again? Who?"

"It's Mother. They said she's been possessed."

"Why didn't anyone notify me?"

Graham glared over at the nurse. "I was only just notified myself."

"Do you know where she went?"

"Not yet. I'm about to take Helena and see if we can find her. She can't have gotten far."

"Check the manor. Do a thorough search. Can you get Seamus to search the grounds?"

"Yes, sir." Graham paused. "Sir?"

"What?"

"I think we need to hire more nurses so this won't happen again."

"That's impossible. Things are tight as it is."

"If you don't do something… something bad is going to happen. The nurses are in over their heads caring for all these patients."

"Don't worry about the nurses. Just tell them to do their jobs. You need to worry about getting a handle on this. We don't want any more *accidents*. Go."

Graham clicked the phone off and shook his head. "Sorry, there's not much I can do."

The nurse nodded. "Aye... Please keep trying. We need help."

"I will. In the meantime, please go back downstairs and take care of the rest of the patients. Is Danny still there?"

The nurse nodded. "He's under sedation."

"Good. Go. Make sure no one else manages to slip by you."

The door slammed as the nurse scurried from the room.

"Is she going to be okay?" Helena asked.

"Who?"

"Your mam."

"Aye. I hope so. This isn't her first possession. She has a weak soul and is easily taken. I should've told you about my mother's problems."

"Why didn't ya?" Helena closed her studier and stood up.

"You just found out about the infirmary. I didn't want to overwhelm you."

"You don't think I deserve to know the whole truth?"

"I wanted to tell you."

"All ya give me is half truths. Why can't ya just be honest?"

Something about her anger made something spark within him. He had been trying to protect her until he was comfortable that she could handle everything he had to tell her. He had tried to be the best man he knew how to be—

and if that wasn't good enough for her... well, damn it, then he would never be enough.

"You want me to be honest? Then why don't you try being honest with me?"

Helena looked affronted. "What're ya talkin' about?"

"Your father told me about your *engagement*," he spat. "Yet you haven't said a word. You know how I feel. I mean... you must know how I feel. But you don't seem to give me a bloody thought."

"Da told you?" Helena sat back down.

"From what he said, your mother's the only one that doesn't want us to be together."

Her face softened. "He... and you... you want us to be together?"

"I... we... bollocks." Graham moved to the table. "I'm doing this all arseways, but to hell with doing this right."

He grabbed her and pulled her close. His breath caught in his chest as she looked up at him. "I want this."

He leaned in and grazed her lips with his. The warmth of her touch radiated through him and quelled the last of his anger.

Her lips moved over his like she wanted this as badly as he had. He reached up and took her face in his hands. Her soft skin warmed as he brushed his thumbs over her cheek. His kiss hardened as a hunger for more raged within him.

Graham's body yearned to take this moment further, but he forced himself back. "We have to stop." His voice was hoarse. "I... I want *this*... and I want you... But I need to find my mother."

"Aye. Right." Her arms dropped from his shoulders. "I... that's a grand idea. Besides, I need to get back to work."

Helena turned away from him, and the simple action made his gut ache.

"No. You don't have to. I talked to Mary. She said you could have the day off."

"You can't keep leavin' Mary with my work. She's gonna fire me," she said, turning back to face him.

The same few strands of hair as before fell into her eyes. He smiled as he took the time to push the wayward lock back behind her ear. She leaned into his hand and let his fingers cup her face.

"Mary is okay with you helping me. She knows who and what you are. And she wants you to help Herb." Graham ran his thumb over the soft pink flesh of her cheek. "He's a channeler."

"What's a channeler?"

"Ghosts talk to him. Sometimes they invade his body and use him to take care of unfinished business."

Helena reached up and held his hand. "I want to help, Graham. I want to help Mary and her husband. I want to help everyone in the infirmary. I do. But I don't have much time. I have to get married."

"You're still getting married?"

"I don't have a choice. I can't disgrace my fam."

"There's always a choice." Graham took her fingers and laced them in his. He leaned in and captured her lips with his. This time their kiss was soft and deep. Her tongue moved against his bottom lip.

Helena leaned back, breaking their kiss. "Let's get your mam."

They made their way around the manor, starting in the kitchens and then moving to the drawing room. The sound of spoons clinking against expensive china filtered into the hall as he peered in.

Graham stepped into the dining room and nodded to the host, who was waiting for the next guests to arrive. The room was packed with plaid-wearing tourists, cameras strapped around their necks and travel guides in their back pockets. He recognized a few of the visiting supernaturals, who gave him curt nods but quickly went back to their menus.

"She's not here."

"Where do you think she would have gone?" Helena asked.

Graham shrugged.

They made their way down the long hallway to the pool. Young children splashed in the water, and their laughter filled the room. Their nannies fanned themselves as they lounged at the tables.

The parlor was empty, and they weaved through the private dining halls set aside for foreign dignitaries and VIPs, which were also deserted. At the front desk, two men stood talking. Their khaki pants were pressed with fine lines, and they wore club shirts from the golf shop at the bottom of the hill. The receptionist was pointing something out to them on a small map.

She looked up and smiled. "Hello, Mr. Kelly. How are you today?"

The men turned and looked at him and Helena.

"We're fine. How are you enjoying your vacation, sirs?"

"Very fine, chap," the man farthest from them answered in a Cork accent. "We just came back from the nineteenth hole. Damn fine establishment. Damn fine." He slapped his friend on the back.

"Yes, damn fine," his friend echoed.

"By chance, gentlemen, did you see a woman out there, walking alone?"

The men looked at each other and shook their heads.

"Thank you, gentlemen. I hope you have the very best of holidays."

The men laughed. "Yes, it's hard to top Adare Manor!" one said.

Graham opened the front door for Helena and followed her outside. The car park was full of Friday traffic. Even more cars would come and go before the end of Feile na Maighe and the summer tourist season tomorrow. Guests would be touring the manor, and reservations would be made for the Oak Room and the private dining halls; the tee-times were probably already filled for the rest of the summer.

This was a fine time for Rose to go missing. She'd been in the infirmary for the last three years, but of course she would have to escape at the worst time to be out of control.

Graham took out his cell phone as they reached a corner of the garden, where there weren't any tourists.

Seamus answered the phone on the first ring. "Wotcher?"

"We have a missing guest. Small woman, about five foot two inches. Gray-haired. Probably not making much sense. Her family said she was having an adverse reaction to a painkiller. We need to find her. The well-being of our guests could be at stake."

"Aye. Will do."

"I need you to do a full search of the grounds. Check the gardens, golf course, archery range, and the villas. We need to find her. She goes by the name Rose."

"Will do, boss. By the by, did ya chat with Helena?"

"I did. She's coming with me to search for the woman."

177

He had a fleeting thought of what he and Helena could have been doing if they hadn't needed to locate Rose, but then shook the image away. "We're headed to Holy Trinity Abbey Church now."

Seamus laughed. "Just because I gave ye a nudge doesn't mean I wanted ye runnin' off to the altar this afternoon."

Graham smiled. "Don't worry. It won't happen. At least not today."

CHAPTER SIXTEEN

It was a short drive to Holy Trinity Abbey Church, which sat just outside the gates of Adare Manor. The thirteenth-century church's car park was empty aside from the church van and a group of pigeons.

"Do you think she'd really come here?" Helena got out of the car and slammed the door shut; the pigeons took to the air in a flurry of flapping wings and spent feathers.

"I don't know, but we have to start somewhere." Graham led the way through the white iron gates and toward the entrance.

The red mahogany door of the abbey stood out against the ash-gray granite that encased it, making it look like a pool of blood in a desert of stone. Helena couldn't help but think of how they would have to pass through the ominous entrance to reach the safety of the church. It reminded her of Chester, and how his murder had been her final trial before her initiation into the supernatural.

"What makes you think she'd come here?"

"This is where she and Mr. Shane got married. If she's possessed, it's possible she might come here to rid herself of the demon." Graham closed the gate behind Helena. "Plus, she's been a longtime friend of the vicar. Before she was sick, she donated money to refurbish the church—she was always passionate about this place."

He crossed himself as he opened the crimson-colored door.

Their footsteps echoed inside the empty parlor. Through the arched doorway was the nave, where rows of carved pews led up to the pulpit. Throughout the main cathedral, columns stood like sentinels, their arms connecting in long protective arches above the pews.

On each side of the altar stood golden-hooded angels. The angels looked down on them as if judging them for their sins. Behind the high altar, the sun shone through the stained glass images of the Holy Trinity, casting long red and green shadows across the floor.

Graham dipped his fingers in the holy water of the font and made the sign of the cross. She followed his lead. Something about the habitual motion calmed her.

A robed vicar made his way down the red-carpeted mezzanine toward them. "Hello, my children."

"Hello, Father," they said in unison.

The vicar extended his hand for Graham to shake and then turned to Helena. "It is nice to see you here. You are always welcome in the house of the Lord."

"Thank you, Father," she said quietly.

"Is there something I can help you with?"

"We're looking for Rose," Graham said.

"I see." The vicar's soft expression turned hard. "I haven't seen her. How long has she been missing?"

"For about an hour. We think she's been possessed."

The vicar shook his head. "I shall prepare myself for a possible exorcism."

"Thank you, Father, but hopefully we won't need your help."

"If you do, please do not hesitate to contact me. You know how demons can be," the vicar said, making the sign of the cross. "Be careful and may God bless you, my children."

"Thank you, Father," Graham answered.

The vicar made his way back up the mezzanine, leaving them alone.

"Where else do you think she'd be?" Helena asked Graham.

He ran his hands over his face, as if trying to wipe away the stresses of his day. "I don't know."

The candles on the altar sent up a tendril of smoke, reminding Helena of the incense in Ayre's havari. "Wait... I know someone that might be able to help, a seer. I could call her."

"Do it."

She pulled Ayre's tattered card out of her purse and punched the telephone number into her mobile.

"Helena, I thought you'd be calling," Ayre's thin voice answered. "What happened?"

"I need to find someone."

"Who is it?"

"A woman, Rose. She's been possessed."

"Aye. I see. There's not much I can do without bein'

there." Ayre took a long breath. "But you should be able to use your shaw to find her."

Her stomach jerked. "How do I use it?"

"Harness the power of intention, ground your body, and then concentrate on the woman. If you can, you might be able to see the future."

"I don't know her well."

"Oh. Is there someone who does?"

"Aye, her son's here with me."

Helena glanced over at Graham.

He mouthed, "Okay?"

She nodded, but her fear grew. What would happen if she tried to see? She'd never *tried* to use her forshaw before. What if the attempt didn't work?

Graham leaned close to the phone.

"Good. Good," Ayre continued. "You'll need to harness his most powerful memory of Rose. Capture the power and use it as you think of the woman. You may not be able to see where she is, but you might be able to see where she's going."

"I'll try." Helena struggled to push down her nerves. "Thank you, Ayre."

"You're welcome, lass. You can always call."

The angels at the front of the church stared down at her with golden eyes as she slipped the mobile back in her purse.

"Did you hear what she said?" she asked.

Graham nodded solemnly.

She laced her fingers between Graham's. "Come on."

She led him to the front of the church and sat down on the pew. "Graham, what is the most powerful memory you have of your mam?"

He exhaled. "It has to be the accident."

"Can you tell me about it? What happened?"

Graham's shoulders fell. "It all started a few years ago. I had just graduated from university. Mr. Shane had recently bought the manor and was getting things in order. We knew there was a power, but we had underestimated it. He and my mother thought they could control it, use it to their advantage…"

The sound of the vicar's footsteps echoed down from the mezzanine. A door clicked shut.

"Have you ever heard of the *Codex Gigas*?" Graham asked.

Helena shook her head. "Nah. What is it?"

"Some people call it the Devil's Bible. It's a collection of prayers, but it also has different books of the Bible—including the Psalms of Solomon. A verse of which is as the manor's words. You may have seen them on the parapet. "Except The Lord Build The House Their Labour Is But Lost That Build It."

"The original codex was written in the thirteenth century by a Benedictine monk, Herman the Recluse, and now it's safely tucked away in the bowels of a museum in Switzerland. What most people don't know is that another monk copied the book sometime after Herman's death, and added in a collection of dark magic and spells."

The words echoed dangerously through the church and reverberated through Helena, making her ears ring. "How do you know there's a copy?"

"Because—" Graham squeezed her hand—"we found it within the walls of Adare Manor."

Helena's heart rose into her throat. "And what does the book have to do with the accident?"

"Danny was young when his visions began, about eight,

and the strain of seeing things he couldn't understand...
Well, at night he couldn't sleep, and during the day he was
like a ghost. When he did finally fall asleep, he'd whimper
and talk about terrible things before they'd happened, things
no one—especially a young boy—should ever have to see."
Graham's hand trembled. "When the visions started, my
mother didn't really understand what was going on, and she
tried every therapy and quack cure. I hated every minute of
it. I hated that I couldn't help. And most of all I hated that I
couldn't stop the chaos around and within Danny."

Helena squeezed his hand. Shutting her eyes, she
mentally grounded her body. She tried to imagine Danny. A
deep sadness welled up within her, but she forced herself to
focus on the power of Graham's memories. "Go on."

"When we came here and began refurnishing the
building, we found the book in a chamber built into one of
the walls. It told of clairvoyance and the different kinds of
psychic abilities, and how to control different aspects of the
different maladies through the use of spells. They started
using the book to help Danny with his visions. He started to
get better and come out of his shell.

"Unfortunately, as Danny started to talk about his
visions, my mother and Mr. Shane realized they could use
him to their advantage, to see things." Graham sighed.

"Soon they were making money from investments that
Danny had helped them to find, but Mr. Shane wanted
more." His hands tensed and he pulled away slightly, but
then stopped, as if forcing himself to continue. "He saw
an opportunity in the codex. With the help of the book,
they could use other supernaturals, covering their greed
with a mask of altruism. They thought they could charge

supernaturals to *help* them with their gifts, but my mother and Mr. Shane didn't understand what they were doing."

Images began flickering in Helena's mind, fuzzy and slightly out of focus, like a television on the brink of getting reception. "Keep going."

"They had me convinced that if we went a little deeper and used more from the book, we could help Danny. We could help him see only the things he wanted, or the things they needed him to see, and nothing else. I should have known better... I should never have gone along with it... I should have known that there is always a price. Anytime there is magic, there is the dark and the light. You can't have one without the other. But I was so stupid. I bought into their idealism. One night, Rose and Mr. Shane began trying some of the Latin inscriptions from the book on Danny." Graham sucked in a breath. "The manor has always been an area with a thin veil between the real and paranormal, but something they said that night, something they read, stretched the barrier even thinner."

The shadows in Helena's mind started to twist and curl, forming images of people she didn't recognize. The shadows moved faster and faster as Graham spoke.

"One of the incantations they read caused a surge of energy, and the veil broke. Lost souls, phantoms, poltergeists, and demons filled the manor. Luckily, we only had a few guests, and they were relatively unharmed thanks to the vicar's help. They thought it was all a big hoax—a séance we had created for their entertainment. The fools."

An image formed in Helena's mind, of Mr. Shane standing over a giant, tan-colored book. The man muttered in a language she couldn't understand. Behind him stood

Rose, with long hair and pale, ghostly gray eyes, echoing his every word. Rose looked over at her as if Helena were there, giving her an eerie smile and then turning back to the book.

Chills rippled down Helena's body. "I see them; they're readin'. Keep goin'."

"That night, Danny's visions were out of control. He saw far into the future. He saw something he could never forget and something he couldn't deal with... his own death. From that moment on, he's been in the infirmary. At first I hoped that he would get better, but it's been so long. I just don't know anymore."

The vision flickered and started to fade, and shadows filled her mind. "What happened to your mam?"

"The spirits took her. She'd never been possessed before. She tried to kill Mr. Shane, but I stopped her."

Helena watched as another image of the chestnut-haired Rose formed. Her pale gray eyes had rolled back into her head, and her lips were jagged where she had gnawed through her own flesh. She looked at Mr. Shane with rabid hunger and raised a knife. Sticky blood dripped down her chin.

Graham jumped between the two of them. Reaching out, he grabbed the demonic woman's wrist and twisted the knife from her grip. Rose hissed and roared. The sound was deep and raspy, the voice of the long dead.

It made Helena tremble.

"Are you okay?" Graham squeezed her hand.

She tried to control her body. "I'm fine."

Her trembling continued.

"That's enough." Graham pulled his fingers from

Helena's grasp, and the vision stopped. "There has to be another way to find Rose. You don't need to go through this."

"No." Helena reached over and took his hand. "I'm okay. I need to do this. I need to learn how to control the gift. I need to help you."

He pulled his hand from hers and lifted it to her cheek. "I can't put you through any more. We'll find her another way."

In a secret compartment, deep in her soul, Helena was relieved. Seeing the woman go crazy, eyes bugging out, blood dripping from her lips as a demon's voice escaped her lips—it was too much.

Helena said a little prayer. Closing her eyes, she tried to envision where they could find Rose, but nothing came to her. A lump rose in her throat as a feeling of icy powerlessness passed through her.

"What's wrong?" Graham touched her shoulder, but she shrugged off his hand.

"Nothin'. I'm grand. Just tired."

"Don't lie to me. Your aura's dark brown..."

"Don't worry. I'll be fine." Helena tried to force a smile. "But I think I need Ayre's help."

CHAPTER SEVENTEEN

A redheaded girl ran across the road in front of them as Graham turned the car into the Traveller campsite outside of Limerick. Following close behind the girl was a young boy carrying a stick. To Graham's left, a boy in a diaper sucked his thumb while his mother hung laundry.

Graham glanced over at Helena. Her aura was a brown cloud, and had only grown thicker after they left the church. "Do you know where Ayre is?"

"Her havari's in the back. Just follow the path." She motioned at a dirt trail that twisted between the trailers.

Graham slowed to a crawl as he drove by more children. Near the back of the camp, he came to a round-topped wagon. "Are you sure you want to do this?"

"Aye." Helena nodded, chewing her nail.

Graham reached out and stopped her from getting out of the car. "What's wrong?"

"I fail at everything I do." Helena looked at him. "I'll

never be of any use to you. And what happens if I make a mistake? What happens if I hurt Rose, or Danny?"

He cringed. "It's worth the risk. Right now, what they're going through, it's no life. You're their only hope." He took her tight fist in his hands. "We'll find Rose. She's a danger, but this isn't the first time someone has gone missing from the infirmary."

Her fist tightened. "If I can't do this, what makes you think I'll ever be of any use? What if I end up like Danny?"

"No matter where you go in life—whether you stay at the manor, or if you choose to marry some Traveller—it won't change who you are inside."

Helena's face softened. "But Danny changed. What if the visions change me, too?"

Graham ran his finger down her thumb and a spark flickered between them. "Danny was too young. Too soft. You know how the world works. There will be death. There will be horrors. But there'll also be things so beautiful we can't even begin to imagine them. You have to accept the bad, move past it and concentrate on the good."

He pressed their palms together.

"You can't just start doing something you've never done before and expect to be the best. No one can build a house the first time they raise a hammer. You saw my memories, yes?"

Helena stared at their entwined fingers and nodded.

"That's pretty incredible. When I first realized I could read auras I was terrible at it. I didn't know what the colors meant. It took me years to learn to read people. You've only known about your gift for a week. It'll get better. It'll get easier." He leaned across the front seat and ran his hand down her soft cheek. "I'll always be here for you—no matter what."

He glanced around to make sure no one was looking, and then leaned in and took her lips. She was tense and rigid as he swept his tongue over her sweet lips. As he kissed her, she yielded to his touch. A wild excitement shot through him as he thought how much their life could change.

There was a knock on the car's window. Helena jerked back, leaving him bent over the front seat. On the other side of the passenger window stood a strange-looking woman with long gray hair, which was matted into thick dreadlocks and adorned with blue and red beads. This must have been the psychic, but if he had seen her anywhere else, he would have thought she was a vagrant.

"I see the Kenaz bone was right, lass." Ayre smiled at Helena. "Ya do me proud."

Graham didn't understand what the woman meant, but her aura was golden, the color of enlightenment and divine protection.

He got out of the car and stepped over to the passenger side. "I didn't mean for us to be snogging in front of your place."

"It's okay, lad. I know you two are in love. It's easy enough to see without the snogging," Ayre whispered.

"No. No, we aren't in love. Nothing like that. We just—"

"Met?" Ayre quietly finished his sentence. "You and I both know better. There are some things in this world that don't have to be spoken out loud to make them true. I can feel it on you. And it ain't of no matter whether you've known her for ten minutes or ten years. Love is love."

The car door clicked open, and Helena stepped out;

thankfully she seemed unaware of what Ayre had said. "Did you tell her why we've come?" she asked.

Ayre took Helena's hand and closed her eyes. "Oh… I see," the woman whispered, as if some secret message had passed between them.

"You see what?" Helena jerked her hand back.

"You didn't find Rose. And you're facing great darkness. Your Thurisaz, an inner demon, is busy at work within you." Ayre turned to the weathered havari as she spoke. "I should've known that would be the form your Thurisaz would take. You are young yet, and have so many roads to choose from."

"It will get better, right?" Graham asked, as they followed the woman up the stairs to the door of the havari.

"I could say it'll get easier. In many ways, it does. So keep your chin up." Ayre smiled softly. The door creaked as it swung open. Ayre motioned for them to enter as the scent of sage wafted toward them.

Graham followed Helena and made his way to an overstuffed velvet pillow thrown upon the floor. Beside them was a well-worn table that stood at about knee height.

"Please sit." Ayre closed the door. She took a small bowl from the shelf, which sat behind the hanging herbs and next to the various bottles of liquor.

"The water bowl is a fickle thing." Ayre set the bowl on the table and looked at Helena. "Just like tapping into memories. That's a difficult skill to master."

"She did it well." Graham said.

Helena smiled tiredly. "I tried. I was able to see into his memory, but it was so dark, so foreboding… It… it made me feel so black. I just can't shake it."

Ayre nodded. "Memories are like quicksand. You fall in and sometimes you can't pull yourself out." Ayre moved to the far end of the havari and pulled one of the herbs down from the ceiling. "Here, chew on this."

Helena took the dried plant. "Thank you."

Ayre took down a small glass and poured a finger of brown liquor. "Drink this when you're done. It'll help with the taste."

Graham looked over as Helena's face pinched while she chewed. She gulped down the amber liquid. The scent of alcohol filled the air as she let out a long, harsh exhalation.

"Are you okay?"

Helena looked at him and smiled. The dullness in her eyes vanished, and a healthy glow returned to her skin.

His shoulders relaxed as Helena's aura changed back to its normal rainbow shades. "What was that you fed her?"

"It was only a bit of dandelion root." Ayre broke a sprig off of a dried bough and set it in a dish in the middle of the table. Striking a match, she lit the herb. Smoke curled up and filled the air with the strong, earthy scent of juniper. "Tonight, Helena, I want you to take a bath with elder bark and hawthorn, and by morning you'll be back to your normal self."

Helena nodded. "Is reading memories always like this?"

"All magic comes at a price. Each person has their own energy, their own pulse, and when you enter their world it can be hard on your body. Going into memories is advanced magic," Ayre said. "Only time will tell what else you will be able to do, but you are already showing great talent."

"But I failed."

"Your abilities will grow. In the meantime, I can help."

The air in the havari stilled as Ayre lowered her head and started to speak in tongues. Her aura pulsed as she extended her hands over the black liquid. Gray smoke and glittering light swirled in the bowl. Her eyes closed, and her cheeks pulled in, revealing her narrow cheekbones. "Spirits of the past, let me see the future. Bring to the light the world that is to be for Rose Shane... Let me see what is to be."

The gypsy opened her eyes and stared into the bowl. Graham tried to concentrate on the water, to take in what she was seeing, but he could see nothing except the swirling glitter of the unknown.

Ayre frowned. "The spirits are showin' Rose to me. It looks like she's in a cottage. White walls. There are pictures. She's in someone's home."

"Where?"

Ayre squinted as she seemed to try to search deeper in the scrying bowl. "I can't say."

"We need to search Adare Village." Graham moved to stand up.

"Wait, lad. She seems safe where she's at. She looks healthy. Maybe you should let her be."

"There's no way she's okay. She needs to be under her nurse's care."

"Maybe she just needed out, to be away from death and sickness." Helena stood up. "Was the nurse sure that Rose was possessed? How could she tell?" She turned to the gypsy. "What happens when a person is possessed?"

"There are different types of possession, spiritual and demonic."

"What happens with a demon?"

"Normally there are claw marks on the body, and

speaking in tongues or in a stranger's voice. It's different for each person and each demon."

Helena glanced at him. "Did the nurse say your mother was doing any of those things?"

Graham tried to recall what exactly the nurse had said, but nothing about voices or claw marks came to mind. "I don't think so."

"Then maybe it's not a demon. Maybe she just got away from the nurses, and that's all."

"The best thing may be for your mother may be to have a little freedom," Ayre offered. "Has she hurt anyone?"

"Not since she entered the infirmary, but she's been medicated."

"It's unnatural to tuck the sick away. They need love and attention—not to wither away in the guts of that manor." Ayre lifted the dish and put it back on the shelf. "Leave the poor woman alone. She needs a taste of living again."

Helena ran her fingers over Graham's, and his mind fogged at her touch.

Ayre looked down at their hands. "You know, lad, maybe what you and Helena need is to do a little living of your own. You've both been through a lot. Go out, have a laugh."

Helena tensed. "I can't. Mam would tan my hide if she found out that I was out with Graham, especially after last night."

Ayre looked at Helena with an air of pity. "I chose to be a Traveller. Soon there'll come a day when you will have to make a choice as to the kind of life you want to lead. There are some great things about being a Traveller, but sometimes tradition is only a weight to drag us down."

Helena tensed and drew her hand back from Graham's.

"Ayre, you must know how it is. My fam is my home. If I give up my fam, I give up everything."

"I understand, lass, but there are far worse things to give up than family."

CHAPTER EIGHTEEN

Helena sat up from her place against the cold passenger window and glanced over at Graham. His fingers were clenched around the wheel.

He must have been so worried about his mother. If it had been her mam who had gone missing, every Traveller would have been out looking for her, but Graham could only tell a few staff members and his stepdad.

In her mam's opinion, the security of the family was enough reason for Helena to marry Brian—the faceless tinkerer who bought her from her family like she was nothing more than a pony.

Helena tried to calm herself.

Maybe Brian wasn't the cad she was making him out to be in her mind. Maybe his family was forcing him into the marriage, too.

"You okay?" Graham's hands loosened on the wheel as he glanced over at her.

She nodded.

"I wanted to thank you for everything back there with Ayre. I was going about half mad, but you're right. Rose needs to find what she's looking for." Graham reached over and touched her leg. A spark of energy twisted through her, and the strange jolt awoke a deep-seated urge.

She closed her eyes and tried to ignore the strange desire that pulsed in time to the tap of his fingers.

Her mind swirled.

She focused on stopping the vision that threatened to take over her mind, but she had no control. The swirling gray fog of her inner sight cleared, and she was met with a vision of a brunette woman. The woman was lying on her stomach on a large white bed, her hair splayed down her back in reckless waves. She laughed as she kicked away the bedding and rolled over onto her back.

Helena sucked in a breath as she recognized that *she* was the woman. What was she doing in bed, naked?

A man's baritone drew her attention, but she couldn't quite make out what he was saying. As she looked in the direction of the voice, she saw a man. His strong chest glistened with a thin sheen of sweat. A droplet formed and slipped down his skin, down to the edge of an easily recognizable red kilt.

Graham smiled a wickedly handsome grin. He unstrapped the black leather belt that held his sporran in place. The belt dropped to the floor. The Helena on the bed sat up, exposing her naked breasts.

Helena's face burned as she tried to force her eyes open. She watched herself motion for him to come to her.

His chocolaty eyes gleamed with lust as his fingers moved to his waist. He took his time unfastening his kilt. The edge of the fabric fell back, exposing the line where his abs melded with his hip. "Are you sure this is what you want?"

"Aye... I think so."

His kilt lowered a half-inch. "You *think* so?"

She nodded coyly.

"You'll have to do better than that."

"Oh, really?" She lifted the sheet around her body and covered her breasts. "What do ya want me to say?"

"Now don't be doing that, love." Graham tugged at the top of his kilt. "Just say that you *love* me... That you *want* me."

The sheet went slack as a smile curved her pink lips. "I want you, Graham Kelly. I want you in this bed."

The side of Graham's kilt dropped slightly, exposing his leg entire left leg and the natural curves at the intersection of his thigh and waist. The muscles of his upper thigh tensed, and she noticed the way the hair grew thicker the nearer it came to the edge of his kilt... and what lay beneath.

Graham growled. He stepped to the edge of the bed, holding the last bit of the red fabric over his front.

She pushed the fabric down, exposing Graham's ample assets.

She ran her fingers up his flat stomach and over his chest. Sitting up on her knees, Helena kissed him. Graham groaned in her mouth and then leaned into her, pushing her down on the bed.

Helena made a feeble attempt to open her eyes. She wanted to watch, but the rules of her culture screamed that what was happening was wrong. Yet it was her, and didn't she have the right to know what *her* future held?

Graham put his arms around her and nibbled at her

lips. His kisses continued down over her collarbone, leaving behind a wet trail that sparkled in the light. When he reached her left breast, he took her small brown nipple in his mouth, making her moan.

She couldn't be with Graham.

Not even in her dreams.

Not when she was promised to another man.

Her vision distorted, and Graham's face twisted into another—a face she didn't recognize. The man who now knelt between her thighs had a strong, aquiline nose, and full, pink lips. His dark brown hair was buzzed on the sides and longer on the top; his chest was narrow, and his arms were pale.

The vision swirled, and the fog took over.

Helena opened her eyes as the car jerked. Out the window, a little cottage flashed by. Graham's fingers were still tapping against her leg.

She glanced up at him, but quickly dropped her gaze. Her cheeks burned at the memory of what she'd just seen.

Helena stared out the window. She wished she had someone to talk to. Someone who would understand what she was going through. Someone who could help her decide if she should follow the path of her culture or the desires of her heart.

A thought struck her. "Graham? Do you mind driving me to Rathkeale?"

"What's in Rathkeale?"

"My sister, Angel."

Graham nodded. "Rathkeale it is."

The drive was quick, and before long they were parked

outside a small white house. A picket fence surrounded a small yard filled with brightly colored children's toys.

Graham parked and then came around and opened her door. "I'll wait out here."

Her cheeks burned as she looked everywhere but at him. "I won't be long."

Helena passed by the house's front window and glanced in. Angel was pouring a bit of bleach in her kitchen sink. She took out a rag and pushed it into the water. Angel wrung out the rag and started to scrub down the kitchen, meticulously working across the surface of a spotless countertop.

Angel was doing exactly what Helena did every morning at the trailer.

Once a gypsy, always a gypsy.

She looked back at the silent yard, filled with discarded toys, and the sadness of this place struck her. Here Angel was, surrounded by things, but all alone. She was left with only her Traveller ways. Ways that belonged to a world in which she was no longer welcome.

Helena tapped on the door.

The muffled sound of footsteps came from inside the house. Angel pulled open the door, the rag in one hand.

"Helena!" Angel grabbed her by the arm and dragged her into the house. "What are ya doin'? Do Mam and Da know you're here?"

Helena shook her head as she shut the door.

Angel ran her hands over perfect dark brown curls and dabbed at the corners of her lined eyes. "I'm glad you're here."

"Where's Duncan?" Helena peered down the short hallway. There were two bedrooms and a privy at the end.

Angel shrugged. "He went out last night. He should be home anytime." She glanced over at the clock.

Toys were neatly stacked in the corner of the living room, and the house was quiet. "Where's Liam?"

"Oh, he's at Duncan's mam's. She wanted him for the day." Angel walked to the kitchen and dropped the rag into the sink. "Why don't ya sit down? Make yourself comfortable."

Helena sat on the plastic-covered white sofa. "I wanted to thank ye for lookin' after Gav and Rionna and makin' sure they got to school."

"Aye. No problem, it's nice to see them." Angel sat down in the recliner next to the sofa.

It had been so long since she had seen Angel, but never in her wildest dreams had Helena thought their relationship would change. Yet sitting there in Angel's cluttered but empty house, she felt horribly uncomfortable.

"How's Mam doing?" Angel perched on the edge of the chair and clasped her hands together, looking as nervous as Helena felt.

"The same as always. Or maybe a wee bit worse. It's hard to tell. Havin' Da home has taken some gettin' used to."

"For all of ya?"

"Da's changed." Helena ran her finger along the edge of the couch. "He misses you, Angel. He's real sorry about everything that happened."

"A pony's tail don't change colors." Angel moved farther back in the chair.

"Nah. I'm tellin' ya, prison changed him." Helena looked up at Angel. "He wanted me to tell you that he's sorry."

"Is that why you're here? To do Da's dirty work?"

"That's not it, I promise you. I think he wants to see ya. You should think about comin' round the campsite."

"Stop right there. I'm not comin' to him. If he wants to have anything to do with me and Liam, he has to make the effort—and he'll need to apologize to Duncan." The chair rocked as Angel fidgeted. She stood up.

"Is everything okay?"

Angel walked to the window and peered out, ignoring Helena's question. "Who's that?" She pointed to Graham.

"That's my friend, Graham Kelly. He's our boss at Adare Manor."

"*Our* boss?" Angel frowned. "What's going on with ya?"

"I got some questions," she said instead of answering.

"I don't got nothin' to hide."

"Do you ever regret marrying a country man?"

Angel paused. "Does this have to do with the man in my drive?"

Helena's cheeks burned. "Mam has arranged for me to marry Brian O'Donoghue. She borrowed some money while Da was away. I was the easiest form of repayment."

"I see. Mam'll never change. At least you're promised to a Traveller boy." Angel looked down at her hands.

A pit formed in Helena's stomach. "What're you sayin'?"

"Look around, Helena. Duncan ain't here. Liam ain't here. Families don't mean nothin' to some gorgers—at least not mine." Angel's eyes brimmed with tears. "Do you remember those nights when we'd sit around the campfire with Da and he'd sing? Remember how happy we were, snuggled together under a blanket, listenin' to him?"

Helena nodded.

"There ain't none of that in my world. Family's just an afterthought."

"At least you got to marry for love."

Angel nodded. "You know, I do love him—even when he ain't showed up after a night of boozin'."

"You know that ain't no different from a Traveller boy." Helena balled her hands into fists as she tried to fight for her dream for the future.

"Listen, lass. At least you know what you're in for with a Traveller boy. Yeah, most of 'em take it a little heavy on the Arthur Guinness, but they all come back to their wives. Gorgers are different. If things get hard, they run away."

Helena thought of Graham. He didn't seem like the type to flee from something hard; he could've given up on his mam and brother, but instead he'd kept taking care of them as he tried to find ways—or people—who could help. He wasn't like the man Angel had married.

"I mean, look out there at your friend," Angel said. "He was uncomfortable and didn't want to meet your scandalous sister, so he waited outside."

"That's not it." Helena stiffened. "He knew I hadn't seen you for a bit. He just wanted us to be able to talk in private. That's all."

"I don't doubt that's what he said. I'm just saying I ain't buying what he's selling. He was uncomfortable—wanted to run away. He ain't no different from Duncan. Country men just show you the best of who they are until they have you roped in, and then they leave ya for some younger woman."

Helena's shoulders fell. She wanted her sister to reassure her, to tell her to break out onto her own path, follow her dreams, and marry a man she loved.

"You go ahead and dream about that man standing out there in his flashy red kilt, but remember that trusting a man is like trusting a stray dog. There ain't no future and there ain't no loyalty. Look what ya get stuck with when they leave." She motioned around her. "I ain't got no family to speak of; I got a house that I hate, and bills I can't pay. This ain't no life for a Pavee girl."

CHAPTER NINETEEN

Helena was quiet. Graham rested his hand on the car's center console, palm up, and waited for her to lace her fingers between his, but her hand never came. If anything, she seemed to move further away.

He brought his hand back to the wheel, but couldn't stop glancing over at her. She wore a tight scowl, which only grew more taut the nearer they came to the manor.

"What did your sister say?"

"Nothing." Helena's gaze didn't budge from the window.

Graham could have sworn there'd been more than a simple spark between them. She'd yielded to his touch, searched for him with her kiss. Yet now, after seeing her sister, Helena was acting as if riding in the car with him were some form of medieval torture.

He pulled the Mercedes up to the manor's gates and waited for the barrier to slide open. "Did I do something?" he asked, no longer able to handle her giving him the cold shoulder.

Helena looked over at him, her eyes glistening. "It's nothing *you* did."

The gates slid open. He let the car control its own acceleration. "What're you talking about?"

"You and I… we can't be together." She looked away from him as her voice quivered with emotion. "I'm sorry."

The words lashed across him like a whip. "What did your sister say?"

"Angel didn't say anything I wasn't already thinking." Helena's face was stern and uncompromising. "You have no business being with a Traveller like me."

"You're not *just* a Traveller."

"No, Graham. That is exactly what I am. I'm a Traveller, and you're a gorger. We're never gonna be right together. Our lives are too different."

"You're wrong." Graham slammed on the brakes. "You're a woman, and I'm a man. That's all that matters. Sure, things won't always be easy. We both will have some learning to do, but that doesn't mean that we shouldn't be together."

"Yes it does, Graham." Her body seemed to tense, as if she were steeling herself to continue. "You'll never learn enough to be a part of my culture, and no matter how much I learn, I'll never really have a place in yours. I'm nothin' but a gypsy. I just need to accept what's expected of me. I can't lose my family. They're all I've got." Helena got out of the car. "Tell Mary I quit." She slammed the door behind her.

Graham threw the car into park and jumped out. "Where in the bloody hell do you think you're going? We aren't done talking. I want answers. I don't want you to run away. Goddamn it, Helena! I love you!"

Helena turned back as tears slipped down her cheeks. "Don't say you love me. *Don't.* It only makes what I'm going to have to do all that much harder. Please."

He ached to take her into his arms and make her forget what she was saying. "You've got this all dog's-arse backwards, woman. Why can't you just accept that I want you in my life—that I need you?"

"Ya mean it now, but you don't know what the future brings." Helena rubbed the tears from her cheeks, but fresh ones took their places. She turned her back on him and sprinted toward the manor.

Graham staggered back to the car and began to drive to the seclusion of his house. He'd tried his damnedest. He'd told her he loved her, for Jaysus's sake.

He should have known what would happen. Mr. Shane had warned him.

Mr. Shane would be upset when he heard they were going to lose Helena—and before she'd even seen her full supernatural potential. His stepfather would take the loss out on him, but Graham would be even harder on himself. He had not only lost the woman of his dreams, but also the only person with the ability to heal his brother.

Danny needed help. He needed to be lifted out of the murky darkness. He needed someone who could work with him, teach him, bring him back to life—he needed Helena.

Then again, the place had trapped them all: everyone who worked there, the people who rested in the infirmary, and those who had given their last breaths to make the manor the hovering behemoth it had become. They were all slaves to the paranormal energy that surged within this place.

At least Helena had seized her chance to get free of

the gasping beast. Yet Danny, and all the people she could have helped, would be the ones who would pay the price for her exodus.

He parked the car in front of his house.

He'd have to find another way to help Danny…

He pushed open the door to the kitchen. Almost everything about the simple kitchen was as it had been when he'd left that morning. Same chipped white cupboards, same little black cooker, but sitting at the round table in some of his ratty old clothes was his mother, Rose.

What the hell was she doing here?

She looked up at him. Her curly hair was uneven and matted, and her cheeks were sunken and limp from lack of laughter. Something in her dull eyes shifted as she saw him. Her lips quivered, but a smile failed to come, and she gave up.

"Ah, my wee lad. I've been missing you. Thought you'd never get home." She stood up and walked to the coffee pot. "I hope you don't mind. I made us a pot. Thought you'd be needing a pick-me-up after your little adventure today."

"You mean our adventure looking for *you*?"

She waved him off with a bony hand. "I saw you all at the church. I hoped you and your friend were there to pray. There's so much evil in this world." Her hands shook against the counter.

He stepped next to her, ready to catch her if she fell. "We were there looking for you. You can't be out here on your own."

She shrugged. "I was doing nothing wrong, only visiting my church. I needed to take confession."

Was she really that confused? The vicar had said he hadn't seen her.

"Mother, you broke out of the infirmary." He put his hand on her shoulder. Her fine bones poked his hand. "We thought you were possessed."

"I know. But I had to hide the codex. People were talking about it. That book can't be found."

"The book is already well-hidden. You can't leave the infirmary, Mother."

"I should've told them where I was going, but they wouldn't have let me go." Rose pulled cups out from the cupboard. They clanked together as she set them down and poured the coffee. "I don't understand who they are to be thinking they can hold me up in that dank old dungeon. I've done nothing wrong. I don't even know why I'm down there. Why hasn't John come for me?"

"Mum, don't you remember what happened?" Graham took the cup she handed him.

He wanted to hate her for forcing this life on him, for using Danny. But seeing how weak she had become, he could only feel pity.

She stepped to the table and collapsed into a chair. Coffee splashed over the edge of her cup, and she tried to mop it up before he could notice. "What are you talking about, baby?"

He took her bony hands in his and spoke as if he were talking to a child. "Do you know how long you've been at the manor?"

"It's only been a few weeks since we moved here." Rose pulled her hands from his and then took a long sip of the coffee. "Have you seen your brother? I can't find Danny anywhere."

"What's the last thing you remember?"

"Well..." She paused. "A couple of days ago we decorated the south wing and we found a room. There was a book. The Devil's Bible. Then I got sick." Her face blanched. "How long was I in the infirmary?"

"It's been almost three years."

She stared at her coffee for a long moment. He wanted to tell her more, but he didn't want to overwhelm her.

"I thought it was only a dream. I didn't... I didn't realize... The book..."

"Mum, it's okay. You and Mr. Shane made a mistake, but you didn't know. You didn't know the power the book possessed."

"Is John... is he alive?"

Graham nodded. "He's fine. Running the manor."

"And the two of you?"

Since the day he'd met his stepfather, they hadn't exactly had a warm relationship, but since the accident they'd been forced to rely on each other—though most of the time they tended to avoid one another. "We're good. Doing the best we can. Do you want me to call him?"

"Is he looking for me? Is Danny?" There was hope in her voice and his heart sank.

"Mr. Shane's been busy with the hospital, but Danny's... he's had a rough time of it." He rested his hand on hers. "When you used the codex to alter his powers it... it destroyed him. The doctors are saying he's catatonic."

"Danny... My sweet angelic boy... What did I do?"

Rose stared down at the table, and the tears slipped down her face.

Graham had done the same thing at this very table, more times than he could count.

"There's hope, Mum. My friend, Helena, she might be able to help Danny... and you. She's a healer."

A knock on the front door made Graham jerk. "I'll be right back, Mum." He stood up and his chair thumped against the floor. "Stay here."

He made his way to the front door, silently begging that the person waiting would be Helena.

Graham unlatched the door.

"What the feck is going on?" Seamus stormed in.

"This isn't a great time." Graham glanced at the kitchen. Rose couldn't be left alone.

"What the bloody hell did you do to Helena? She came to me crying. Sayin' she quit." Seamus pressed his furious face into Graham's. "I gave my blessing and ya made her cry? What the feck did you do? You better not 'a laid a single finger on my gra."

Shite.

"I didn't touch her." They'd only shared a handful of kisses, and that didn't have anything to do with what had transpired between them—no, that had all been thanks to Angel.

"Then why's she upset?"

"You need to talk to Angel. We went to see her in Rathkeale. Then the next thing I knew, Helena was quitting."

The door from the kitchen opened. Rose poked her head out. "Helena?" his mother asked in a dazed voice.

"The woman from the church... my friend," he answered.

"We need to find her. She needs to go to the infirmary."

Graham's heart leapt into his throat. He shook his head at Rose, silently imploring her to be quiet.

Seamus glared at Graham. "I thought you said you didn't touch her."

"It's not what you think." Graham's stomach twisted into one solid knot of fear. Seamus couldn't know the truth. "This is my mother, Rose."

She stepped out from the kitchen and proffered her hand, as if she felt none of the tension that ran between him and Seamus. "We need to find Helena."

Seamus shook Rose's hand briefly. "I'm sorry, but why do you need Helena?"

"She needs to go to the infirmary," Rose said matter-of-factly.

"Mother, stop."

"No." Seamus put his hand up to Graham. "What infirmary?"

"The infirmary under the stairs." Rose walked to the loveseat and gracefully sat down.

"What's she talkin' about?" Seamus asked.

"I'm sorry about my mum, Seamus. She's confused. I need to get her back to the facility."

"I'm not going back!" Rose shook her head, and a matted curl fell into her face, making her look every bit a mad woman. "You can't make me go back!" She trembled. "I hate that place."

"This isn't a good time." Graham put his hand on

Seamus's shoulder and led him to the front door. "I'll talk to you in the morning."

Seamus stopped and turned. "Is that the woman you had me looking for?"

Graham answered with a tight nod.

"We have to find her," Rose urged. "We have to help my son."

"Wait. How does all this involve my gra?"

"Adare is involved with a local infirmary," he said, trying to lie in order to cover his mother's slip. "I tried to find Helena a job there, but she passed."

"She didn't mention no job."

"Maybe you need to talk to her."

"There's something you ain't telling me. She wouldn't be that troubled over just passing up a job."

Graham maneuvered Seamus to the front door. "Like I said, you need to talk to your daughter. One minute, Helena and I were doing pretty good and the next… well, you saw her." He opened the door and Seamus stepped out.

"I'll get to the bottom of this. If you did something to hurt my gra, I'll be coming back for your head."

"I would expect nothing less."

CHAPTER TWENTY

The campfire crackled as its orange and red fingers tore away at the embers. The flames coalesced on the wood, burning away the outer flesh of the tree, only fulfilled when they had taken everything the wood had to give. It struck Helena how much she was like the ash, with all of her life sucked from her, destroyed by the force of another's will.

Gavin's laughter, and the sound of the neighbor kids' voices, echoed from the line of trees next to the trailers. Rionna slammed the door of the trailer shut and stomped out to the fire.

"What's wrong?" Helena asked.

Rionna dropped into the little camp chair next to her. "Mam said I ain't gonna go back to school."

Even if Helena fought to let Rionna stay in school, it would do no good. It would only get Rionna's hopes up for something more, something better. She would end up like Helena; hope would lift her up, and life would beat her down again.

Rionna picked up a stick and poked at the fire, playing with its deadly force. "Do you like it, Helena?"

"Do I like what?"

"Do you like traveling?"

"Sometimes." Her thoughts flashed to Angel.

"When do you think we're gonna be moving again?"

"Why?"

"I don't know." Rionna stabbed at the fire. "I guess I like it in Adare."

Tightness grew in her gut. "What about school? Don't you want to keep going?"

"It's all right. I wouldn't be staying in too much longer anyways, I guess, so why worry about it. You know?" A bit of ash flew up into the air and got caught in the light evening breeze.

Helena wanted to shake her.

The door to the trailer opened behind them, and Da stepped outside. "Rionna?"

"Aye?" Rionna asked, putting the stick down.

"Go look after your brother."

Rionna stood up, brushed off the dirt from her knees, and walked in a wobbly line toward the tree line. For a moment Helena caught a glimpse of Rionna's future— looking after children.

Da sat down next to her. There was a brown paper bag in his hands. "Mary asked me to give you this." He handed her the bag.

Helena pulled open the top and peered inside. She was met with the faint scent of onion and tomatoes: the smell of the kitchen. Inside the bag sat the book Graham had bought her.

"How'd ya get home, gra a mo gris?"

Helena put the paper bag down on the ground. "I walked. It felt good to stretch my legs."

"Graham told me about the infirmary." Da nodded and took a penknife out of his pocket.

"What... what did he tell you?" Helena stammered.

He scraped the blade under his fingernail. "Is there something you need to tell me, gra?"

Her heart leapt into her throat. Graham must have revealed her secret.

"I'm sorry, Da. I should have told you before. Ogak Beoir told me I had the gift. I should have told ya, but I'd been hopin'... I guess, I thought maybe the forshaw would go away."

Da looked up from his hands. "You thought *what?*"

Her heart dropped as she realized she had outed herself. Her mouth opened and closed as she tried to find the right words to make things go back to the way they had been only moments before.

"You have the fecking *shaw* and you didn't tell me?" He pitched his pen knife into the dirt.

The silence sat between them like a thick kettle of soup, just waiting to boil over and burn them.

"Why didn't you tell me?" He looked up, and where anger had been only moments before, there was now understanding.

"I'm sorry, Da."

"You don't got to be sorry, gra. This has to be hard on ya." He waved her off. "But tell me, does Graham know about... your ability?"

She nodded.

His face was contorted with confusion and worry. "I shoulda known... No wonder they wanted to hire us both."

"The forshaw had only just started, but Graham knew about it... He knew that I had the gift. He wants to teach me how to use it, Da."

He scowled. "Do you trust him? Really trust him?"

Helena looked down at her hands. "I do, Da. Besides, they need my help."

"When you saw Ogak Beior, did she speak of this?"

She nodded.

Da gave a resigned sigh.

A mud-covered lorry pulled into the campsite, kicking up dust. Da stuffed his penknife into his pocket. At the sound of the car, Rionna and the rest of the children poked their heads out from the trees.

The lorry came to a stop next to their car. An older man stepped out. "Ya got the banknotes ya be owin' me, O'Driscoll?"

Da stiffened and a look of pinched anger returned to his face. "Aye. Come inside and I'll get ye what I got."

"Don't got all of it, eh?"

"I've only been working a week. These legit jobs don't pay like your business, O'Donoghue."

The man gave a deep, dangerous laugh. He leaned down and looked into the car where a boy waited. "For someone on the dole, ya'd think they'd be a little more thankful. We could've taken all they got, but no. We just got a girl. They ought to be kissing our feet. Isn't that right, Brian?"

Helena leaned as far forward as she could in her chair. The door of the lorry slammed shut as the young man got out. He had a narrow chest and thin arms. She recognized him as the man from her vision, the man who'd taken Graham's place. He had full lips and well-kept hair. Most women would probably slobber over the man, who was thin but good-looking, but not her; instead she felt only the bitterness of dislike.

The old man stepped beside Da and, for the first time, seemed to notice her. "Is this the lass we traded for?"

"If I pay you the whole amount, with interest, do ye think we can call the deal off?" Da's expression hardened. "Her mam was off her face when she agreed."

The old man snickered. "Already pullin' out of the deal, are ye? I shoulda known. You and your fam ain't nothin' but beggars."

Helena stood up. "We ain't no beggars."

Brian stepped around the lorry and peered at her. "Helena?"

"I don't know if you want this filly. She's got a mouth on her." Brian's father glanced down at her chest. "But she ain't a bad looker. If you want, you might be able to train it out of her."

"Don't bite her head off, Pap," Brian countered as he smiled at her.

"This boy..." The old man huffed. "We've been living near Dublin and he ain't done a lick of hard work in months— yet he's thinking he be some kind of man. That he knows better than his old pap." The man motioned threateningly at his son, but Brian didn't seem to notice. "You two'll make a good couple. She's got a big mouth, just like you."

Brian didn't speak again.

"O'Driscoll, why don't you go get me that roll of

banknotes you owe me and a glass of scotch? We have business to discuss about the dowry."

The man looked back at Brian. "Why don't you stay out here, visit with your bride a bit." He snickered as the door slammed shut behind him and Da.

"I'm sorry about me Pap." Brian motioned to Da's empty seat. "All right if I sit down?"

"Aye, go ahead." The ache in her gut tightened the nearer he came. "Do you want a cup of tea or a bit of beer?"

"Nah, lass. I'm fine." He motioned for her to sit back down.

She was a mix of emotion. It was wrong to share a campfire with her enemy, but then again, the enemy was going to be her husband—soon they would be sharing far more than the flames.

"So you've been livin' in Dublin?" Helena plucked up the courage to start a conversation. If they were to be married, she should at least know who he was on paper.

"Aye, we were working up there on a construction job. I don't much like construction."

"Is that right?"

"A while back I wanted to go into business for meself. I wanted to open my own shoe shop, but my dad didn't think that was a fitting profession for a Pavee man." He shrugged.

A twinge of empathy flickered within her.

"Were there many women where you lived?"

"Aye, there were a few Traveller girls, but none as fine as ya. And oh, Dublin was filled to the gills with country girls." A wide smile spread over his lips. He leaned in as if he wanted to tell her a secret. "Half of them don't even know what a mop looks like." He chuckled and shook his head in disbelief. "What's a man to do with a woman like that? They ain't of no use if ye ask me."

He gave her a smug grin as he leaned back. "I wanted to get me a nice Traveller girl." He looked over at her with a gleam in his eyes. "So Pap set this meeting up, wanted me to get started like a *real* man. I'm just glad you're a fine thing. I didn't want to be getting married to a woman with a face like a pig licking piss off a nettle."

He could call her beautiful all he wanted, but it wouldn't change the fact that he was the real pig.

"I bet you're pretty excited about gettin' off wit me. Your mam made it sound like you've been planning the wedding since you were a lass."

"Mam must have been mistaken. My sister Angel was the one who wanted to get married." Her admission sounded angrier than she had intended. Her face flushed. "I mean... I'm..."

Brian's smug smile brightened. "It's okay. I know you're nervous around me. Most girls are."

Helena bit back a laugh.

Brian reached over and touched the top of her hand. She held back the urge to recoil. "I was thinking about goin' to Feile na Maighe. Do you want to go with me? It might be fun."

Only that morning, she and Graham had been talking about the same festival and what it meant for the manor. Her heart ached as she thought of Graham, his rich brown eyes and the perfect cleft in his chin. Now she was going to the festival with another man. It was all so surreal.

Brian pointed at the brown paper bag on the ground next to the legs of her chair. "What's that?"

Helena grimaced. "It's my… it's a bit of refuse." She pushed the bag further under the chair with the heel of her shoe.

The book had only been hers for a few days, and it had already gone from a treasured gift to something she couldn't bring herself to look upon.

Brian smiled. "I was thinking we could live at my family's campsite for a bit. Then maybe we could head over to England. I got a line on a real good job from a friend who owns a construction business. The pay would be good and the work's steady. We could make a real good go of it for ourselves."

England? "How long would we stay?"

Brian held his palms up to the fire, warming his hands. The damp sweat on them reflected the sunlight that had managed to break through the dark evening clouds.

"I'm thinkin' we'll stay for at least a year. Hopefully by then we'll have a little lad runnin' around, keeping us busy. Then we can go from there."

A year? Da couldn't leave the country. That would mean he wouldn't be around for the birth of her first child.

She thought back to her vision, the one with Graham standing naked in front of her, his muscular chest glistening with a thin sheen of sweat. Her gaze swung to Brian. Maybe if she imagined Graham, the experience, her first experience, would be bearable. Maybe she could even come to enjoy it.

Brian picked up the stick that Rionna had thrown on the ground and prodded the ebbing flames, teasing them back to full strength. Their orange tips whipped back and forth in the faint evening wind, burning faster.

Helena tried to choke down the lump in her throat, but it was no use. She was already turning to ash.

CHAPTER TWENTY-ONE

Feile na Maighe was in full swing when Helena and Brian arrived. The throaty sound of bagpipes echoed down the street, bouncing off the yellow, blue, and pink houses of Adare Village. The distinct aroma of freshly baked bread and the oily scent of street food vendors wafted through the air, mixing with the sounds of the much-anticipated festival.

Lydia and Jimmy stood by a coffee shop, waiting for them.

"Hiya, Helena!" Lydia beamed. "I'm glad ya and Brian could meet us. I thought I was gonna have to take my sisters. Now it's like a real double date!"

Jimmy walked up to Brian and extended his hand. "Wotcher. I'm Jimmy. I hear we're gonna be cousins of sorts."

Brian shook his hand. "Aye, good to meet ya."

Helena adjusted her purse on her shoulder and leaned in, so only Lydia could hear her whisper, "What does he mean, they're gonna be cousins?"

Lydia shoved her hand in front of Helena's face. "Look! He did it!"

On Lydia's ring finger was an oversized solitaire diamond on a yellow gold band. It was beautiful. Helena ran her thumb over her naked ring finger. Strangely, she didn't feel upset or jealous, only a sense of disappointment. Unlike Lydia, she wasn't getting married for anything as romantic as love—with her and Brian, the arrangement was nothing more than familial business.

"Congratulations, Lyd. I'm real happy for you." Jimmy may not have been a prince, but if this was what Lydia wanted, it had to have been better than being sold off.

"Well, congratulations to you too." Lydia slipped her arm through Helena's. "Are you happy?"

Helena forced a smile. "It'll be okay."

"At least you don't have to take those shite exams."

It might have been pointless to take the exams now, but a part of her still wanted to complete them and to do well. It could be the last gift she gave to herself—the last selfish thing she could do. After the wedding, her life would revolve around Brian.

"Who knows, maybe Jimmy and I can stay near you all for a bit. I hear you're going to England. Do you think Jimmy can find a job in tarmac there?"

"It would be grand to have ye round." The idea of having Lydia near her in England made it seem almost bearable. "I'm gonna have to give up so much."

She thought of her job in the kitchen. Mary had to be upset that Helena hadn't returned to work. But she'd been *forced* to turn her back on Mary's kindness.

Helena tried to push any thoughts of Mary or Graham

from her mind. She hated to admit it, but she wanted to catch a glance of Graham today, to have the chance to say she was sorry, to thank him for the opportunity he had given her at the manor and to tell him goodbye. Yet she shuddered at the thought of seeing him. It was so much easier to keep moving, to not look back, to ignore all the things that could have been. Live for today, look to tomorrow, and follow the Traveller way.

Brian and Jimmy walked ahead of them, weaving through the crowds of villagers and tourists. The two Traveller men wore tight white shirts with sparkling patterns up the backs, finely pressed trousers, and shining black dress shoes. Their hair was perfectly shaped and gelled into place. Among all the tweed- and khaki-wearing villagers and tourists it was easy to pick them out. Lydia looked beautiful; her hair was half-up, and curls cascaded down her back, ending right above the crystal-studded angel wings she had meticulously added to her bright pink tank top. She pushed up the straps of her purse and held them in place on her shoulder, strategically, to show off the oversized diamond on her left hand.

All the roads were shut down, and the streets were filled with people. Kids clutched balloons in their little fists as they chased after each other, while others licked at steadily melting ice cream cones. Their parents stood in circles, visiting with their friends or sitting at the base of the fountain in the center of the little town.

The men stopped and waited for the girls to catch up. Brian extended his hand and waited until Helena slipped her fingers into his. His skin was warm and, though callused, still boyish, a far stretch from Graham's strong and well-worn hands. Brian lifted their entwined hand to his mouth and gave her a kiss.

She reminded herself to smile.

Brian led her toward a group of people in front of the windows of a pub. Standing in the center were three women doing a traditional Irish step dance. Their feet whipped through the air, up, down, right, left, while their arms and chests remained still. They smiled brightly as they twisted and tapped in time to the music issuing from a radio that rested beside them.

Amongst the crowd were the two golfers she and Graham had questioned at the manor. They were gabbing away. Maybe it wouldn't be so bad to move away from this village—everything reminded her of Graham, and what she had to give up.

"Jimmy and I are gonna go and grab a pint. You want a fizzy drink or something?" Brian asked.

A fizzy drink wouldn't numb the emotions that filled her. "Nah, why don't Lydia and I come with ye? I could use a pint."

Brian's eyebrows rose. "Is that right?"

He was going to have to get used to the fact she wasn't like other Traveller women. She would do her best to play the role of the perfect little Traveller wife, but there were going to be times when she wouldn't be able to hold her tongue. Brian would either have to grow to like it, or hate her for it.

They walked into the busy pub. Men filled the counters, and a few couples were seated at the booths. Brian and Jimmy found an empty table at the far end.

"Ladies." He motioned his thumb at himself and Jimmy. "We're gonna get a start on this piss up."

Lydia perked up. "Would you get me a fizzy, love?"

Helena would have to be a rebel on her own. Brian

looked at her, but this time she didn't have to force the smile that played over her lips.

The boys made their way to the packed bar. The folk music seemed to grow louder, as if the owner were trying to tune out the drone of his patrons' voices.

Lydia leaned across the table and motioned toward the front door. "Who's that?"

She turned and looked toward where Lydia was pointing. Graham was walking toward their table, but his gaze was focused on Jimmy and Brian. There was a tight expression on Graham's face—a look reminiscent of jealousy. He had no right to be jealous, but then again, in a strange way it made her feel wanted... really wanted. Brian never made her feel that way, and she doubted he ever would. To him, she was nothing more than an accessory, a plaything to be used and then ignored when it no longer suited him. Everything would be so different if Graham were the man in her life.

Graham weaved toward them through the tables. He looked at her and, catching her gaze, motioned for her to meet him outside.

This was her moment.

The vinyl stuck to her skin as she slid to the edge of the bench seat. "Lydia, cover for me."

"Wait." Lydia reached out for her. "What am I gonna tell Brian if he comes back and you're away?"

"Just tell him I had to use the facilities."

"What if he notices you followin' that man out?"

Helena shrugged. She didn't really care.

Standing next to the circle of people surrounding the dancers was Graham. He stared at her like a lost child—alone, scared, hungry for love.

"I wasn't sure you'd meet me."

Helena's stomach tightened. "I just came out to say goodbye. I'm sorry. I shouldn't have left the way I did. Ya know. When ya said…"

"That I loved you?"

"Aye, that."

Graham's shoulders fell. "If you don't feel the way I do, you just don't."

A lump rose in her throat as she thought about the man waiting at the bar for her. There was only one choice she could make if she wanted to stay part of her family.

"I don't, Graham." Helena pushed back the tears that threatened to spill down her cheeks. She couldn't be weak. If she cared for Graham, the best thing she could do was let him go. It might hurt him in this moment, but eventually he would be happy again, and fall for a *country* woman.

Graham's gaze never wandered from her face, as if he were trying to remember every line there and every expression she made. "I know you don't believe me, but you have a special gift. You have more power than you know. If only you could see it. If only you could see what an incredible woman you are. You don't deserve to be held back—not by me, not by your family, and especially not by that eejit *Brian*. He wouldn't know the difference between his arse and a teapot. You can't marry him, Helena… you just can't." There was an edge of desperation in his voice.

Graham was right. Brian wasn't the full shilling, but he was the safest option. She would get exactly what she needed to have—her family, a life she knew. Maybe she could even ignore the forshaw and avoid using her clairsentience. Life would be simple. She'd cook, clean, travel, have children, and please her husband—nothing more.

"He's not as bad as you're makin' him out to be, Graham. He'll take good care of me." Graham reached out for her hand, but Helena stepped back. "Why did you come here? You are only making this harder on the both of us."

"I wanted you to know that Rose came back. She hadn't been possessed. The nurses were wrong." He dropped his hand. "She found me, but she's gone missing again. She didn't remember what happened. When I told her about Danny, she didn't take it well. I think she went looking for you, but she also said she hated the infirmary—she may just be hiding. She was so confused and upset."

"Maybe Ayre can help you." Her gaze moved down to his empty hand.

"Aye." Graham exhaled as if he had expected the answer she had given him. "I still need you, Helena. I know you don't love me, but I know you care about Danny. If you don't come back…"

Her heart ached as she thought back to the sickly boy who rested in the bed beneath the manor. She had pushed Danny from her mind as much as she could, but it pained her that she could do nothing. He was only a boy… an innocent child.

"All I can do is sense his illness with my ability. I can't do anything to change what is goin' on with him, Graham."

"You just need to strengthen your gift. Exercise it, and it'll get stronger. I don't expect you to be able to help him right away, but maybe if you keep trying, you can get through. You can't just leave him there. You're his only hope."

Graham reached out to touch her. This time Helena let him hold her for a moment before she pulled away.

The crowd around them shifted. She stepped back as she tried to see what they were looking at. From behind a stocky brunette man, Gavin stepped out. Tears ran down his ash-covered face.

"Helena?" Her brother's voice was hoarse and weak.

She dropped to her knees and pulled his quaking body into her arms. His tears wetted her shirt as he gasped for breath.

Helena lifted Gavin into her arms and rushed away from the crowds of people. "What happened, Gavin? Are ya okay?"

The boy smelled like a campfire and sweat.

"What are ya doin' here?"

The boy shook as he whimpered on her shoulder.

"Gavin, what's goin' on?"

She pushed him back so she could look at him. His eyes were red with tears, and she could see that some of the hair on the side of his head was singed, as if he had been too close to the fire. "Are ya okay?"

She grabbed his shoulder and spun him around as she searched him for burns. His neck was red, but nothing a little ointment couldn't cure. "What happened? Are Mam and Rionna okay?"

Gavin hiccupped as he tried to stop the tears. "I... I... They were in the trailer... Mam..."

"Mam what?" Helena shook his shoulders as if the action would dislodge his answers.

"Mam was... was drinking..." Gavin stammered. "I dunno know what... what happened... She was in the trailer with me and Rionna. Then the fire started."

CHAPTER TWENTY-TWO

The crowd swelled around the smoldering remains of her family's trailer. The smoke rose up like a giant fist, as if even God were smiting her for wanting more in her life—for wanting anything that wasn't the traditional gypsy way.

The center of the trailer moaned and collapsed with the screech of hot, twisted metal. Everything around Helena pulled in and succumbed to the pressure of an angry fate.

She wiped away the tear that slipped down her cheek, almost surprised she had any left to shed. Her family had lost everything. Their jobs, their home, and all the hope she held for a future.

An icy wind blew against her back and encouraged the flames that licked at the sides of the charred trailer. The ashes surrounding the burning skeleton lifted up and scattered in the air. The crowd shifted, as if they were afraid the ashes of her family would defile them, the flesh of their flesh.

She hated them all. She hated every person who stood there. They'd done nothing but watch as her family's life crashed to the ground. They didn't care. All they wanted was a show, a bit of gossip to spread around the town and the Traveller campsites.

Rionna stood next to her, her arms pulled loosely over her chest. Helena hugged Gavin to her. Da sat on the ground, his face in his hands, broken. Her chest ached as she watched him falling apart in front of the world.

Brian stood with his father, talking quietly.

Maybe he wouldn't want her now. She and her family would only be another drain on their resources—and they had nothing more to give.

Gavin looked up at her. "Is Mam gonna be okay?"

Helena glanced over at where the ambulance had sat only an hour before. Mam was lucky to be alive. She had been burned across her arms and upper body, but a few days in the hospital and she would likely be back to her old self—drinking, angry, and forgetting all about the disaster she had caused.

"She'll be fine, gra. She'll be fine," Helena said, but it was only a half-truth.

"My hands hurt." Gavin leaned against her.

She took the boy's hands. There was an unmistakable circular burn, as if Gavin had grabbed the searing door handle of the trailer in his escape.

She let go of his hands and turned to Rionna. "Are ya okay, girl?"

Rionna lifted her arms. The undersides were covered in yellow blisters.

Helena gasped.

A flurry of emotions filled her: hate, love, anger, resentment. She couldn't hold back the tears that slid down her cheeks. She'd never been so furious, so hurt. Her mam had not only ruined her own life, she'd also done her damnedest to ruin the lives of all of those around her.

She couldn't be allowed to do any more damage, or to hurt another person Helena loved.

"Come with me." She strode into the trees, away from the prying eyes of the crowd that milled around the campsite.

Rionna and Gavin followed her until she stopped next to a gooseberry bush. A small stream gurgled past their feet, slipped around a boulder, and disappeared in the direction of the Maigue River. "Stick your arms in there."

Downstream was an old pine. It stood crooked and bent like an old crone; its bark was split, and pitch oozed from its wounds.

The kids dipped their arms into the brook. She tore some of the branches from the gooseberry bush and stripped the bark. Dipping her hands into the water, Helena lifted out a handful of the black mud. It stuck to her fingers as she folded the strips of bark in. She kept mixing the concoction until it was the consistency of pudding.

"Gras, come here. Let me see your burns."

They lifted their chilled arms. Rionna's shirt was singed at the edge of her sleeves. Helena took the mixture and gently dabbed it onto Rionna's hot flesh, careful to barely touch her blisters. Amazingly, the girl didn't budge.

"What happened, Rionna?" Helena asked, trying to take her sister's focus off the pain.

Rionna shook her head and looked over at the stream, unable to speak. Helena patted the last bit of Rionna's arm then pulled her into her embrace. Rionna stuck her arms out, unable to hug her back, but Helena didn't care. "I love you, sweet gra. I love you."

Rionna pulled away. "You shoulda been here."

"I know. I'm sorry. I should've been there to stop Mam. I should have stood up against her. I knew somethin' like this would happen. I knew it and I hadn't stopped it. I wish I coulda seen it—maybe I could have used the forshaw…"

She stopped.

What had she said?

Hopefully Rionna hadn't understood what she meant, or thought it was only a slip of the tongue.

Rionna's mouth opened and closed. "What?"

"Nothing." Helena turned to Gavin and started to apply the salve to her brother's hands. "I just wish Mam hadn't done what she did."

"Don't lie to me." Rionna eyed her suspiciously. "I'm not a child, Helena."

Helena let go of Gavin's hands. "Don't play with the mud, gra." She stood up and wiped off the dirt from her knees.

"You can just tell me if ye got the forshaw," Rionna continued. "It would make sense. I mean, ya always get everything. It would be only normal if you got the gift too."

Rionna's words bit at her. "It's not as great as you're makin' it sound."

"Oh really? The woman I met with the gift could heal. She could read palms. She could make money. People loved her."

"It can be a gift, but—"

"It's fine. Knowing you, you're probably lying. If you

really had the gift, you'd use it to heal me and Gavin, but no… All you ever care about is your bloody self."

"Come with me." Helena walked over to the pine tree and put her hands to its gnarled surface as she tried to control her anger. Every choice she had made had been made with them in mind, but her resentful sister couldn't possibly understand those sacrifices.

She closed her eyes and let the magic within her be her guide.

She was the tree, her roots planted deep in Mother Earth's bosom. Her body tingled with the power that radiated up from the earth below her.

I am like this tree; firm in my beliefs, strong in my intention, unwavering in my path.

Gavin and Rionna stopped beside her as she repeated the silent prayer.

A wave of calming energy rose within her, and suddenly it was if she held all the power of the earth within her hands. Helena opened her eyes and turned to Gavin. She took his arms and traced her finger over his wounds. The energy flowed through her, invisibly passing from her fingers into his marred flesh. The mud dried instantly.

"What?" The little boy's astonished voice bounced between the trees.

The heat of his burn circulated over her arms, as if the injury were upon her own flesh. She grimaced and let the pain fill her senses. Using her power, she surrounded the pain in her arms and hands and tried to force it to collapse. Wisps of pain tried to force their way through the tendrils of her energy, but she held them back. The orb shrank smaller and smaller the harder she pressed.

The pain abated in her arms.

Helena opened her eyes. The mud on Gavin's arms dropped to the ground in chunks. The burns had disappeared without so much as a pink dimple where the heat had defiled his flesh.

She turned to Rionna and extended her hands. The power pulsed inside of her, and she didn't dare speak for fear that it would diminish her strength.

Rionna reached over, and Helena took her hands. She closed her eyes. The heat of the burns drew a whimper from her lips, but just like with Gavin, Helena didn't allow the pain to control her. She collected all her sister's pain. She imagined the power of her own body dousing the burn with healing energy. As she tried to manipulate her power, there was a sensation of cool water running down her arms.

Rionna gasped.

After a moment, there was no more pain. She released Rionna's hands.

Rionna's mouth was agape as she stared at the fresh skin on her arms. "You do. You really have the gift."

Helena put her hands to the tree and grounded the last bit of energy, silently thanking Mother Earth for the gift from which they had all benefited. "Now that you know the truth, I need to know I can trust you. You can't tell anyone what I've just done. Do you understand?"

"What else can you do?" Rionna asked.

"I don't know, but I know I can heal, and see things others don't."

"Why do you have the gift and I don't?"

"I don't know. I don't want this…"

Rionna pushed her arms over her chest. "You have

everything. Da loves you the best, you got your schooling almost done, and now ya got a gift that everyone would love. Why don't I get nothin'?" Rionna spun on her heel and rushed out of the trees, leaving them behind.

CHAPTER TWENTY-THREE

"Rionna?" Helena called. Gavin hugged her legs.

She needed the chance to explain herself. Helena didn't have it easy. Maybe it appeared that way to Rionna, but her assumption couldn't have been further from the truth.

The branches drew back, and Graham stepped into the opening.

"Graham?" she said with a shocked breath. "What're ya doin' here? I thought I told ya to stay at the festival. We can't…"

"I couldn't stay away. I had to come. Are you okay?" He motioned to Gavin. "Are the kids okay? They didn't get hurt, did they?"

"Are you by yourself?" Everyone who stood around the fire must have noticed him coming back here to see them. "Where's Brian?"

"I think he's out there talking to his father."

She stepped through the mess of trees. The branches pulled at her body like needy fingers. Helena reached for one of the sticks poking at her. The bark was rough in her hands as she snapped the twig in half.

The mass of people that had filled the campsite had started to disperse, and her betrothed was talking animatedly to Da while his father, beside him, took a pull from a pint. She moved deeper into the trees, until she was back by the calm little stream. Graham shushed Gavin as Helena drew near.

Gavin looped his arms around her leg and popped his dirty thumb into his mouth.

"Everything okay? How's your mother?" Graham asked. "I heard they took her to the hospital."

"She'll be fine. Some burns, but she'll make it through. She's tough."

Helena glanced down at Gavin's chubby little hands, which had, only minutes ago, been covered in angry red burns.

Gavin loosened his hold on Helena's leg. She leaned down so she could look him in the eyes. "Gav, would you check on Da? Make sure he's okay, aye?"

The boy nodded and ran off through the thicket, glancing back only briefly before leaving them alone.

Graham stepped nearer to her, close enough that she could make out the sweet smell of his skin. She resisted the urge to pull his intoxicating scent deeper into her lungs.

"Are you going to be okay?" He pushed a lock of hair behind her ear.

"What?" She tried to focus on something other than his luscious pink lips and the place where his fingertips had brushed against her skin.

"Where are you going to stay tonight?" His breath whispered across her skin, awaking a deep need within her.

"I... I don't know." She hadn't thought that far ahead—there had been so much going on. The children couldn't be without a home, but Da had to pay the O'Donoghues the money that was owed before they could buy another trailer. Their debt left them with nothing.

Graham took her hand in his warm grip. "If you ever need anything, I'm here."

He pulled her hand up and brushed his lips against the backs of her fingers. The heat of his skin made her draw closer to him, and his other arm wrapped tightly around her waist. "I want this hand. I want you, forever."

"I... I can't. I got to marry Brian—more now than ever. He and his family control our future." She halfheartedly tried to move out of his grasp, but he would let her go nowhere.

"No. You don't. You don't have to marry that rat bastard." There was a sparkle in his luxurious brown eyes. "I can help..."

"I appreciate that, but there's a price for everything in this life."

"I want you to walk away from Brian."

"And ya mean my life as a Traveller..." Helena stared at him. "Have ya thought of what'll happen to me if I take up with ya?"

"I thought we could finally move past our differences. You and I are more than what our cultures have labeled us. We're both people. We share the same feelings, and I think we share the same mind." Graham placed her hand on his chest. "I told you before that I *love* you. I want you to know that I meant it. I love you, Helena. I'd love you whether or not you were ever able to help Danny. I'd love you even if you chose to stay with your family and Brian. My love for you isn't going to go away."

"If you mean what you say…" She paused. "If you love me… Prove it."

Graham smiled, the dimple on his cheek making Helena's chest ache with the love she carried for him. "I think that's a grand idea." He pulled her closer and took her lips in his.

She swam like a lover lost in the sea of his kiss. She held nothing back and let their passion take control, as if it were the only thing keeping her afloat. She pulled her hand free of his fingers and trailed it down his chest. He drove his kiss harder against her lips, matching her fury. His body rubbed against hers—only making the need within her grow more desperate.

The pressure of his kiss lightened, and he drew back. "I want you to be mine."

She wanted him too—but she didn't want to leave her life behind. Not now. Not when her family needed her so much.

Graham lifted her chin with his hand and slowly slid his lips down the tender skin of her neck. She couldn't hold back her quiet moan. Graham jerked at the sound, then pulled her even tighter against his responding body. She forced herself to move away from him, her cheeks aflame.

"I…" She tried to speak.

His lips stopped their descent. "Hmm?" His eyes were glazed over with lust.

"I have to go."

He leaned back and nodded resignedly.

She moved in and stole another kiss. His hungry lips searched hers with unrestrained passion. Her chest pressed against his as his lips melted into hers. She clung to his shirt and could feel his pulse through the thin fabric. Her heart beat in time with his, as if they were connected, one being, one need, and one shared craving for the other's touch.

His hands moved up and down her back as their kiss slowed. A strange urge rose within her as his touch warmed her chilled skin. She pushed her body against his and felt the hardness that he had revealed to her in her vision.

No. They couldn't do this—not here, not now.

"I..." Her voice came out in a squeak. "I need to get back. They're going to start wonderin' where I am." She wiggled out of his arms, hating the cold dampness that soon overcame the residual warmth of his touch.

"I want you." He reached out for her, and she let him touch the slight curve of her waist.

She wanted him too, but other things needed tending. There was so much up in the air. The only fact she knew with any certainty was that she loved him but was promised to another man.

"I need to figure out my life before I can think about *this*." She motioned between them. "I need to find us a place—Gavin and Rionna can't be without a home. My da's da, he might be able to take us in. They're camped up near the North Coast."

Pain filled his eyes.

She couldn't stand to look at him. "We are at the mercy of others, and my da won't be on the dole any more than we already are—the O'Donoghues are asking for more than what is owed. And what'll my family do to settle the debt if I walk away from the engagement?"

Graham dropped his hand from her side. "The vicar has

a little place where your family can stay until you get back on your feet."

Helena paused. She had expected Graham to offer them a place at the manor, which she would have needed to refuse. But this suggestion was different. They had tithed to the church for years. It wouldn't be like being on the dole.

"I'll talk to Da."

"Grand. I'll tell the vicar to expect you and your family. And, if you want, you and your da can come back to your jobs. This way you can save up your money and pay the O'Donoghues whatever they're asking."

Helena smiled at the thought. She could get back to *her* life, but Brian would never go for this. He wouldn't let them break their agreement.

"The O'Donoghues won't be happy. This is about money—this marriage is business to them."

"If you let me, Helena, I could help. My family has money. We could pay them off—anything to make them leave you and your family alone."

"If I allow you to pay, we would only be shifting our debt about. It's not right, Graham."

"I want to help, Helena."

"I know, but this is something I think I'm gonna need to take care of on my own." Helena thought back to her job in the kitchens. She missed her freedom and the life she had started to create for herself. "Does Mary know what happened? Did she notice I was gone?"

Graham shook his head. "She didn't mention it, and I didn't tell her that you'd quit. I think she assumed you were still working with me."

"Aye, good." She hated to think of the look of

disappointment on Mary's face. "Da and I'll be to work Monday morning. Six o'clock sharp."

Graham stole one last kiss before she moved toward the trees. "I can't wait to see you again. And if you need anything... money... anything... to help break your engagement, I'm here."

"I know. Thank ye, Graham." She took off through the trees and into the campsite, where hungry flames still licked at the carcass of her former life.

Brian stood by the fire. The sweat on his face reflected the orange glow of the greedy flames. Standing at his side was Rionna. Her sister glanced over at her, drew her arms over her chest, and lifted her nose up in the air like she was an angry French poodle.

Helena glanced over at Da. His black eye had started to fade to a sick yellow, and there was soot smeared over his forehead. The black ash had sunk into his wrinkles, giving him a fearful look.

She made her way through the last of the crowd toward Brian, his father, Da, and Rionna. "Brian, do ya think we can have a talk... alone?"

His father threw his head back and laughed, making the pint in his hand shake violently. "You can't be getting him alone just yet, lass. I know he's a strappin' lad, but those types o' things'll have to wait 'til after your wedding."

She coughed lightly. "That's actually what I want to be talking about. I don't think I can go through with this."

"Whatcha mean by *this*?" Brian's father's voice dropped its playful edge.

Da looked up at her with a worried expression on his soot-covered face.

"Brian, I appreciate what you're trying to do for our family. I do. But I can't marry you." She reached for him, but he recoiled. "I don't think we'd make each other happy. I don't love you."

His cheeks flushed with anger and embarrassment. "You daft woman—"

"You got this all wrong, girl. You don't have a choice." Brian's father interrupted with a wave of his hand. "You and your fam have a debt."

"I'll pay you what we owe."

His father lunged at her like he wanted to strike her down.

Rionna stepped between them. "I'll take her place. I'll quit school and marry Brian. I mean, I'd be proud to marry him." She smiled at him.

Everything Helena had ever done was to protect her family, and Rionna was doing the one thing Helena feared most. Rionna was giving away her chance to follow her passion, to learn what was really out in the world—all for some good-for-nothing boy who wanted nothing more than to please his father.

"No." Helena reached out for her sister. "You can't."

"I can do whatever I want." Rionna gave her a sharp glare. "I'm my own woman. You have no right to tell me what to do."

Helena moved to speak, but Brian's father cut her off.

"Are these acceptable terms, lad?" he asked.

Brian leaned back and gazed down at Rionna's backside, then motioned for her to turn. Rionna obliged with a smile.

"Aye," Brian said with a nod. "I'll take the younger one. I think I'm getting the far better end of the deal."

CHAPTER TWENTY-FOUR

The morning sun spread its fingers over the granite headstones that lined the grass as Helena peered out the front window. Death and decay seemed to follow her wherever she went. Goose bumps rose on her arms as a faint draft moved through the vicar's guest cottage. Helena turned away from the window and glanced down the hallway toward the closed bedroom doors, where Da and Gavin were still fast asleep.

After their fight Rionna had gone to the hospital with Mam, and refused to consider coming to the house or being within twenty meters of Helena. Helena didn't mind her sister's absence, not after the blade Rionna had plunged into her soul.

There was a rap on the door.

Who would be calling on them at this early hour?

Helena straightened the long cotton shirt the vicar had given her. She would need to get more clothes.

The door opened without a sound. Standing on the other

side was Angel. Liam was asleep in her arms. His sweet little blond head was on her shoulder, his thumb in his mouth.

"Did I wake you? I heard what happened last night." She stepped in, and Helena shut the door. "Are you okay? What about the kids?"

"The kids are fine." Helena couldn't make sense of Angel's presence.

"Grand... That's just grand..." Angel set Liam down and covered him with a blanket.

She made her way into the kitchen with Helena close on her heels, and collapsed into a seat at the little square table. The morning sun settled on her face, highlighting the thin lines around her red eyes.

"How about ye, Angel?"

Angel looked back through the kitchen door toward the couch and, once assured that Liam was asleep, she turned back. "Are Mam and Da here?"

"Mam was admitted to the hospital. Da's in the back bedroom, asleep."

"Is Mam gonna be okay?"

"I'm going to go see her later." Helena paused for a moment. "You don't want to go with me, do you?"

Angel shook her head. "You got any coffee?"

"I don't know." Helena moved to the cupboards and shuffled things around until she found a small tin of grounds and a filter for the automatic brewer.

"I... I know that you'll have to say no, but Liam and I... we need a place to stay." Angel wrung her hands and peered back out at the sleeping boy. "We can't go back to Rathkeale—to Duncan. He and I, we're getting divorced."

She whispered the last word, as if she were afraid Liam would hear.

"Are ya okay?" Helena filled the pot with water.

"Yeah, I'll be fine. It's for the best. There are some things that we couldn't get past; we're just too different." Angel dropped her face into her hands. "I tried to make our marriage work. I swear. I know I shouldn't have come here, but you're the only people I've got to turn to." Angel's voice was choked with tears. "Is it okay if we stay? It would only be 'til I can get a job and get a few shillings."

The vicar had said that all of their family was welcome, and Angel was in a bad position. Helena thought of Da. Even a few months ago, she would never have believed he'd allow Angel to live with them, but he'd changed. If he loved Angel as he said he did, than he would give her another chance.

The same couldn't be said of Mam. Cora would never allow her shame-causing daughter to come back. Jesus himself would have to come down to save Angel from the vile words Mam would undoubtedly have in store for her.

They would just have to deal with the fallout.

"You're welcome to stay."

"Thanks. Yer savin' me arse."

"Aye."

Helena turned the faucet off, picked up the filled carafe, and carried it to the machine.

Angel rubbed her hands over the knees of her jeans. "I think I owe you an apology… For before. I shouldn't have been so hateful. I was just upset when you stopped by. I've felt just awful since you left. I was acting like a prat. Duncan and I had been fightin'. And Da… As usual, Da was at the center of our row. Then when you got there I just..." Angel stopped wringing her hands and rested them on the table. "I love Da, and I miss you and the kids. I wanna be part of my fam again."

"I know what it is to want to be a part of the family. You've never stopped bein' my sister and you never will."

Angel stood and wrapped her thin arms around Helena. "I love ya, gra..."

Helena's eyes filled with tears as she wrapped her arms around Angel. "I'm glad you're home."

"Thank you, gra." Angel stepped back and, smiling, wiped away the tears that wetted her cheeks. "What happened with that boy you were supposed to marry?"

Helena shifted uncomfortably as she searched for the right words.

"Brian is the worst kind of git. I told him I wouldn't marry him, but before the words had even cooled, Rionna had offered herself in my place."

"Rionna has always been a pain in the arse. She'll get what's coming to her."

"I just hoped she'd do more. Maybe at least get her schooling done before she ran off with some boy."

"Not everyone is like you, gra. Just look at me—I tripped over myself to get to Duncan. What an eejit I turned out to be."

"You got Liam. You ain't no eejit." Helena paused. "To tell ya the truth, there was another reason I couldn't marry Brian."

"What's that?"

"I'm in deep with Graham."

The scent of the hot coffee filled the tiny kitchen.

Angel looked down at the counter and sucked in a long breath. "Follow your heart, gra—even if it isn't the easiest path to take. If the road turns out to be full of ruts, you'll always have a place with me."

. . .

Rionna crouched in the farthest corner of the hospital room, her back against the yellow wall, which was the only thing that kept her from moving farther away from Helena. Rionna had said nothing of what had happened between them, but she was staring at Helena like she was a traitor to her, the family, and their traditions.

Mam groaned from the bed. Her hands and arms were covered with thick white gauze, stained yellow from the wounds that lay beneath. Mam's eyes flickered open.

"Mam?" Helena asked.

She looked over at her, but then her gaze swung to Rionna and Gavin. "Where's your da?" She tried to sit up, but instead she grimaced in pain and fell back.

"Here, let me help you." Helena stood up and moved to reach under Mam's arms to lift her.

"No. Don't touch me, girl. Rionna told me all about your black magic. I don't want to be manked up by your gammy touch," Mam spat. "Your sister can help me. Isn't that right, Rionna?"

Helena dropped her hands.

Mam shunning her hurt worse than she could have ever expected.

"Aye, Mam. I'll help ya." Rionna pranced over, her tall heels making out-of-place clicks against the sterile white floor. "I'll always be there for ya, instead of runnin' off like a cow with her arse on fire."

"What're you talkin' about? I've done nothin' of the sort. All I've been tryin' to do is to help the fam—to pay the debts, work hard, and make you all proud. I gave up my dreams to help you. I'm not even gonna take the exams."

"You lie. All you ever do is lie." Rionna pushed Helena out of the way as she lifted Mam higher in the reclining bed. Mam bit her lip, and her eyes shut as if she were trying to hide the pain.

"If you really cared about this family you wouldn't be running away from your duties," Mam said between breaths. "You're just damn lucky you have a sister who actually cares about me and what I look like to our people."

"That's not true. Da and I care."

"If that's true, then where's your da? Why ain't he here? He couldn't stand to be near me, could he?"

"He had to work this morning. The festival's goin', and they needed him at the manor—one of the tables was broken in a guest's room."

She held back the fact that Graham had offered to give Da the morning off, but Da had refused.

Mam huffed angrily. "I ain't surprised. He's never done nothin' for me, or any of us. He's been nothing but a dirty louse. Sucking the blood right out of this family every chance he gets, and the one time I need him, he ain't here. He's hidin' out, tryin' to act the part of a country man."

"That's shite."

Mam's eyes bulged in surprise. "What was that, girl?"

"You heard me. You're talking shite. Da's been nothing but a saint since he's gotten out. The only time he did anythin' away in the head was when allowed himself to be bullied by you."

"Shut your mouth, girl. You don't know what you're talkin' about." The monitors around Mam started to give off shrill beeps.

"No. I'm sick of ye and the way you're actin'."

"Mind your manners, girl. I didn't raise you to be talking to me like this. If I could get up, I'd give you a right whippin'."

"You have no right to treat me like a child."

"As long as you're livin' under my roof I'll treat ye as I want."

Helena couldn't control the wild smile that broke free of its reins. "Then, thanks to you, none of us have to put up with your gammy arse anymore."

"You ungrateful little prat. You will—"

Helena put her hands up, stopping her mam's tirade. "All you've done my whole life is beat me down, but no more. Ye ain't gonna tell me what to do anymore."

Gavin stared at her with fear in his eyes.

Helena turned to Rionna. "You listen to me. I know why you're acting like ya are. I'm sorry. There's nothing I can do to change who ye think I am, or how easy ya think I have it. I know ye hate me."

Rionna crossed her arms over her chest. "I don't *hate* ya."

"Then don't be jealous. I only want the best for you. And the best thing you can possibly do is put off this marriage and finish your schoolin'."

Rionna stared at her. "How can you tell me what to do? All you do is follow Da around like his little lap dog. Ye don't think for yourself."

"You don't know what you're talking about, love." She

tried to ignore the pain that radiated through her at her
sister's words. She knew they weren't hers. They were well-
planted lines that had been seeded, watered, and fed by
Mam's bitterness.

"Rionna." Helena tried to keep the hard edge from her
voice. Her sister was only a puppet; if she was patient, maybe
some of what she had to say would seep through the cracks.
"Da is a good man. He's made mistakes, as we all have, as
we all *do*, but he's done more for me since his release than
Mam's done in me whole life."

"That's shite!" Mam screeched. "I've clothed and fed
you and kept you out of the streets. I've paid a heavy price to
keep you under my roof, don't ya forget. I'm the one who's
taken care of you when your precious Da was away."

"All you did was use us to get on the dole. And when
the government's dole wasn't enough, you used us to take a
shilling from anyone else who would give it, even if it meant
selling your daughter in the process."

"I don't know what you're talkin' about."

"You knew the O'Donoghues would want a high return
on their loan, but you did it anyway. You knew they had a
son who was close to my age. You've had this planned since
the moment you took their money."

"So what if I did? So what if I wanted somethin' better
for ye? I didn't want ya to end up like Angel. She brought
nothing but shame to this family. And it was a damn fine
plan if ya ask me... We win back a little bit of face and you
get married to a good enough bloke. You're lucky any man
would take a woman like you... Took quite a bit of sellin'
before they would buy."

"You don't own me, and I don't want to be the wife of a

good enough man." Helena walked to the door, but turned back to her mam one more time. "I'm done bein' your puppet." She pointed at Rionna. "Hopefully she'll figure out what a banjaxed old cow you are before it's too late."

"Shut your fecking mouth, ya little bitch!" Mam screeched.

Helena stepped back from her. "You may be my mam, but I don't need you anymore."

"What's wrong with ye?" Mam tore at the IV's that protruded from her arms. "You ain't no daughter o' mine!"

"There's nothing wrong with me, Mam. I just can't be happy settling for this life. I want to learn; I want to be more than a wife. Even if that means that I can't be your daughter."

"Get out of here! Don't you dare come crawling back to me! We're done. You're done. Who'll want you... you, a stupid little prat!"

Helena moved to the window and pulled Gavin to her side. "I'm takin' Gavin with me. You aren't a fit mother. When you quit drinkin' and tryin' to burn yourself to death, you can come see him. I'm not letting you put this family in danger anymore." Helena looked up to Rionna. "You're welcome to come with us."

Rionna's gaze snapped to Helena and a sneer puckered her childish lips. "I'm not leaving Mam's side." She put her hand on the burnt woman's shoulder.

"That's fine. You should stay here." Helena smiled dangerously. "I love you, but if you don't watch yourself, your jealousy and hatred will turn you into Mam." Helena looked over at the pickled, bandage-covered woman on the bed. "Family or not... she's a foul woman. And Rionna, you're better than her—you still have a heart."

CHAPTER TWENTY-FIVE

"So how did the festival go? Did the guests enjoy themselves?" Mr. Shane sat across from Graham in his office, his fingers tented in a perfect triangle. The morning light poured through the window behind him, casting shadows throughout the room.

"It all went off without a hitch," Graham said.

"That's grand." Mr. Shane was too nonchalant for Graham to read his expression. "I heard you didn't stay until the end."

It had been less than twenty-four hours since Graham had shown Helena, Seamus, and Gavin the cottage at the far end of Holy Trinity Abbey Church. The entire time, Seamus had overflowed with appreciation and assurances that they wouldn't "overstay their welcome." He'd sounded so adamantly against the help that Graham secretly wondered if the family would still be there by the week's end.

"No. I had to take care of some additional business."

"Like?" Mr. Shane prompted.

Graham could only oblige him with the truth. "There was a fire at the Travellers' campsite. I had to help them find another place."

Mr. Shane tapped his fingers against his chin. "You should've told me you put up our employees on the church's grounds. I had to find out from the vicar this morning."

"Why did you talk to the vicar?"

"It is my job to know what's happening on this estate." Mr. Shane gave him a predatory smile. "And, amongst my many duties, this morning I received a complaint from one of the guests."

"What's it this time?"

"Yesterday we had a staff member fixing something in a guest's room. Yes?"

Graham nodded. "I sent Seamus up to the Lady Caroline Room to fix a broken table. It was nothing major, why?"

"He's the gypsy with the gift of sight, yes? Is his ability strong enough to help with Danny and your mother?"

"He has a gift, but I don't think we can use it. Why?"

Mr. Shane dropped his hands down to his desk. "If that's the case, and we won't be able to use his abilities, you're going to need to let him go."

"Go where?"

"You know what I mean."

"Why? He's done nothing wrong. He's been a damn fine employee."

"I'm afraid not." Mr. Shane slid open his desk drawer and removed a file. "Apparently, he has sticky fingers."

"No, not Seamus."

Mr. Shane flipped open the file to a picture of a diamond

necklace. "He was in the Lady Caroline Room, and this necklace went missing. Do you know anything about it?"

Graham shook his head. "When did the guest say it was taken?"

"Sometime during the festival. The woman is convinced he took it from her nightstand."

"Are you sure she didn't lose it?"

"Her husband remembered seeing it there before they left, and it was missing upon their return—after Seamus had been in to fix the side table. They wanted to call the police, but I managed to control the situation. You know the last thing we need here is more bad press."

Nothing—not a single item—had been stolen from Adare Manor, with the exception of hand soaps and the occasional guest towel. Who would have broken into the room and stolen the woman's necklace? It had to have been someone who knew what the woman had, and someone with access to the room.

"Was there any sign that someone had forced their way in?" A part of him hoped there was a chisel mark to the door—anything to indicate that it wasn't Seamus's doing.

Mr. Shane shook his head. "I've been asking around and, besides the cleaning staff, the only person who was reported to have been seen near the room was that gypsy. I know you have a soft spot for him, but think about it. His trailer burns... and then a necklace, which is worth more than his yearly salary, goes missing. It has to be more than mere coincidence."

It wasn't possible. Seamus had said how much he regretted his time in prison. There was no chance he would risk being sent back.

"He didn't take the necklace."

Mr. Shane tapped his fingers against his chin and the chair squeaked as he shifted his weight. "What proof do you have?"

"Seamus's a good man. He wouldn't steal."

Mr. Shane tapped. "Graham, let's be frank. He's a Traveller and an ex-con. We should've never hired him in the first place. Since he and his daughter have been working for the manor, it's been one problem after another."

"You know we couldn't have gotten Helena here without getting Seamus. I know he wouldn't have stolen the woman's necklace. He's been a model employee."

"The woman wants us to pay to replace the necklace. I can't say I blame her, but I'm not looking forward to footing the bill. If you think he didn't do it then you need to find the person who is responsible."

"I'll see what I can do."

"Now, have you had word on Rose yet?" Mr. Shane asked. "The vicar said you had stopped by when you were looking for her."

"No one has seen her since yesterday."

"When she was at your house?" Mr. Shane flipped the file closed. His cold gaze clung to Graham. "You don't have to pretend you didn't see her. I already know. Why did you let her go? Why didn't you insist that she return to the infirmary?"

Graham sighed. "I tried, but she gave me the slip."

"Don't you *think*, Graham? First the gypsies, then her, and now the necklace. Can't you do anything right?"

Mr. Shane hadn't been there, staring at his mother's face, listening to her cry as she realized what had happened to

Danny. If he had wanted Graham to handle Rose differently, then he should have been out there searching, just as Graham had been. Instead he'd been holed up in his little castle, entertaining guests and doing promotion for the manor. All he cared about was business, always business. And now… now he wanted to tell Graham how to handle his mother?

"You once told me you would do anything for this place, for your family." Mr. Shane's fingers curled around the armrests of his office chair. "Yet, from what I can see, the only people you really seem to care about are some gypsy and his daughter. When it came to your own *mother*, you dropped the ball." Mr. Shane shook his head in disgust. "I thought I could trust you like a son."

"Helena might be a just another gypsy to you, but you don't understand. She's a great woman."

"Look here, I said you could hire them in the hope that you could help Danny. Danny's gotten no better—maybe it's time we call a spade a spade and cut our losses. Hiring them has been a poor business decision."

"No one ever says no to you, but you know what? I'm saying no to you. I'm not firing her or her dad. You can fire me, but I'm not doing it."

"You know you don't mean that. You could never walk away from this place, from your brother." Mr. Shane glared at him. "I think I've put up with enough of your feeble attempts to be open-minded. Gypsies aren't to be trusted."

"You're blaming Helena and Seamus for something that has nothing to do with them. You're the one who got greedy and read from the codex. This is your fault."

"Maybe you need to go take a look at your brother to see where your loyalties should lie."

Graham jerked to his feet, knocking his chair to the ground. He put his hands on the edge of the desk and pressed his face toward Mr. Shane. The man didn't move.

"Don't you dare use my brother to force your hate on me. I'll never hate Helena or her father. They did nothing wrong."

Mr. Shane smiled. "Then prove it. Prove to me they're not thieves, that they were worth taking a risk on—or you're all going to be gone, and I will take things into my own hands."

Graham slammed his fists down on the table. "What's wrong with you?"

Mr. Shane scowled. "I'm not wasting any more time on this crazy idea that this gypsy is the answer. If I find Rose first, I'm putting her in a restrictive institution." Mr. Shane turned his chair toward the window and away from Graham. "I hear that Hollow Oak Park Mental Health Center is taking patients. If I pay them enough, they've assured me that they are willing to do *whatever* it takes to make her comfortable. They are well practiced with neurosurgical procedures— even lobotomies for the right amount of money."

"You wouldn't—"

Mr. Shane's chair squeaked. "I didn't say I wanted to take things this far, but something must be done. What happens now is up to you and your little gypsy."

CHAPTER TWENTY-SIX

Helena walked into the kitchen and was met with the sounds of whisks and electric mixers. Mary had her back turned as she worked away, washing fresh strawberries next to a stack of gold-rimmed glassware.

"Mary?" Her voice was thick and scratchy from the long morning of talking with Angel. She lifted down an apron from the stack of freshly washed linens as Mary turned from her work on the counter.

"What're you doing here?" Mary looked shocked; the little mole under her nose even wiggled with surprise. "Your mother better?"

"She'll be fine."

"Your first wages are over there." Mary pointed to a bin of sealed envelopes. "Graham told me you might be taking this week off."

"I gotta work." She drew the strings of the apron tight. She rifled through the plastic bin until she saw her name. Then she pulled the envelope from the rest and stuffed it in her purse. A slight sense of relief passed through her as she thought of how badly she needed the money.

"What in the bloody hell are you doing here? Don't you have tests that need taking?" Mary frowned.

"I need to work. I can't afford to take the tests right now. Maybe next year." She tried to keep her emotions in check—after the row with Mam and Rionna, she had nearly forgotten about her girlish dreams.

Mary put down a strawberry and dried her fingers on her apron. Around her neck was a beautiful gold necklace Helena hadn't noticed before, but as Mary moved it disappeared beneath her uniform's collar. "What're you thinking, lass? Do you think you're gonna be working in these kitchens forever? That I'll let you do that?" Mary reached into her back pocket and pulled out her mobile. "What time do your exams start?"

"I don't know. Eight o'clock? Eight thirty?" Helena tried to sound dismissive, but for months she had known the time, right down to the minute. They were supposed to be there fifteen minutes ahead, find a seat, and have two pencils and a calculator for the mathematics portion of the test.

Mary punched the buttons on her mobile. "There." She stuffed the device back in her pocket. "Now, I don't care whether your trailer burned down or not. You can't be here when you need to be taking those exams."

"I can't, Mary. Like I said, I need the money." Helena turned her back on the kitchen matron and stumbled her way to her station. There was work to be done. She pulled a knife from the butcher's block.

Mary stomped over to her. "I hired you so you could see what it was like to have your own money, and to be able to

261

make your own choices. Don't you understand that? I know what it's like to be in your shoes."

"How do you know what it's like bein' a Traveller?" She sat the knife down, letting it clink on the metal counter. "I appreciate you givin' me this job and all, but ya don't know what it's like."

"I may not have been a Traveller like you, but I grew up Catholic in a Protestant town. We were poor, some days barely able to keep the clothes on our back or the shoes on our feet. There were nine of us children and each of us had a job, all in an attempt to keep food on the table and a roof over our heads. I can see that's what you're trying to do for your family. I just want to help you, to keep your family from having to go through what we did… to keep you from having to do the things we were forced to do…" A tear came to Mary's eye.

Helena put her hand on the woman's arm. "What happened?"

"At sixteen, I was forced to quit school and marry a man twenty years my elder. He used me as his wife." Mary's cheeks flamed and a thin veil of sweat drew on her forehead. "After a while, I wasn't enough and he started going to other women.

"Who would've thought a man in his forties would need more?" Mary said as she waved off the thought. "After a while he saw me as nothing more than a drain on his finances, a waste of time and space, and he put me to work. It started out easily enough, meeting men at the local pub for a friendly conversation, but soon he was forcing me to do things, to act in ways that God himself couldn't have imagined."

Helena shivered at the thought. What if this happened to Rionna after she married Brian?

"That's how I met my Herbert. He was so sweet and kind. He saw me at the pub waiting for one of my clients. We chatted for a bit until the man arrived, but then Herbert, being the jealous type he is, wouldn't hear of the man taking me away from him. That man ended up in the hospital with thirty-five stitches." She stuck out her chest with pride. "And I never went back to my first husband."

"So you and Herbert aren't married? Or did you get a divorce?"

"We're married in our hearts, and if God is just, he'll see the union as we do." She crossed herself. "I didn't tell you all this to scare you, but you need to take risks… Let your head be your guide, but don't forget to follow your heart. If you always follow the easiest path, it will only lead to a life filled with disappointment."

The door to the kitchen opened. Graham walked in, his red kilt glaringly out of place in the sterile grays and whites of the kitchen. "Are you ready to go?"

Helena stared at the kitchen matron, then at Graham. Her hands shook as she pulled the apron from her waist. "One thing first." Helena checked the clock on the wall. There was just enough time. "Graham, can you take me to Danny?"

Mary smiled like the mother of a beloved child. "That's a good lass. I knew you had it in ya."

Graham followed closely behind her as they made their way into the basement infirmary. Danny lay on his back, his silver hair damp with sweat.

Graham stared at her. "You can do this. I know you can."

She'd helped Rionna and Gavin, but it was still hard to believe she could have the power to help a boy who had far deeper wounds than the burns upon her sibling's flesh. His wounds were more complex, more psychological.

The air of the infirmary hung on her, humid and foul. Closing her eyes, she grounded her body, then laid her right hand on Danny's chest and her left on his forehead.

"*A libha sarog. A karkn lugil. A dha ogaks moniker, d'umiik a libha nalks, dha karkn fhas, dha lugil kuldrum.*" She repeated the prayer in English. "The blood is red. The flesh has pain. In the old one's name let the blood dry, the flesh grow, the pain sleep."

Danny's breathing steadied.

The energy in her sparked and tickled her hands slightly. She could feel the silvery tendrils of energy as they moved up his body and then down to his feet. There was pain in his back from the bedsores of the long-ill, but as she searched there was a deeper pain too. She tried to force the energy there, to that unknown place, to that deep need. Almost as if she had hit the limits of her power, the energy retreated back to her hands.

His heartbeat slowed beneath her palm. The movement of his chest steadied in the rhythms of sleep again.

Her hands fell down to her sides as she opened her eyes. The boy's flesh was a shade pinker, but it could have just been wishful thinking. Aside from the hue, he was the same.

"Danny?" Graham asked, his voice horribly hopeful.

"Don't." She reached out and rested her hand on Graham's arm. "I couldn't reach him."

Anger and guilt coursed through her. She was so weak. So useless.

"Let's go." She turned away from Danny and moved toward the door.

"Wait. Just another second," Graham called after her.

She turned. "Graham, I'll try again. I prom—"

She stopped mid-word as Danny's face twitched. His eyes fluttered open. Danny blinked a few times, and his mouth trembled as if he wanted to speak.

"Danny?" Graham cupped his brother's face with one hand.

The boy looked up, and there was a shimmer of light in his eyes. The boy gave him a glimmer of a smile, and then his eyes closed and he disappeared back into his mind.

• • •

The room was filled with people fiddling with their hair and tapping their yellow pencils. A woman wearing a khaki suit stood at the front of the hall, holding a thick stack of papers in her arms. Another woman, the moderator, sat at the table staring at her watch.

Another of the test-takers, a man, leaned over to a girl in the desk next to him. "Thank Mary it's almost over, right?"

"I know," the woman answered with a flick of her hair. "I've already started the paperwork to attend Limerick University. I don't know what I'm more nervous about: passing the test or starting school again."

Helena sank down in the hard wooden chair and pulled at her uniform pants. She wasn't the only one who was nervous about what the future held.

The man glanced over at her, and Helena smiled. The woman he had talked to lifted her nose as if, even though

Helena was in her work uniform, the woman could tell that she was out of her element.

The moderator coughed, bringing the room to attention. "The exam will begin in exactly fifteen minutes. You'll have four hours to complete the compulsory Irish exam. We will then break for lunch, after which you shall all return and take the second half of the Modern Language exam. Tomorrow, we will be administering the Applied Sciences, followed by…" The woman's monotone voice carried on in the background as she warned against cheaters and the like.

All Helena could concentrate on was the white booklet the woman set down in front of her and the way the letters on its cover seemed to blur.

• • •

After two days of exams, Helena was relieved they were nearly over. As she stood in the kitchens and waited for Graham, a few cooks worked away at early morning preparations. It felt strange not to be working beside them, but truth be told, after the last few days she was knackered. She had been seeing Danny each day after her exams, trying to make him open his eyes again, but nothing had happened. It was almost as if the stress of the exams had weakened her powers.

Thankfully today was to be the last day of exams, albeit in her worst subject—economics.

She fiddled with her hair and made sure all the loose ends were tucked away. Helena glanced down at her mobile. 6:45.

Where was Mary? She was always in before six o'clock.

Leaning back against the steel counter, Helena tried to

slow her breathing. The time would come for the test, and then she'd never have to deal with the pressure of the exams again. Her foot tapped against the tiled floor.

Helena glanced back down at her mobile. 6:46.

A flat of spuds was waiting to be peeled and chopped in the dry storage. Unable to sit still, Helena put one hand on the counter to steady herself as she reached up and pulled down an apron from the stack above her station.

A necklace fell with a clatter upon the counter and landed on her fingers. The diamond pendant was covered in blood, making it look like a bloody tear. An unchecked scream ripped from her throat.

CHAPTER TWENTY-SEVEN

It had taken almost fifteen minutes for Helena to speak. The kitchen was full of staff members. Graham had his arms around Helena, protecting her from the probing questions of the people that surrounded them.

"I'm telling ya, I saw Mary wearin' the necklace yesterday. Now she's missin' and there's *blood*," Helena said, her face buried in his chest.

"Don't worry." He couldn't stop the fear in his voice. "I'm sure there's an explanation."

"Graham, Mary's never late to work. You know it as well as I do somethin' is wrong."

"I haven't checked the infirmary; maybe she's down there with her husband. It's hard to say. You don't need to worry. I'll handle this." Graham leaned to whisper in her ear. "Besides, you need to go. You have to finish your tests."

She gave him a simple nod.

"Hey!" Graham called out, trying to get the attention of

the staff above their chatter. The noise briefly lessened, and then started up again.

Helena let go of him, stuck her fingers in her mouth, and gave a sharp whistle. "Aye... Listen up!"

The stunned crowd stopped and turned to face her.

"Thanks." Graham put his hand to the small of her back.

"What happened?" one of the waiters asked, as the crowd around him quieted.

"It was nothing... I only saw a spider." Helena's hand balled up tighter.

"*Jaysus*. Are you putting me on? I didn't finish my morning prep for a pissy spider? I'm gonna be behind all day."

Another man stepped to the front of the group. "Don't talk bollocks. There ain't no way she's screaming like that for a bleedin' spider. Tell us what's goin' on."

Helena's skin was hot under Graham's touch, and he tried to reassure her with a light pat of his hand.

"We might as well tell them." Helena whispered. "Maybe someone has seen her."

"All right..." He turned to the mass of people. "Has anyone seen Mary Margaret this morning?"

The crowd shifted, and everyone shook their heads.

"If no one has seen Mary Margaret, it is my belief that we have a problem."

"What's the problem?"

"Mary Margaret's missing. And she was last seen wearing this." Graham lifted the bloody necklace, and a gasp rippled through the crowd.

• • •

The university hall's doors were closed, and students were milling around, anxiously checking their watches, as Graham escorted Helena to her exams. A woman in a khaki suit opened the doors, and the students milled in. Graham gave Helena a quick peck on the cheek, and she made her way into the exam room. She must have had the strength of a thousand women to be able to pull herself together to do what had to be done. Any man would be lucky to have her— even if the man wasn't him.

Graham made his way back to the car.

His mobile rang from his sporran, and he pulled it out. "What's it about?"

"Mr. Kelly?" a woman asked timidly.

"Aye."

"I'm calling you about the infirmary," the nurse said, her voice trembling. "Herbert's missing. He musta snuck out sometime this morning. I'm sorry to tell ye this, but in our search, we found Chester's wallet under his mattress... right next to a knife covered in dried blood."

The woman was quiet on the other side of the phone line as he struggled to make sense of exactly what she meant.

"Why does he have Chester's wallet?"

"Well, me and the other nurses have been talking. We can't be sure Herbert was accounted for the morning that Chester was murdered."

"You're saying that you think he is responsible for the chef's death?"

"From what we have found, I'm thinking so."

A sickening ache grew in his gut. "Have you seen Mary Margaret?"

There was a long pause. "I'm afraid not, but as you

know, Herbert has been channeling the spirits more and more lately—he's been jealous of Mary and talking about the incident with the codex. If Mary's missing, then I'm afraid that it's possible he has something to do with her disappearance."

"That son of a bitch."

He hung up, furious.

Graham drew the diamond-encrusted necklace from his pocket. He wrapped the chain around his fingers, letting the metal dig into his flesh. The blood, which had been smeared across the surface of the diamonds, had rubbed off in his pocket.

He started the car and, as the air kicked on, the floral aroma of Helena's perfume wafted toward him. He closed his eyes and took in the soft scent. She'd looked so nervous outside the broad doors of the exam room.

If so much hadn't been going on, he would've done more for her. Maybe brought her a dozen of the freshest red roses he could find—anything to help her keep her nerves in check and show her his love and support. Instead he was in a rush to go find the owner of one blood-stained necklace, two missing women, and a killer.

His mobile buzzed in his hand. "What's the problem?" Graham grumbled.

"You need to get back here," his stepfather ordered. "I can't believe you left."

"I had a prior engagement."

"I heard." Ice clinked against a glass.

Graham ran his free hand up and over his forehead. "The nurse just called. Herb's missing."

"Bloody hell. Not another one. These types of events

are not acceptable. We can't put our guests or our staff in harm's way. We already had one murder... Do you know how much that cost me? Paying off the police doesn't come cheap."

"You knew? You knew that there was a killer on the loose and you didn't say anything?"

"What was I supposed to do, Graham? I know the infirmary is important, but I still have a business to run. I can't have a murder happening on our grounds. We'd be finished."

"Who cares about the damn business? The people who needed help would still come to us."

"You think people who are scared of what they are and the curses they must face would come to a place where they may be put in even more danger? You can't be that daft. Besides, we can't have cops all over the property... Think about it. Think what they would find." There was a pause. "If you don't hurry up and get Herb, Mary, and your mother back, it's hard to say that there won't be more deaths."

His stepfather was right. They couldn't risk having the guards nosing around the manor.

"How long's Herb been gone?" Mr. Shane asked.

"He's been missing since this morning. One of the nurses found a bloody knife under his mattress along with Chester's wallet."

"First thing I want you to do when you get back is return the necklace to its rightful owner. Say it was found in the laundry. Whatever you do, you need to keep this all under wraps."

Graham started the car. "I'll be right there."

He sped all the way to the manor, but it still took almost

an hour to reach the estate. Upon his return, there were extra security guards posted at the gate. A man stood at each post, wearing black sunglasses, black suits, and little white earpieces. Another two waited on the other side, presumably to check cars on the way out.

Graham slowed to a crawl, and the men waved him past. He found a strange comfort in the awareness that no one would come or go without them knowing.

He pulled the car into his spot. The car park was almost empty. Thick clouds rolled over the green grass of the lawns, blocking out what little sun there had been. A light breeze carried the scent of rain.

A few of the wait staff stood quietly in the drawing room. When they saw him they nodded in welcome.

"Have ye found Ms. Mary Margaret?" one of the waiters asked.

"No… No word yet."

The man at his side glanced worriedly out the massive windows that lined the dining room.

"Don't be fretting, boys. I'm sure she'll turn up." Graham forced a smile.

They didn't look reassured.

In the main hall, the receptionist waved him over. "Mr. Shane said he would like you to use this to return the necklace." The woman held out a black velvet box.

"Thanks."

The owner of the necklace was staying in the Lady Caroline Room, the finest of the manor. He knocked on the door and waited until it was cracked open. A thin man in a black suit opened the door; Graham recognized him as the golfer he had seen chatting up the receptionist. "May I help you?"

"I believe we've located a necklace you reported missing." He held out the box.

The man nodded. "My wife will be so pleased." He took the box from him and opened it up. "Where did you find it?"

He thought of Mr. Shane's orders. How would the man react if he told him they had found the necklace covered with blood in the depths of the kitchen? The reputation of the manor would be ruined.

"One of our staff found it in the laundry. I'm sorry for any inconvenience this may have caused you or your wife."

"I suppose some type of reward is in order?" the man continued.

"No," Graham said with a bit too much force. "Seeing you all during your next visit will be enough reward."

The words rolled off his lips with professional grace, but they left a bitter aftertaste. When had this place turned him into a version of Mr. Shane?

CHAPTER TWENTY-EIGHT

The pencil fell from Helena's tired fingers, rolled off the table, and bounced onto the floor with a wooden sound. Clothes ruffled as people turned to look at the Traveller making all the noise. Helena smiled at their gawking faces. She was done. Done with exams. Done with being forced into a life she didn't want.

Grabbing the pencil and her purse, she stood up, letting the chair scrape against the ground. Let them think what they wanted. This would be the last time she'd see their sneering faces.

She dropped the test on the table in front of the two stone-faced women in charge.

"Good luck," the thicker woman whispered.

Nodding, Helena turned and walked out.

She sighed as the door closed behind her. Never again would she have to go through the pressure and stress of these exams.

Whether she passed with high marks or skimmed the

bottom, she had done the one thing she had wanted to do. Now she could move forward with her life knowing that she'd tried her damnedest, that she'd given schooling everything she'd had. She was the first woman in her fam to finish. She could be proud.

Graham wasn't in the car park, so she made her way to the main building. A few of the little cafes were bustling with students, and she passed a window full of university books and souvenirs. On a hanger, just inside the shop's door, hung a green jersey like the ones worn by the Republic of Ireland Footballers.

Helena smiled.

She owed Graham a thank you for showing her that there was more to life than she could have ever expected—he'd shown her love. It was time she shared one of her loves with him—the Boys in Green.

She picked out the shirt and brought it to the girl at the counter.

She made her way back out to the car park and waved as she spotted Graham. He smiled, but he had a worried expression on his face. It all hit her at once. For the last few hours the realities of life had been gone from her mind, but seeing him brought it all back—Mary, her mam, Rose, and Danny.

The bag slipped in her fingers, but she forced a smile to her lips. For one more moment, she wanted to savor the feeling of accomplishment that swelled within her. She had done it. The roadblocks scattered throughout her life had almost stopped her from finishing her exams, but with Graham's help and reassurance she had made it through.

She opened the door and sat down next to him. "I did it."

In his lap, Graham held a dozen long-stemmed red roses. He smiled and handed them over. "Congratulations, my love."

"What are these for?"

Graham reached over and ran his hand through her hair. "I'm proud of you."

"They're beautiful." Tears threatened to spill over.

"Don't cry, love." He kissed her cheek. She put her hand up to his face and ran her thumb over his light stubble.

"Thank you. For everything."

His lips were strong and firm as hers caressed them. Her tongue explored the edges of his mouth and pulled at the contours of his full lips. He held her tighter to him, owning her. Her heart thrashed with unbridled excitement. She was his, and he was hers in this stolen moment.

He reached up and pulled the pencil from her hair. "Did you forget this?"

A giggle slipped from her lips. She took the yellow pencil and dropped it in her purse. "Here." The plastic bag crinkled as she picked it up and thrust it at him. "I got you something too."

He opened the bag, and his eyes grew large as his laugh filled the small car. "Oh nay, love. I won't be wearing this!" He pulled out the emerald green shirt.

"If you want to be with me, you have to cheer for the right team." She giggled.

"Is that how it's going to be?" He raised an eyebrow.

She answered with a wicked grin.

"If you say so," Graham said. He reached down and

drew his work shirt over his head. The bare muscles of his chest tensed as he grabbed the jersey.

Helena drew in a ragged breath. Every part of her wanted to reach over and touch the rippling muscles of his body. She thought of her vision, his naked body standing before her. A need pulsed up from deep within her. "Graham..."

"Aye?" He gave her a sexy smile.

"You need to put a shirt on."

"As you wish." He laughed as he pulled the shirt on and ran his fingers over the smooth fabric.

What she wished for was something far different from him putting his clothes on... rather, her fantasy ended with his clothes on the floor.

• • •

Graham parked the car in the spot farthest from the side door of the manor, near a row of well-trimmed hedges.

There was a tap on his window. A gray-haired woman with sunken cheeks and wild eyes frantically gestured at them. From the waist down, she was dripping wet and covered in green algae.

"Mum?" Graham pushed open the door.

Helena gasped. She had seen Rose in the hospital, but the wet, skeletal gray woman who stood before her was sicklier-looking than she remembered.

"I tried to stop him. He wouldn't listen." There was an edge of terror in her voice. "He wouldn't stop holding her under the water... The woman... she's dead."

"What happened?" Graham took his mother's hand and wrapped his arm around her shoulders.

"Herb... he was channeling a spirit. He said something about Chester... how he tried to take Mary away. He said the spirits told him to find the *Codex Gigas*—that if he didn't, they would kill him and Mary and condemn their souls to roam the earth forever... He said he'd been looking, but couldn't find the book... He said he couldn't let them take her... he was going to take matters into his own hands... I tried to stop him, but he just went crazy." Rose pointed at the gardens. "They're by the river."

Helena raced around the garden with Graham and Rose close on her heels. Mary had done so much for her—she'd given her a job and a purpose, and pushed her when she had needed pushing. She couldn't be dead.

Two bodies lay on the bank of the river. Herbert's feet floated in the water like black bobbers.

Mary's face was ghostly white and her eyes closed; a droplet of water dripped from her wet hair and slipped down her face. There was a slash on her neck, near her collarbone. A gray-haired man with heavy lines across his forehead and an overly large nose lay on the ground next to her. His face was limp and mottled.

Helena knelt down and pushed her fingers against Mary's thick neck. No pulse. She pressed hard, willing herself to feel the rhythmic whoosh of blood.

Helena put her hands over Mary's heart. The buzz of energy started in her core, stirring the will inside of her. It built up, spilled over her heart, down her arms, and out every pore in her skin. The pulse of energy moved through her body as if she and Mary were no longer separate people, but one shared being.

Mary's pain became hers. Her head thundered like a

thousand drums. Helena pushed her energy into Mary's head. Focusing on the pain, she wound the energy around the pulsing mass of red pain that ran along the inside of Mary's skull. She pulled at the tendrils of red and drowned them in silvery light, smothering them one by one until the pain abated.

The energy moved down into Mary's body, warming the river-soaked flesh with its ethereal fire.

Mary shifted beneath her hands, and Helena moved toward the pale, mottled Herbert. Her fingers trembled as she moved them to his throat. As her flesh touched his, his body jerked. Helena gasped and looked down. A slimy, scale-covered green hand protruded from the water, grasping Herb's ankle. The same hand that had tried to claim Charlie—the Glashtyn. The river spirit reached up, her yellow hair flowing in the direction of the moving river like a grotesque doll.

Herbert's body jerked, and he slid into the water up to his waist.

"Stop! You can't have him!" Helena yelled. She tried to grab the man beneath the arms, but she couldn't get a firm hold. "Graham, help!"

Graham sprinted to her, but it was too late. Herbert disappeared into the green water of the River Maigue, his body becoming property of the spirit world.

CHAPTER TWENTY-NINE

Graham lifted Mary into his arms and made his way to the service entrance at the back of the manor.

"Why?" Mary repeated over and over. Her eyes were bloodshot, and tears streamed down her face as she looked up at Graham. He forced himself to look away.

They all came to the painting of the men with their nets. Helena feathered her fingers around the edge of the frame and pushed the little button, and the door to the basement swung open. Graham took the lead, making his way carefully down the steps. He looked up the stairway to Rose.

"I can't," Rose whispered. "I can't go back there."

Of course his mother wouldn't want to enter the prison which had held her for so long. "Mum, Mr. Shane wants to see you. Why don't you—"

"Why doesn't she what?" Mr. Shane interrupted Graham as he stepped into the doorway beside Rose. "Hello, my dear."

His mother looked at the man. Her gaze reminded Graham so much of the way Helena looked at him.

"John?" She reached up and took his face in her hands. "Is it really you?"

Mr. Shane's lips curved into a tight smile. "I've been looking for you, my Rose." He lifted his hands to hers, and lowered them from his face. He turned to Graham and Helena. "Is Mary going to be all right?"

Mary's eyes had finally closed, and her body had relaxed in his arms. "Thanks to Helena, she'll survive, but I need to get her to the infirmary."

"What about Herb?"

Helena shook her head. "He belongs to the Glashtyn."

There was a greedy gleam in Mr. Shane's eyes. "So, you've harnessed your abilities?"

Graham moved between Mr. Shane and Helena. "Stop right there. Whatever ideas you're getting, you need to stop."

Mr. Shane took a step back, but the triumphant look never left his eyes. "I completely agree, but she'll come to see that there are many rewards for helping those that need it the most."

Mr. Shane turned to his wife.

"Don't send me back down there, John," she begged. "Have your guards stay with me, do whatever you need to do, but don't send me back to that place."

Mr. Shane pulled her into his arms and kissed her head. "I won't, my love, as long as you promise to never run away again. We can help you. Right, Helena?" Mr. Shane sent her a questioning glance.

Helena nodded.

"Aye, Helena can help, just as long as she's allowed to stay here," Graham interrupted, "and so is her *innocent* father."

Mr. Shane nodded. "The necklace has been returned."

Graham shifted Mary in his arms. "And there'll be no more threats. Aye?"

"Fine."

"And you will hire ten new nurses. We need more hands on deck."

"That is going to cost us a fortune... You'll need to think about other ways to start generating revenue for our business if you want to make it work." Mr. Shane looked at Mary, but his arms never left Rose.

"Is that a yes?"

Mr. Shane's face pinched into a scowl. "Fine."

• • •

The infirmary was filled with the sounds of nurses and the shrill beeps of IVs that had run dry. A nurse carrying a clipboard rushed toward Graham as he moved to the nearest empty bed. The nurse's hair sat half undone on top of her head. "Mr. Kelly, we've been trying to get in touch with you. We haven't been able to find Herbert."

"I'm aware," he said, laying Mary down on the bed. "We had to move him to another facility."

The nurse frowned. "I thought we were working to rehabilitate?"

"He was beyond our help." Graham drew the blanket up over Mary. "But there is some good to come of his escape and *relocation*. I've convinced Mr. Shane to hire ten new nurses for your staff. You are responsible for hiring those who can be trusted."

"Thank you, sir... Thank you so much." The nurse stared at Helena. "What about *her*?"

"I'll start next week." Helena said with a wide smile. "But I'm just learning."

The nurse reached over and squeezed Helena's hands. "God bless ya, love."

Graham stood up and looked at Helena's bright smile. "Are you sure, Helena? What about school?"

She stopped him. "When I was taking my exams... my power weakened. Everything I truly am, is all because of this place." She motioned around the room. "I finally know who I am, and where I belong... If I learn how to control what I've been given, I can do more good here than I could ever hope to do by goin' to school. The nurses here can teach me what I need to learn. Aye?" She looked toward the nurse.

The woman nodded. "Absolutely."

"As long as I'm welcome here... I will use my gift to help people like me."

"If this is what you want. We need you."

She smiled nervously. "We're going to have a lot of work to do."

Helena moved to Danny's bed and bowed her head as she mouthed a silent prayer. Danny's cheeks were gaunt and pale, and his chest rose and fell as he slept.

Her hands trembled as she reached out and placed one on Danny's forehead and the other over his heart. Helena hovered over Graham's silver-haired brother.

Her aura glowed as a rainbow light streamed from her head and between her fingers. Tiny atoms filled the air and buzzed as they moved toward Danny, just as they had done with Mary.

For a moment, nothing happened. She looked up, and shook her head. "I don't know if it's going to work. I'm sorry, Graham."

"Keep trying... It has to work." He stepped closer and ran his fingers through her hair. "I love you. I know you can do this. I believe in you." As he spoke, her aura brightened. "Please, love... Try... Try hard."

She nodded. Closing her eyes, she mouthed what he assumed was a spell. The air around her buzzed with electricity, and her aura flexed under the force of her will.

Danny shifted, and his fingers trembled.

A bead of sweat trickled down Helena's temple.

Danny's chest rose and fell with a deep breath. His blue eyes opened.

"Danny? Danny?" Graham said, rushing to his brother's bedside.

His dry pink lips pulled into a weak smile. "Graham?"

"Aye, boy." Graham smiled wildly and pulled Danny's hand across the sheets. "How're you feeling?"

"Tired..." Danny looked around the room. His gaze wandered to his body.

"I'm so sorry, Danny," Graham said, breaking down. "I'm so sorry for ever making you go through this. I'll make it up to you."

"This... isn't your fault," Danny said, his voice weak after years of silence.

"Aye. It was, Danny. I should have never let them use you. I should have taken you away from this place."

Danny reached up and took Graham's hand and gave it a light squeeze. "Graham, no…"

Helena weakly dropped her hands from his brother and slumped down on the bed beside him and Danny.

"Helena, are you okay?"

She nodded, but her face was pale.

"Oh, love, thank you…" he said. "Thank you."

He leaned over and kissed her lips. In that moment he had it all—family, life, love—and none of it would have been possible without his gypsy girl.

EPILOGUE

Two weeks later, Lydia stood at the front of the Holy Trinity Abbey Church. The red and white crystals that adorned her princess-like wedding dress glimmered in the bright lights. Flowers lined the aisle, and red rose petals dotted the runner that ran between the pews. Lydia's mam and da sat at the front of the church, dabbing their eyes and nodding as the vicar spoke.

"Ye are blood of my blood, and bone of my bone..." The vicar continued on, but Helena's mind had wandered to Rionna and her mam. They would have enjoyed the wedding, but no one had been able to reach them after they disappeared from the hospital.

At the end of the pew sat Gavin, Angel, and Liam, who stared at the bride and groom. At the far end was Da. His face was drawn, and his wrinkles deeper.

Helena felt guilty, but she was secretly relieved Mam and Rionna had disappeared—along with their cutting words and the fights that came on their heels.

In Lydia and Jimmy, and in Graham, Rose, Danny, and John, two families had come together while another, hers, had fallen apart.

Further down the bench sat Danny. His cheeks were pink and had filled in over the last few weeks.

The Travellers around Helena and Graham turned and whispered, undoubtedly condemning her for bringing a country man into their world. Yet Helena remained strong. She loved this man. She would protect him.

Sitting there, looking at the people who were watching her, Helena realized that maybe at one point in her life she had seen things as they did—those who went against tradition were strange, weird, and deserved being exiled. Yet she had found a home and a future beyond the limits set by the traditions of her culture.

They could judge her, but she would not cower. She wasn't ashamed. She had made a promise to herself and, with Graham's help, she would continue to fulfill her dreams.

The vicar stopped, and Helena looked to the couple at the altar.

Jimmy swayed a bit as he held onto Lydia's hands. "I vow you the first cut of my meat, the first sip of my wine, from this day it shall only your name I cry out in the night and into your eyes that I smile each morning. I shall be a shield for your back as you are for mine, nor shall a grievous word be spoken about us, for our marriage is sacred between us and no stranger shall hear my grievance. Above and beyond this, I will cherish and honor you through this life and into the next."

Graham's hand tightened around hers. He leaned close. "Don't you want me to say that to you?"

Helena ran her thumb over his skin. The warmth of his touch reminded her of why she had fallen for such a man. Their love was a sacred love, but a bright future waited—a future that didn't depend on her being married. "Maybe someday, my love."

Graham let go of her hand and pulled her against him. She looked into his eyes. "I love you, my Helena," he whispered, his breath brushing against her skin like a lover's hand.

Helena took his free hand and lifted it to her lips. "I love you too, my Graham."

She thought back to the moment she had stood behind the spiked bars of Limerick Prison. Just like those gates had opened for Da, the gates to a new future had been opened—she was no longer limited by the thoughts and judgment of those around her. For the first time in her life, she was truly free.

CPSIA information can be obtained
at www.ICGtesting.com
Printed in the USA
BVOW11s1120230916

463078BV00003B/4/P